LONE WOLF

SAM HALL

Nail 'Em

Lone Wolf © Sam Hall 2021

All rights reserved. No part of this book may be used or reproduced in any manner whatsoever without written permission except for in the case of brief quotations for the use in critical articles or reviews.

Cover art and design by CJ Romano

The characters and events depicted in this book are fictitious. Any similarity to real persons, living or dead, is coincidental and not intended by the author.

 Created with Vellum

Author Note

This book is written in Australian English, which is a weird lovechild of British and American English. We tend to spell things the way the Brits do (expect a lot more u's), yet also use American slang and swear more than both combined.

While many people have gone over this book, trying to find all the typos and other mistakes, they just keep on popping up like bloody rabbits. If you spot one, don't report it to Amazon, drop me an email at the below address so I can fix the issue.

samhall.author@gmail.com

Trigger Warning

This book does deal with the death of a parent, which may push some buttons for people. There's an extensive scene that deals with the grieving process that's designed to be emotionally moving, but you'll need to assess if you're up for that. As always, talk to someone you trust about content that might be potentially upsetting.

Chapter 1

They say you should never go back. Well, sometimes you didn't get a choice.

"Hello...?" My voice was a combination of a grumble and a moan, having rolled over in the middle of what the fuck o'clock to grab my phone off the bedside table.

"Paige."

Just my name, that's all he said, but it was enough, more than enough. I recognised that deep voice with just a hint of growl like I would my own, but mine didn't have me sitting up straight in bed.

"Mase?"

"He's in the hospital, Paige. It's time to come home. A decision has to be made."

And that was that. The object of all my teenage fantasies, my father's beta, hung up on me. I just stared at the screen, unable to decipher what sorcery was at work in a simple device that it could create a temporal rift in my room and yank my mind, if not my body, to five years ago.

"*Paige, a decision needs to be made,*" *Dad growled as I shoved clothes into a bag, not really caring what I packed. Actually, I did. Those dumb floofy gowns they tried to make me wear to pack meetings were not coming. If anything, I'd* like to take them out the back and set them on fire. I grabbed jeans, T-shirts, jumpers, socks—

"Paige!"

My spine was jerked up straight, I lost my grip on a handful of socks I'd been holding, and my body became taut as a plucked string.

"I know you're hurting, love, but Spehr's don't run from their problems."

His voice was all warm, reassuring Dad, but the effect was ruined by the fact he was keeping me pinned to the spot by the dominance in his voice. I quivered with the need to go, to get the fuck out of Dodge and away from all of this. Away from men who could freeze me with just a snap, who could push their will on me at their leisure, who could force me to listen to their fucking bullshit.

I remembered this moment because it was the last time I saw my dad. I remembered it because for the first time, I managed to move when Dad pinned me, just a small twitch of my finger. Dad's voice was being drowned out by the smash of my heart in my ribs as I watched it jerk, then curl under my direction.

"Are you listening to me?"

The order snapped me back to what he was saying and the moment was lost, but it was a memory that sang in my mind, long after this ended.

"Speak freely," Dad said, finally seeming to realise I couldn't do shit unless he gave me permission.

"I don't want this."

"You're my daughter."

"Disown me. I'm leaving anyway, so adopt one of the cousins or something. A woman of our blood has to claim the next alpha, not me specifically. Aunty Nance is dying for—"

"No." I stood there silently, unable to suggest anything else while his will beat down upon me. "You know I could force this. I could make you stay, keep you here until you make your decision. Plenty of other alphas would do the same."

"But you won't," I said, half whisper, half hope.

"But I won't. Paige, run off to the city if that's what you think you have to do, but, honey, you gotta know it won't make a difference. This is your pack, these are your people—people you'll rule over one day as alpha female."

No, no, no. No. I never felt further away from my father than when he spouted this shit. We'd done our best after Mum died, rubbed along as well as an alpha and his only daughter might, but I made no mistake. My father had never understood me. That went when Mum did.

"If it doesn't matter, then it won't hurt if I go," I said, my chin raising despite the instinctual beat inside me that screamed for me to lower my eyes.

But he didn't exert his dominance right at that moment. Alpha Spehr fell away, and right then, there was only Dad. A man disappointed, a man at war with himself, because irrespective of what he thought he knew, he did love me and he did want me to be happy and it killed him I couldn't be happy here.

I jumped when those big arms wrapped around me, making my own considerable height feel like nothing as I was swamped by my father's massive frame. As I closed my eyes, I was hit hard by my dad's reassuring scent. I was a little girl again, running to Daddy with my boo-boos, feeling like any problem in the world could be solved by him. But that had stopped after puberty.

I pulled away, something that hurt us both, I knew, but I had to. It beat, loud and true, my own instinct—get away, get away.

"I love you, Dad, but I need to leave for a bit. I'll be back, when I'm ready."

But that moment never came, despite everything I tried and achieved away from the pack. I'd toss the idea of going home around in my mind, and it never felt right.

It didn't feel any better now as I hauled myself out of bed and started shoving clothes back into that same bag, as well as everything else I needed to take. Luckily, I had a big car. I'd need it to take all this shit...

I looked around the apartment I'd lived in since I got here, the crisp white walls, the high ceilings, the large windows that filled the place with a diffuse light that made it OK to ignore the dodgy plumbing and ancient fittings. I'd built something here, something that was going to have to be packed away and returned to sender.

But there was no point in dwelling on it. This was always the way. Our kind lived in packs and had no time for lone wolves.

Chapter 2

"So you're going."

It should've been a question, but it wasn't, Zack standing in the gym we'd both worked in since I got here.

"Thought I better give you the keys rather than send them to you."

He'd met me downstairs readily enough when I texted. Probably thought I just had an itch to scratch like I sometimes did. And who wouldn't? He stood there in nothing but a pair of grey sweatpants that hung low on lean hips, giving me a damn good outline of Not So Little Zack. Massive muscled arms crossed a bare chest that would've had Brad Pitt having a little sook about his body circa the *Fight Club* era. Those smouldering dark eyes took me in, the heat now irritation not sexual, but it didn't seem to make a difference. My vajayjay was trying real hard to convince me that just one more for the road, or maybe two, would be a good idea. Except coming home stinking of another wolf shifter, right when the three ring circus of choosing another alpha male was on the agenda, was a certain way to have one of the idiots from my pack driving down here to 'defend my honour.'

Would Zack be able to take them? I wondered. I shook my head, trying to clear it of yet more bad decisions. Fuck, Dad was in hospital… I'd boxed up my feelings about that a lot like my junk in the back of my car, not to be opened until I was at home, if ever.

"Anyway, here they are. Consider this notice given. Take my last pay as compensation for last minute bullshit."

My hand hovered in the space between us, holding out for him the cluster of keys to the gym I'd used every day since I started working here.

"I'm not docking your fucking pay, Paige. You're good here. We're good here, and you're gonna throw it all away on—"

"Familial bullshit. I know, but that's how it goes. You knew this when you took me on."

"I don't know shit." He raked his fingers through that raffish shock of dark brown hair. "Other packs don't adhere to this archaic crap. Plenty of people live lone or make their own packs—packs built on mutual respect, not hereditary shit."

I put my spare hand up, not having time for the patented Zack Gillespie vision for the future, trademark pending. As it was, I'd be guzzling coffee all the way to get home in one piece.

"Keep them." A big warm hand closed my fingers over the keys, then used that to draw me forward.

"Zack, I can't—"

"I don't give a shit what those fucks in your pack think. You're not walking out of here without this."

I might have protested, but he knew I couldn't say no. Not to the hiss of his breath as he came closer, giving me all the time in the world to make good on my objections and pull away. Not the feel of his other hand on my chin, tilting my lips up, and not the feel of his pressing to mine, firm, persistent, not stopping until mine parted and his tongue surged in.

The keys lay forgotten on the ground as we clawed at each other, the hunger that always rose when we spent too much time together roaring to life. His hand fisted in my hair, forcing my mouth hard against his, the other pressing me firmly against him as I felt Not So Little Zack become a fucking raging anaconda. He smiled against my lips at the guttural sounds I was making as his hand went to my waistband to pull it down.

But god fucking dammit, I jerked away.

"No…"

"Baby, when you run, it just makes me harder," he said as I shuffled back to the door.

"Zack, I can't."

"See, I hear what you're saying, but your scent is telling a whole other story."

"Scent's not consent, Zack. You told me that."

And that was exactly what I needed to say to stop things cold. My boss, my sometimes lover, my friend, froze where he was, nodding for a moment as he processed his own words.

"I can't let you walk out of here without one last taste of you, Paige. You know…"

His words fell away. We'd had this conversation, going around and around, but my objections stopped it cold each time. I walked up to him, feeling the weight of that, the finality of this gesture. When my arms went around him, when I was pressed against that big broad chest and breathed that sweet, spicy essence of Zack in, he went way deeper than if we'd given in to our urges and he'd fucked me on the floor of the boxing ring.

I would miss this. Pain surged up, having already been battened down once tonight, loss a ravening ghost inside me, wanting to suck every part of me down into it. I kept my eyes down when I finally pulled back, trying to hide the tears welling there, but he brushed a thumb across my cheekbone, capturing a stray one.

"Just remember everything you've learnt," he said in a low rumble I felt down into my toes. "None of them will be able to take you if you do."

I nodded, scooped up the keys, and shoved them in my pocket, then walked out without saying goodbye. I couldn't, a howl building in my chest. I might have refused his offer to form a pack here, but my beast, she didn't acknowledge that. As far as she was concerned, we were walking away from that bond, again, and she wasn't happy about it.

Chapter 3

I'm not going to describe the drive home, because I don't really remember it. There was coffee, long roads, the flicker of sunlight through the pale trunks of big gum trees, and endless rolling hills of farmland. And dread. That rose the closer I got, until I was driving down the road into town, passing paddocks of sheep before the first houses appeared. The farther your place was from the centre of town, the lower in rank you were, so in I went, past houses, car yards, shops, a McDonald's, the big ceremonial garden, and then past the ANZAC memorial to the 'big house.' A big old stone Federation style building complete with decorative pilasters; tourists coming to Lupindorf assumed it was the town hall, and in some ways, it was. I drove the car around the back, the automatic gate recognising me, and on the back steps, there they were—the contenders.

Men in their twenties and thirties. Big strong men, lounging upon the stone stairs. Men I'd grown up with. Men who were waiting for me. Mason, Mase I called him, pushed away from the pack and approached the car, bending down when I wound down the window.

"You made it OK?" he asked, leaning on the car door. One look at those muscles, that too long scruff of dark hair, those piercing brown eyes, and you could see what the draw of Zack was for me. He'd been the latest in a long line of Mason substitutes, though I liked him best out of all of them.

"Yeah. Fine."

"So you know the drill? You're gonna run the gauntlet, let them get a smell of you, then we get you inside and you shower and change clothes to get the stink of another shifter off you. Then I'll take you to see your dad."

My eyes jerked up to meet his, something that drew a growl from him, but for once, it wasn't hostile. He shifted against the car, brows frowning then smoothing as he watched me stare back. This was a threat, a slap to the face, a throwing down of a challenge in my pack, but right now, Mason Klein just seemed intrigued that I could. Something inside me flared hard when he was the one to look away first.

"They can't touch you, can't make overtures, can't do a fucking thing without your say so, and I'm here to make sure that's how it goes."

I opened the car door, waiting for him to back off so I could get out, and didn't mention the fact I could probably put any one of these pricks down if they started anything. *Don't declare your hand early*, Zack always told me. *They'll misjudge you for being a woman. Use that to your advantage and take the bastards by surprise.* So I didn't use any of the holds or throws on Mase as I got out, not while he kept backing off, keeping a respectful distance. Something that was about to change abruptly.

'Running the gauntlet' was a tradition our pack had brought over from the old country. The next alpha was always chosen by a female member of the old alpha's family, preferably his daughter. The man who became her mate took the position as head of the pack when they were ready. Running the gauntlet was supposed to be something our beasts naturally did. Strong males pushed forward, scented her for receptiveness and then put themselves forward as contenders if she was. So why did my wolf whine unhappily inside me at the prospect? I didn't let that show as Mason escorted me over to the stairs.

"No touching, no getting in her face. Be respectful, or I'll show you how to," Mason said as we approached.

But they didn't pay attention to him, just me. Familiar and not so familiar faces were directed my way, hot eyes raking down my body. Some eyebrows jerked up. So they should, I was in a helluva lot better shape now than I'd been when I left. Working with Zack, I'd honed my body just as they did theirs. They'd tell themselves they didn't like it, that they liked their women sweet and soft and pliable.

Like I gave a shit.

But that wasn't what got their hackles up. My pack liked to talk about dominance like it was a fixed quality, that some wolves had it and some didn't and that was the end of that. Well, I'd left Lupindorf and learned just how malleable that concept was. Dominance allowed you to psych out an opponent. Dominance let you push your will on those weaker than you, in theory to keep the peace and avoid every conflict between our snappish animals turning into a physical one. But what they didn't know was that dominance was a lot like confidence—it surged and fell in response to your actions and your reception from others. I'd left this weird little hothouse I'd grown up in and become an unruly weed like everyone associated with Zack's gym.

Every day you walked in that door, you tested yourself against others, found out what they could do, what you could do, and every single one of them was a discovery. I'd learned a lot about me, about others, and particularly about wolf shifter men. I saw former school mates, men I'd seen at my dad's council table, men who'd come sniffing around his door the moment I turned eighteen. I met their eyes and they came clustering in, a wall of masculine flesh, all so well muscled and taut, it took some effort to keep my hands to myself. But I did, and they took their long breaths in, getting my scent and Zack's.

"Who was he?" growled Aidan. Tall, good looking of course, with a shock of dark blond hair and hazel eyes, he'd been king of the school when I was still a student. It was odd to see that intense gaze turned my way this time, not to the popular girls that had hung around him.

I smiled, feeling my teeth sharpen. "Just a hookup. Nothing important. Now, gentlemen, if you'd excuse me?" I spoke with a confidence I didn't feel, pushing past them with an abruptness that made my heart race, old memories of what doing something like that to men who considered themselves dominant over me flooding my mind. But maybe because Mason was at my side, the group parted and let me go by without comment.

Well, not entirely.

"We need time to pay court," Aidan said, eyes shifting from Mason to me and staying there, taking in the sweatpants and spaghetti string tank I was wearing like it was fucking couture. "Don't think because you're ensconced in the house, you get a leg up on the rest of us."

"The alpha's not even dead yet. I haven't had a chance to explain what happened. Show some fucking respect."

Well then, Mason always did have a way with words. My eyes slid sideways, just watching those big hands form fists, the wolf tattoos that ran up his forearms dancing as the muscles shifted. He wanted them to step forward, I could smell it. Sharp, acidic, it was a stink that filled my nose and coated my tongue. Grief, anger and…

"The courting season will be announced once Paige has had an opportunity to see her father and settle in. Now, you've got what you wanted, so piss off."

I jumped when Mason slung an arm around my waist, steering me inside the house, the cool calm settling over me as soon as the door was slammed shut. But the men weren't here when he directed me upstairs with his hand on the base of my spine, burning through the thin spandex of my top.

I can't, Paige!

The memory of his shout rang in my mind until I pulled free, scaling the steps up to the bedrooms and stalking down the hall. My room was right next to Dad's, and for a moment, I stopped and stared at his door, closed now. He wouldn't be in there. They'd have taken him to the hospital out on White Road. Would he be lying on one of their beds, stiff, still, cold, lifeless? I remembered that was the way Mum looked. I swallowed and put my hand on the doorknob.

"Paige—"

"Have a shower and get changed. I've got it," I snapped back.

I heard rather than saw the long sigh. "I'll bring up your stuff from the car."

"Thanks." He paused on the step at my words, and I listened to the creak on the stairs before opening the door and walking inside to a museum piece.

Nothing had changed in here, I realised as I looked around the room. It'd been cleaned, the same bedspread on the bed, but I could smell the scent of lemon washing powder and sun. My books had been dusted, my photos still in the same frames, my cupboards full of all the clothes I'd rejected when I left. *Home, family, pack…* They pulsed inside me, something I wasn't willing to let in just yet. My head jerked around when the door creaked, something Dad refused to fix as it alerted him to any attempt of mine to sneak out. Mason filled the doorway, eyes meeting mine as he brought my stuff in, dumping it on the bed.

This was the stuff of my teen dreams—Mason Klein in my room in an empty house. He had to know what I was thinking, catching a whiff of my scent, something only male shifters could do. Did he detect the sadness and the pain as well as the arousing thrill? It was a knee jerk reaction that had been conditioned into me throughout my adolescence, but this time, he didn't scurry out like the rat he was. No, he placed the items down with undue slowness, then turned to face me.

It'd take three steps for him to close the gap between us. He knew it and I knew it, because we both sucked in air, as if that was enough to stop us. My fingers twitched, remembering the feel of that soft hair between them like it was yesterday, and his eyes jerked down to note the movement. His nostrils flared, his brow creasing as he watched and listened to the faint sound of my fingertips rubbing together.

If I was dreaming, this would be the moment he remembered

what it was like, the feel of his hot mouth on mine, the dark stubble of his jaw scraping across my skin as he fought to suck down every stolen taste he took of the alpha's daughter. He'd remember the thrust of his tongue, tangling with my far less experienced one, dragging sensations from me I'd never really known until I left town, but then just registered as a deep throbbing between my legs, one I felt right now. He'd shove that thick thigh between mine, drag me onto it, force the pressure right up against my—

"Have a shower, Paige," he said instead, all cool, calm, and collected. I smiled to see the beta mask resituated so thoroughly. "Meet me downstairs in your father's office when you're done. We need to talk."

And with that, I was dismissed, the soft click of the door my only goodbye.

Chapter 4

So it's bad to admit I rubbed one out in the shower, right?

My body, my mind was a riotous mess when I stepped under the water, and the heat helped relax my muscles but not much else. None of what was happening was unexpected, except it was. Dad wasn't a young man, but dying? We had more time, I'd been sure of it. Time for me to come home of my own volition, to show him what his little girl had become. I slammed a hand down on the white tiles, claws forming to scratch at them as I gasped. I'd had it stolen from me, the reconciliation, that moment when my dad saw me and not his heir standing before him. When he finally told me—

Mason... The guys... I insisted, redirecting my thoughts sharply. In my mind, I was running the gauntlet again, but this time, I was using that time honoured technique for managing anxiety—imagining them all naked. That wouldn't have been hard to achieve. Shifters aren't as funny about nudity as humans are. If I'd asked for it, if I'd requested them all to strip down, even Mase, there was a fair chance they would have. To show me what I was missing if I didn't pick them. To show me what they had to offer.

I was compartmentalising, dissociating. Well, that was what Zack called it. I packed up thoughts and feelings and boxed them away for later, much later. Mase was gonna give me the deets when I went downstairs, then he'd take me to the hospital. I'd find out exactly what had happened in my absence, everything I'd missed. I'd see my dad lying there… I shook my head under the water, grabbed the soap, and began working it across my body.

It became them, their hands skating across my skin. I didn't want the contenders per se. Well, none but… However, I replaced the actual guys with a faceless bunch of muscular bodies. Yeah, I could get behind that. Zack had told me one day, when he was psychoanalysing me again, that the thoughts we give energy get bigger, more powerful inside us. He'd meant the scripts I'd learned from growing up in this pack, but I'd twisted that idea to my own ends. Because the soap slipped between my thighs, the foam made my fingers skate over my folds, giving me friction but nowhere near enough. Because as my nails raked the tiles, as I worked myself up, quickly, efficiently, I blanked my mind. For a few hot moments, I could feel all those hands, those teeth, that skin against mine, and it yanked me out of here, away from my problems, to just feeling.

Then it was him pushing his way through all those bodies, a wolf where everyone else was a pup. He shouldered his way through the pack until his body pressed against mine, filling me with that scent of smoke and moss. His mouth brushed mine, his stubble scraping, then his teeth as he took my bottom lip between his. I knew that taste, sharp and sour from a beer as it'd been last time, then all him, and my tongue flicked out to capture and savour it.

"Paige?" A couple of knocks on the door had my eyes jerking open, flicking over to the door knob, but it stayed still. "Don't think you can hide in there. We need to get this done."

I heard the growl in Mase's voice, felt the sharp tone of reprimand on my skin as my fingers moved.

"Paige?"

I pressed my arm against my mouth to stifle my moans, but with his hearing, he probably knew what I was up to. Could smell it too. I heard the faint sound of him shifting on the other side of the door, his low sigh, the slight creak on the door as if a body leant against it. I closed my eyes again and remembered what that had felt like, when it was my body he leaned into. I felt the claw of his fingers, the way he yanked me tight against him, his eyes going silver as his beast rode him hard.

Just like I'd hoped he'd do me.

"I'll meet you downstairs in ten," came his much more muted voice, right as my hips jerked, as my pants filled the air. My body twitched with a short, sharp orgasm that rushed in and then left just as fast, leaving me just aching for more. Then reality shoved its way forward moments later. I opened my eyes, staring blindly at the tiles, at the water running down them, at my own shaking hands.

What the fuck was I doing?

I grabbed the soap and started again, washing myself as quickly and efficiently as I possibly could, paying special attention to cleaning my fingers thoroughly.

IT DIDN'T MATTER. After I'd dried off, plaited my hair back from my face, and put on clean sweats and a long-sleeved compression top, I padded downstairs to Dad's office and Mase was waiting, sitting in the chair he customarily did, opposite to Dad and on his right side. His eyes slid down my body, a quick automatic thing he corrected swiftly enough, forcing them to stay with my eyes. But when I went to sit down on the other side of him, his hand whipped out and grabbed the one I'd been using to get myself off unerringly, drawing it, and hence me, with it. He brought the fingers to his nose and breathed in deeply, no doubt past the scented soap and body lotion and perfume I'd slathered on before staring up at me. I yanked it back, tilting my head at him before sitting down in an ungainly sprawl.

"You wouldn't bring me back here, not unless it was bad, real bad. So tell me what's happened."

Chapter 5

"You're just going to pretend—"

"Yes," I replied sharply.

"You were—"

My eyes jerked up, and I met his head-on, pausing for a moment to watch the inevitable look of surprise spread across his face, and bing, there it was. I held his gaze, the second most dominant guy in the whole pack. I held it and kept it without too much effort. When I was ready, when I was done watching his jaw lock down, the muscle quivering slightly, I dropped my eyes, looking across at Dad's desk. Big, beautiful, and carved from a richly polished mahogany with a million little mysterious drawers and cubby holes, it'd been a whole other world to me as a child.

"I know you believe a woman's pleasure belongs to her suitors or her mate. I know you don't like what I was doing, but I'm tired, worn out, and needed to blow off some steam before we go to the hospital. I don't expect you to understand."

"And the guy you came here stinking of? He does?"

"Zack," I said, meeting Mase's hot gaze for a moment, then looking away again. "And yeah, he does. He took me under his wing when I got to the city, helped train me, helped me shake off some of the small-town bullshit I inherited from here."

Mason paused at the sound of the man's name, his jaw tightening. "I just bet he did."

"He encouraged me to find my pleasure where I wanted, didn't try to constrain me in any way. Didn't tell me what to do or get jealous or hem me in."

"So he didn't give a shit about you."

"Maybe. Maybe he just knew if you love something, you gotta set it free, and if it comes back, it's yours." I grinned toothily at the cheesy cliché, but I knew what we were doing—fencing rather than dealing with the hard truths, as per usual. "It doesn't matter who I fucked or didn't fuck—"

"It will if he comes here."

"I need to know what happened with Dad. The kind of fucking bullshit that this place runs on, all of this…posturing and crap, Dad trumps that. What happened, Mase? Last chance, or I just get in my car and go to the hospital and find out myself."

I watched him pack all that tall, dark, growling beast up behind his human façade and settle back in his chair.

"He had a stroke, Paige. I found him early last night. He'd hit the emergency button in the alpha's bedroom, the one that lets us know if there's an attack or something. His speech was slurred, his face was all… You'll see. By the time the ambulance arrived, he was in a coma. He still is. There's not much to see." He paused, looking down at his hands. "He's in a hospital bed, covered in tubes to keep him breathing. I'm sorry, Paige."

AND IT WAS TRUE. We drove up, walked down the halls, a nurse getting up to stop us until she saw Mase and realised who I was. I froze in the doorway, taking in the glaring lights, the sterile white and steel surfaces, the steady whoosh of the respirator, the *ping* of the vital signs monitor. And there, under a pile of pale blue and white blankets, was Dad. At least, I thought it was. I crept closer, feeling the same trepidation I'd felt as a young girl, creeping into his room when I was having a nightmare, though this time, it was multiplied exponentially.

My shower antics seemed hollow and ridiculous, as they often did when I felt like my back was against the wall. *Reactive rather than deliberate*, Zack always said. But he also told me to meet any challenge head-on. I forced my feet to move, one after the other, until I sank down into the chair placed by his side. I reached out carefully, cautiously, allowing only my fingers to touch a hand that seemed gnarled now, knuckles swollen, skin heavily lined with age.

"Dad…?"

I didn't say the word, it just came out on an exhale, the barest of whispers. This was not my father, that idea took root quickly, my brain firmly, solidly rejecting the reality before me. My father was alpha, held this town through will alone, strode into meetings, barked out sharp, succinct orders, expecting to be obeyed, and he was now…this? This was someone so much smaller, older, weaker. I didn't know who it was, but it wasn't Dad. I frowned, my fingers grabbing his and squeezing, probably too hard. Weakness didn't work well in the pack, and for the first time in my life, I felt a rush of something completely alien—protectiveness. People would see this, see him down, see me having just returned, and be ready to make a play, a major play.

"Get the family together. We need to meet tonight," I said to Mase, but I didn't look away from my father.

"Done. I started calling them straight after I called you. They're just waiting for my call."

"Have everyone in the house by nightfall, especially any of the girls or unmated women, or anyone you think is likely to be a target. They move into the compound."

"You think someone's going to try and force a bond?" I watched Mason stiffen, eyes beginning to dart around the room, as if rogue 'suitors' would jump out from behind the curtains.

"That doesn't work. You have to want someone on some level to form a bond, that's something I learned. I just don't want any of my cousins getting attacked by any ill-informed mouth breathers and being hurt."

"I'll get the enforcers onto it, get them to pass the word around."

"And you better tell them you're stepping up temporarily too."

"No." Mason's reply was sharp, definite. "No fucking way, Paige, I can't—"

I watched the fear, the anger, the animal need to escape a trap rise and rise inside him. That fear of being connected to me.

"No one's going to force you to take a mate. We'll explain that this is a temporary situation, that you're stepping up until this is sorted. You have to until we work something else out." I stared into those hot, angry eyes, already bleeding to silver, his fangs dropping in the face of a threat. "Mase, no one can beat you. That's how you've held this position for so long." I looked back at Dad, embracing that cool tone he often used when he didn't want excuses, just results. "It's only temporary, Mason. I promise I won't lay a finger on you other than what's necessary. It's just to provide a united front."

"Fucking high-handed Spehrs…" I heard him mutter.

"Yeah?" I snapped back. "Well, you fucking Kleins seem pretty determined to serve under us."

Silence stretched out between us, filling the room, dampening all sounds until…

"I'll make the calls."

"You do that."

And while he obeyed my order, I held my father's hand, felt the thready pulse under my fingers, watched a machine force him to keep breathing. I'd thought I had time and I was wrong, so bloody wrong, and now there was nothing else I could do but wait. Wait for him to take his own breaths, rip the cannula out of his hand, and start roaring to be taken home and given a big feed of bacon and eggs. Wait for my dad to open his eyes and take up the mantle of alpha again, before we were forced to.

Chapter 6

You're deflecting again, Zack's voice said in my mind. That was eerie, hearing the voice of someone who was still alive and kicking and, if the missed call notices on my phone were anything to go by, wanting to actually talk to me. *A warrior does not hide or push away a threat. She assesses the danger, then finds the best way forward. Accept, then act.*

I'm halfway there, I thought as I watched the familiar streets pass by. Mason was driving us back to the house, not one word or sound escaping those thinned down lips, but it wasn't until we stopped at the traffic lights, my head turning at the raucous sounds coming from the pub on the corner, that I knew where I needed to be. Stevie's bar.

"I'm getting out here," I said abruptly, hand going to the door, then I was opening it and getting out before Mason could reply.

"Paige!" he shouted, having wound down the windows.

"I'll be back in time for the meeting, but I need to relax for a bit or I'm gonna scream."

"Don't fucking do it, Paige. You said it yourself, this leaves the family open to an attack." A beep from the car behind him had his head whipping around before he wrenched on the wheel and stopped the car half in and half out of the street side carpark.

Not in Stevie's. It was neutral ground, always, something I think he hoped I'd forgotten. I wasn't arguing with him. Spehrs didn't argue, which was autocratic and high-handed bullshit, but that was how it worked here. I walked up the steps, hearing the steady thump of music coupled with the low hum of voices inside that just got louder as I pushed open the doors.

Until they didn't.

Heads turned, conversations stopped, barflies peeled themselves away from the counter, but my eyes all skated past them. She smiled when she saw me, cocking her hip and throwing down her tea towel, then she grabbed the remote for the jukebox and flicked through songs until I heard the familiar bars of an old standard in the pub. Sheryl Crow started singing about her neighbourhood going to shit, and people picked up the lyrics quick enough, warbling along as I shook my head and approached the bar. But I didn't get far, as Stevie vaulted over it and landed on the ground for just a second before launching herself at me. She wrapped me in her arms, those slim limbs possessing a hidden strength, pinning me to her chest as her mouth went to my ear.

"You said you'd never come back."

I pulled back, disentangling myself, standing on my own two feet, as I would have to now. I met those catlike green eyes and saw her hair was almost the same colour as them now. It always changed.

"You know why I had to."

"I don't know anything of the sort," she said, then sniffed, turning back to the bar and getting behind it in the more conventional way this time. She pulled down the top shelf tequila to the sounds of whoops from the patrons, but she just stuck her finger up as she poured out two shots, pushing them towards me before pouring her own. "So you need some fortification before you deal with that bloody family of yours?"

"Just came from the hospital." Stevie's hand froze midway to her mouth, a look of concern on her face. "I think I just wanted to see a friendly face before it begins."

"Think I see why," she said, nodding over my shoulder. By the chill in the air and the stiffening of the patrons' backs around me, I knew who had joined us.

"Stevie," Mase said in a curt voice.

"No crap in my bar, Mason. The alpha agreed this was to be neutral ground. Beta or not, you don't cause shit here." As a sop to his pride, she poured another shot and pushed it his way, watching to see if he'd pick it up. His muscles bunched, his T-shirt sleeves riding up as he leaned against the bar, something several ladies took note of as he reached for the glass. I lifted mine, saluted Stevie and then the onlookers, before downing one then the other.

"You little beauty!" came the refrain, the music and the noise picking up where it had left off, cloaking me in a cocoon of familiarity.

"I'm safe. You can keep an eye on me from by the pool table. No one's gonna do shit here," I told Mason, swivelling around to face him.

He didn't reply straight away, typical dominance bullshit, but he could no more stop himself than cease breathing.

"I'm not holding your hair back this time. You spew alone and not at all in my car."

Old me would have been creaming her panties at all that big, growly, bossy, shifter bullshit, but new me just smiled and waved, though she wasn't above getting a little damp in the knickers. I'd been fantasising about Mase ever since I was old enough to work out what the achy feeling between my legs meant, but it didn't mean I had to fall straight into that crap again.

"Fine, now off you toddle. Play nice with the other kids. I haven't spoken to Stevie for ages, and I need to update her on a lot."

There was a stillness about Mason that had always transfixed me as a teen. When I was at my most ratty, he just was. Daddy issues, I figured. Like my father, he carried around with him a kind of quiet power. Big dick energy, as Stevie liked to say. But I'd never gotten the chance to confirm or deny, and that pulled at my attention. I could do literally anything and he would remain unmoved. I felt a sharp pang at that, watching his eyes narrow as he considered what exactly Stevie and my conversation might entail. Well, I was done getting caught up in that monolithic macho bullshit. I just shook my head and turned back to her, watching her pour out the tequila.

"So big, tall, and delicious you sent me the photos of when you were in the big smoke? He seemed promising. Where is he?" she asked.

"I left him where I found him. We never had anything permanent going. It was nice, y'know? Not being pressured to mate forever and choose the next alpha. He just was, I just was, and sometimes, we just were, together."

"And when you were?" Her eyes sparkled as she smirked, just a hint of silver staining them.

She, the bar, the crowd, the music all faded away for a moment, and there was just him.

He moved like a fucking panther in the ring, sparring with me, doing everything he wouldn't do outside the ring. Tracking me, hunting me down, pushing me up against the ropes until I came back twice as hard. I struck with fists wrapped in tape, elbows, knees, feet, forcing him back, back, back, until finally, I got the fucking drop on him. My leg swept out and hooked behind his muscular one, yanking on the knee before he could react, and down he went. I got exactly half a minute to look down at the big body sprawled out on the canvas, eyes wide as he panted, staring blankly at the ceiling. My grin spread, my fist going to the air.

And then he yanked me down on top of him.

"Don't let your fucking guard down," he said with a grin, holding me easily pinned in this position. Fighting wise, this was exactly where I didn't want to be, sprawled out, unable to use physics or momentum to break his hold.

But I didn't really want to, did I?

He'd smiled, slow and cocky, then did that thing wolf shifters do—took in a long inhale of my scent.

"Scent isn't consent, Paige," he'd said, running a hand down the side of my face, watching me shiver. "Sometimes the blood gets up. Sometimes fighting's a bit like foreplay for shifters, feels like a mating fight." I couldn't move, couldn't say anything, my entire focus on his finger as it moved now to trace the shape of my lips. He smiled when they parted, letting the pad of one finger slide in a little to touch my tongue. Our breath sounded so damn noisy right then. "Tell me you want this. Tell me you want me, and I'll—"

I cut him off with a kiss, because what else could I do? I couldn't say it.

The words of the alpha's daughter had a weight to them, even all the way out here in the city. So I showed him, like he showed me, shifting until I was straddling him, feeling the fucking great lump underneath that let me know just how into this idea he was. And then I bent down and kissed him, long and sweet, the way I'd wanted to since we met, when I watched those full lips tell me about gym procedures.

"Fuck, yes…" he hissed, pulling back for a moment as his hand slid to my hair, yanking free my ponytail holder and then burying his fingers in it. He crunched up into a seated position, unable to just lie there and take it, then dragged me down hard against him. His mouth, his hands were hungry, eating me up, wanting more, more…

My eyes jerked up when I heard my friend's chuckle, Stevie and the pub all flooding back. I swallowed hard, blinking for a moment, still able to feel Zack's fingers on my skin.

"That good, huh?"

My eyes dropped down to the countertop, fingers going around the new shot and downing it without a thought, needing that harsh burn. Anything to assuage the ache.

"Hey, I'm sorry. I shouldn't have pried. I figured we weren't talking about your dad if you were in here."

Beep… beep… That bloody machine making that rhythmic noise, him lying there looking so—

I jerked my head up and forced myself to smile. I'd be doing that so much in the next few weeks, until things were settled.

"So where is he? Mr Tall, Dark, and Handsome and frighteningly similar looking to a certain beta we both know and love," she charged on.

"I came in here to drown my sorrows?" I asked with a snort, but I'd known the drill when I got out of the car. Stevie was a straight shooter, didn't bullshit around, and if I wanted soft words and my hand held, this was not gonna be the place for it. "I couldn't let things go too far. It just wouldn't be fair. He was looking for a mate, and I…" I looked around the pub, which was starting to fill more, being Saturday lunchtime. "I get to play pack princess and kingmaker all in one. Zack wouldn't want any of this bullshit, was certainly never gonna wanna play the stupid games that involve becoming alpha."

As if in response to that, my phone started to ring. I fished it out, moving my thumb to accept the call, when I saw who it was. Stevie shook her head when she peered at the screen.

"You sure about that? Doesn't look like he's ready to let you go, if the…seven missed calls are anything to go by. Answer the phone, Paige. You're going through shit, your dad is sick, and I'm shit with sad stories, you know that. Talk to the man, even if it's just to tell him how things are gonna go. Don't leave him hanging. No one needs that."

She pulled away from me, moving to pour the beers of those people milling around the bar, leaving me to stare at the phone. My thumb hovered as I felt the vibrations all the way down my hand, through my body, like Zack was reaching out physically as well as via phone. I swore silently at myself as I thumbed the green icon, feeling that surge of need, to hear his voice, to hear that growly rasp of concern, to hear him dissect my fucking life and help me put together a plan.

"Paige."

I'd put the phone to my ear, Zack's words an echo of Mason's the other night, but the tone so different. It was like dropping into a warm bath when you were cold, cocoa in hand, feeling all that heat just wash over you. Stevie shot me a mischievous look as I answered, waggling her eyebrows before turning back to her patrons.

"Hey, I'm sorry—"

"Are you OK? How's your dad?"

I let out a long sigh, feeling like I'd been unconsciously carrying a heavy weight and not noticing it until I laid it down.

"It's not good. He's had a stroke and is on a respirator. I…" Don't think about that yet. Not yet. "I'm not gonna be back, Zack. I should've left those keys for you. I'll mail them."

"No need. I'm halfway to Lupindorf. Be there in a few hours."

"What?" The bath turned ice cold and filled with sharp icicles. "No, turn around, go home. Fuck, Zack!" Stevie frowned, looking over at me with concern as she worked.

"I know what this means, Paige. I came from an old-school pack too. I'm not gonna get in the way of anything or try and stop you from taking whoever you think is your best choice for mate, but I'm not leaving you alone to deal with this. You been hiding again?"

I swallowed fiercely, trying to dislodge the massive lump there but not succeeding. It just swelled and swelled until my throat was closed shut.

"Thought so. Some burdens, they're too much for any one person. You don't have to fight every battle by yourself. I'll be there soon, just hang tight."

"Zack, I can't put you up at the house. The contenders will see that as a challenge. Every single one of them will want to take you on."

He laughed at that, a low rumble that did interesting things to my body, despite the almost total wave of fear rushing over me.

"Never backed away from a fight before, babe. Not gonna start now. I won't cause shit with any of your suitors, but I ain't backing down if they do."

"Zack!" I hissed his name, trying to inject all the pain and fear and frustration I felt in that one word and failing. "Please…"

"It'll be OK, Paige. If I have to, I'll find somewhere else to stay. You're not alone, you hear me? None of my fighters go through something like this without someone by their side. Now, I gotta get off the phone before I put my pedal to the floor and speed all the way there. Just know I'm coming."

What I felt for Zack was always a complex tumble of intense friendship, need, desire, but it all just got more and more pressing as I said goodbye. So much so, I just hung my head and breathed for a few moments, trying to ride out the maelstrom of sensation inside me and come back to the here and now.

I wasn't sure how long it took for the sounds—people talking shit, the occasional shout, the regular beat of the music—and the smells—sour, yeasty beer, the sharp chemical scent of the tequila—of the bar to come back to the fore. *Be here, be now*, I told myself.

"You ready to go?"

My head jerked up to see Mason standing beside me, staring

down. His eyes got so hard sometimes, they looked like polished jet. I met his gaze for several heartbeats, getting the waves of irritation from him, even if I couldn't scent him like he could me. I picked up my last shot and downed it, nodding to Stevie as she sauntered over.

"You've got a place here," she said as she watched me ready to leave. "Know that. Whatever goes down, I got a spare room above the bar with a comfy bed and—"

I cut her off by reaching across the bar and wrapping as much of my arm around her shoulders as I could.

"Thanks. I needed to hear that today." I pulled back, then reached for my wallet, ready to pay for my drinks.

"Oh no, you don't." She curled her fingers over mine, shoving the money back in. "If I'm really hard up, I'll just send a bill to the alpha's office. Come back, Paige, even if it's just to sink a few drinks or to play a game of pool. Mason."

He returned her nod and then did something surprising—put a hand on my shoulder to steer me out of the bar. While I'd spent so many years waiting for this man to touch me spontaneously, today, I wished he hadn't. It burned through the tight Lycra of my top, setting my flesh alight in ways that were intense and confusing right now. Zack and I were in a weird place between friends and lovers, and he was coming into a hostile environment I couldn't help but want to protect him from. And Dad... But I let the beta wolf lead me outside, waiting for him to open the door like he wanted before piling into the car.

"It'll be OK, Paige," he said so gently, I wondered if I'd misheard him. But I didn't get a chance to ask as he turned the key in the ignition and drove us home.

"SLEEP FOR AN HOUR OR TWO," he said when we got home, the quiet of the building almost tangible, despite being situated in the middle of town. "The family won't be here until sundown, and you look tired."

"Thanks," I said with a wry sniff. "That bad, huh?"

"What's coming, it'll be tough. You need to be rested to deal with it."

He was, of course, right. He usually was. But as I climbed the stairs, ready to return to my childhood room, I looked down the hall, moving to my father's on automatic. I opened the door a crack, that inbuilt fear of pissing off the alpha too ingrained, even though logically, I knew he wasn't there. And then it hit me.

That woodsy tobacco scent that was all Dad, the old western novel left facedown on the bedside table, open to where he was up to. The lamp, giving off a faint glow in the afternoon light which streamed through the big picture windows. The deep burgundy satin bedspread that was usually spread neatly across the bed, now rucked up and half off. It was the feel of that which drew me down. Initially, I was going to straighten it up and then go to bed, but the feel of it, false, fake, silken texture had me falling down into the dent Dad had left in the mattress.

"You can't fight this stuff like you can a bout," Zack had said, tapping my forehead. *"The more you push the thoughts and feelings away, the harder they come. There's no grapple, no hold to keep them at bay, Paige. All you can do is face them down head-on and know they, too, will pass, like every other feeling or thought you've had. Now, let's do the mindfulness exercise I showed you."*

He'd pulled me against him, knowing that right then, I needed that physical reminder to anchor me in the present, to disengage my mind from all its constant chatter and just be. I breathed when he breathed, our chests synchronising, growing slower and calmer with each breath. I felt the thoughts and feelings clamouring at the edges of my perception and then did what scared me the most —let them in.

And in they rushed, all pent-up repressed energy, and my discomfort rose higher and higher until I started to stiffen, feeling like I'd be swallowed whole by them.

"Ssh…" he'd said, rubbing circles on my shoulder, helping me tolerate the feeling until what he always said would happen and I always feared wouldn't— my mind adjusted and settled, letting the clamour inside it just exist, which somehow quietened the roar. Then, as the rush subsided, my breath, my body came back into focus, especially where it slumped against Zack's. He held me *close, sheltering me within that massive body, until that last long breath shuddered out.*

But when they came now, they weren't so measured. I was still fighting what was coming, always did without Zack to ground me. But I knew what to do, had been practising it for so long. So why did it hurt so much? I curled up in a ball, my chest burning with pain as silent sobs racked it, every muscle screaming with the effort to hold it all in. Tears streamed down my face, blinding me to everything but the blurry sight of my father's bed, soon to be replaced by his current one. *Beep…beep…beep.*

"Daddy…" I whimpered like a little girl, but I couldn't stop it. We had more time. *We should have had more time*, my brain insisted, even while my heart knew otherwise. There were no shoulds, only what is, and the reality of that hit me, one-two, a devastating combination I couldn't block, not now. My mouth opened in a long loud cry, my wolf needing to howl her pain to the world. But I didn't. Spehr's didn't. I just screamed silently into a pillow that smelled of my father's aftershave until I could scream no more.

Chapter 7

"Paige."

Again, his voice jerked me from sleep, Mason standing in the doorway, a dark shadow with soft eyes and a firm voice. I rolled over from where I lay, and he took it all in, my dishevelled look, my swollen eyes, the stain of my tears on the pillow, and just nodded in response.

"It's time."

I jumped out of bed with a speed that seemed to surprise Mason, but I needed to put distance between me and that bed. The time for being a little girl was over, I had a role to fulfil and I had to get it done. I raked my hair back, plaiting it tight and neat as my father's beta watched.

And what does he think? I wondered, those eyes giving little away. But they stared, oh, how they stared, taking everything in until I went to move past him. This wasn't how it was supposed to be, as my father had worked damn hard to make sure I was not left alone with any man, let alone his beta, and especially not in his bedroom.

Which is perhaps why Mason didn't move. I knew right then, as those tensed muscles made a lie of his casual slouch against the door frame, as I brushed past him while he didn't give me an inch of ground, that there was more going on here than Mason wanted to give away. I paused midway out of the door, hovering in the space that pressed our bodies together, my legs on either side of one of his, and met the beta's gaze. A smile curled my lips, something just made his eyes glitter all the more dangerously, those firmly crossed arms starting to loosen the longer I stayed, but to do what?

"Paige, honey? Are you up here?"

I heard my aunt Nance's voice coming up the steps, so I stepped out into the hall with a mocking little smile and then went to meet her. That disappeared as soon as she got to the top. Only Mum's family mattered to the pack, since the alpha line was passed on matrilineally, and she was Mum's only sister.

"How are you, sweetheart? You must be devastated. I know you've only just got to town, but…"

I looked over my shoulder to where Mason still lurked, then followed Nance downstairs. It had begun.

"YOU REALLY THINK the contenders will want to declare an open contest?" Uncle Alan asked, settling back in his chair in the meeting room. All my cousins filled the chairs around me, along with my aunty and my two uncles.

"Wouldn't have if Paige hadn't run off to the city," Bryce said. We were of close enough age that he'd proposed himself as a potential mate when we were growing up. Ew.

"Well I did, and if we toss around might have beens and should've's, we'll still be thrashing this out long after Dad's…" I'd been about to make a flip statement about Dad's mortality, but I couldn't now. My jaw tightened for a minute as I saw Nance and several of the older cousins lean forward, ready to deliver their own opinions, but I was about to put a stop to that. "I thought I had more time. The agreement between my father's beta and myself was that if it looked like Dad was becoming seriously ill, he'd let me know and I'd come back. I know it would have been better if I'd stayed here, taken a mate and settled down, but I…"

My voice trailed away as Mason and ten of Dad's enforcers filed in the door. My harem in waiting, Stevie used to call them. Enforcers were a way for the strong young men of the pack to find a place in the hierarchy, rather than fomenting rebellion against it. Every woman's eye was drawn to the men as they came into the room and leaned against the wall, and some of the guys too.

"Well, the quickest way to solve this problem is to choose from your father's men," Nance said.

"Now, Nancy—" Uncle Bill started.

"No, Adam was one of our father's enforcers, and our grandfather was his alpha's beta before him. It's the natural way of things. Paige simply reacquaints herself with Adam's men and makes her choice…quickly."

"So, it's that easy, is it?" I asked with a snort. "You haven't even asked any of the guys if they're interested. None of them were there when I ran the gauntlet."

"Yeah, why was that, Mase?" A really tall man with a shock of reddish-brown hair and a thick Ned Kelly beard looked down the line at the beta, but not for long. Whiskey coloured eyes flicked back to me, crinkling in a smile before he said, "Well, you know I'm in, Paige."

"Declan?" I got to my feet, something that drew hisses of censure from the women around the table. "Oh my god, you look so…"

"Yeah, the beard came in and I went with it. You look so…" He gestured vaguely to me, then watched me closely as all the memories came flooding back in. He'd been a boy when we were dating back in school, no beard back then. But those freckles that scattered across the tops of his cheekbones and his nose, I'd spent a lazy afternoon kissing each one when we were in Year Eleven, which then led to…

"You finished?" Mason snapped.

"No, he isn't, beta," Aunt Nancy said in her ice princess tone. "I forgot you had a prior connection to young Declan. Perhaps you should pursue—?"

"Nance, there's no need—"

"It's important a—"

"We need to—"

I raked my eyes across the guys as my family argued.

"So who you gonna choose?" I turned to see my cousin, Bridget had flopped in the chair beside me, shooting me a conspiratorial wink. I smiled back, I couldn't help it. She was always a picture of mischief, usually just before we got in serious shit. "They all look pretty tasty. I wonder if there's a 'try before you buy' option. As your loyal cousin, I would, of course, help you sample—"

"Stop it, Bridge," I hissed, seeing the lazy smiles go up along the group of men. Well, not all of them. Callum, often touted to be the next in line for beta, looked around uncomfortably.

"Hey, we can't just dump this on the guys," I interjected. "There's a process, and some of them may have already found mates or be in the process of doing so."

"If he's unmated, he's a potential choice," Nance said primly.

"I'm not breaking up existing relationships," I said, looking around the room sharply when more people went to argue, waiting for silence. "Work out who would be the next single females in line, especially the ones you think people might want to throw their weight behind." I scanned the faces of my female cousins, including Bridget. "That's who you need to watch out for, who guys might make a play for to take the role of alpha. We also need to work out who steps up if I can't."

"Paige…" My name was warning, reprimand, and threat.

"Maybe we should make it an open call," I said. "Maybe we should let any guy who thinks he's got the chops to put his name forward make his case to the people like humans do. Maybe us retaining a stranglehold on this town isn't such a great idea." Well, I got silence at that, didn't I? I shook my head, then said, "Collect a list of the contenders, and I'll work my way through them."

"Yeah, you will," Bridget muttered.

"But we also need to work out who's second and third in the line of succession, and they should be moved here until things are decided." I felt a flush of shame identical to the one I'd felt as I swept out of here five years ago. "To make sure nothing happens to them."

"Well, that'd be—"

"It's not you, Nance," Alan said. "They need to be of child bearing age."

"I'm well aware of that, Alan. I was going to say it'd be Bridget and Selma. My girls." Her smile was smug. It'd have been so much easier if Dad had agreed to one of my cousins taking the role I didn't want.

"My daughters were born before yours," Alan said

"But not of the female line," she replied snippily. "Jade and Fern are lovely young ladies who would make beautiful alpha females" — the two girls did what we all did and looked bloody uncomfortable as the 'adults' spoke— "but the role passes to my daughters first."

"Something I already spoke to Dad about before I left," I said, getting everyone's attention real quick. "I didn't plan for this. I wanted him to pass the mantle on, but he refused." For a moment, I didn't see my family, I just saw my room, my bag, Dad… But I blinked and brought myself back to the now. By the look on their faces, I'd managed to surprise them, even Bridget. "Look, maybe that's something we can look at, going forward."

"Not me," Bridget said, pushing herself away from the conference table. "Like, I'm sorry, Mum, but being alpha female is not in my future."

I wasn't surprised at that. Both of us had talked about this whole process being total bullshit when we were kids.

"Selma?" Nance asked tightly.

She sat forward slowly, then looked down the table. In some ways, my cousin was the best possible candidate. Only a year or so younger than me, she was dressed in a smart pantsuit, her blonde hair cut into a sleek bob. I thought she was working in finance or something? We were never close, not like I was with Bridget. Where we were a couple of scrapping cubs, she seemed like the perfect poster girl for safe, sane, wolf shifters. Especially if we ever went public to humans.

"Mum and I have talked about this," Selma replied. "Apologies, Paige, but with you out of the picture for so long, we needed to look at what our options were. We broached it with Alpha Spehr, and while he certainly wasn't supportive of the idea, he did acknowledge it as a necessary step to be taken if Paige was unwilling or unable to take on her duties."

"So, what?" Uncle Bill asked. "Selma looks at the contender list as well?"

Selma's face barely registered a response at that, the perfect oval remaining serene. Had she had Botox? Surely not at this age.

"If she wants. Is there anyone you've decided to take as a mate?" I asked, knowing what I hoped she'd say. If she had a suitable guy in the wings, ready to step forward into the spotlight, it could solve all of my problems.

It was there, I could just taste it. Freedom was in my reach. Selma would be exactly what the pack wanted. She was smart, beautiful, professional—everything a modern alpha female needed to be. I found myself tugging my sleeves down over my hands, sliding my thumbs into the holes.

"I haven't really explored that with anyone while the succession was up in the air. It didn't seem fair to get into a relationship with someone without knowing what roles they'd be expected to play."

Bridget shot me one of her patented 'whoa, baby!' looks. She and her sister were…different to say the least.

"So you'd be amenable to meeting and engaging with the contenders?" I asked.

"Of course. Whatever the pack needs."

"As long as it's clear that the title only goes to Selma if you're unable to find someone suitable," Uncle Alan said, crossing his arms. "Nance, I know you've got your heart—"

"I would never try to circumvent the rules," my aunty snapped back. "Paige is just being sensible. Not every heir wants to be the alpha female. Why, our great aunt—"

"We all know about Great-Aunty Joy," Alan said with a dismissive shake of his head, "and that was no walk in the park either. Think long and hard before messing with the succession, Paige. We maintain control over Lupindorf largely due to tradition. Stuffing around with that starts people thinking about what else could be changed."

He looked around at the walls, as if imagining them disappearing just like that.

"Mason, can you talk to the enforcers and make it clear that anyone who wishes to put himself forward as alpha needs to do so through you?" I asked, looking at the beta but not really.

I couldn't meet those hot, dark eyes, not here, in front of my family. Because the thing was, I'd tried to be a good little heir, take a mate I thought would be a good contender for alpha, and got knocked back for my troubles. There was still a small scar on my bottom lip where his fang had scraped that night, slicing it as he'd cut me open, my heart, my body aching for his as we…

He didn't reply, which was rude in this context, but while this raised grumbles around the room, I knew why. He didn't trust himself to speak, I could see that in the tight muscles of his jaw, but when I stared into his eyes, I knew what was on his mind.

He remembered it, he still felt the ghost of his mouth on mine, his hands on my skin. All that lovely forbidden heat. My tongue flicked out, moistening my bone-dry lips, and Mason followed that movement. But a buzzing in my pocket dragged my eyes away, and when I pulled out my phone, I felt a much deeper, more welcome flush as I answered it.

"You're here?" I said in a much smaller voice. There was no point, everyone in the room would have heard me, but a part of me wanted to keep this, him, to myself.

"Just rolled into town," Zack said, and I could hear the exhaustion in his voice. "Tell me where to go, babe, and I'm there."

"Go onto Commercial Street and drive until you find the biggest building."

"A castle for the pack princess, huh?" He chuckled. "Yeah, I think I see it."

"You sound fucked. Pull over and tell me where you are. I can come and get you."

A grunt pulled my attention away from the call, from the welcome rasp of Zack's voice. Mason had taken half a step forward, something I didn't think he'd realised.

"Don't worry, nearly there. I better get off the phone before the cops sting me, but yeah, I'll need to crash when I get there."

"OK, well, see you soon."

I was met by a wall of interested eyes when I put my phone down, their collective gaze oppressive. Nothing I'd done had gotten me this much attention since I'd left. Well, almost nothing.

"So you've got a visitor coming?" Nance asked brightly, the tone only a little forced.

"A friend of mine, Zack. He was worried about me, so he came down to see if I was OK." Something I realised none of my family had expressed. I frowned for a moment, staring at the table. "He's just a friend. There's no way he'd want to be pack alpha, so I expect everyone to treat him with respect while he's here."

"Of course," Nance said, dropping me a nod, just like she would have done for Dad.

I got up and walked out of the room, ending the meeting, and didn't feel like I could really breathe until I was out the big ceremonial doors at the front of the building. Standing on the main street, I felt the breeze in my hair, tugging at it as I waited for Zack's big ute to arrive. But I wasn't alone for long, Mason's face like thunder when he appeared beside me.

"Who's the guy? This the one you came here stinking of?"

I just stared at him for a moment, trying to read that inscrutable face, but a beep of a car horn stopped that in its tracks. Something lightened inside me when I saw the car pull into one of the reserved carparks, even though I could see Zack looked like shit through the windscreen. I was down off the footpath and around to his door in moments, then he was jumping out and sweeping me into his arms. My eyes closed on automatic as I felt and smelt home. My fingers dug in deeper, my arms wrapping tighter.

"It's all right, babe. I'm here now."

I held on way too long, hearing the beat of my heart in my eardrums, marking the time I spent hugging Zack, but I just couldn't let go. That muscular body, those solid arms. I felt like I was being sheltered by a huge boulder or a massive tree or something. Something eternal, that could never be taken from me. A ragged sigh clawed its way out of me as I exhaled something I'd been holding onto since I left the city.

Zack closed that small gap, holding me so tight, my ribs ached, but I didn't want him to let go. My hand slid up, tangling in the longer strands of hair at his neck before he dropped his head down and kissed the top of my head.

"This is him?" The voice took a while to register, but it soon became clear. For some reason, Mason was pissed. "This is the guy you came back here reeking of?"

Zack didn't want to let me go, I could feel the reluctance in his arms and felt the same, but we compromised when I turned around, his arm snaking around my waist and pulling me in close as we faced the beta down together. That, I expected. What Zack said next? Not so much.

"Long time, no see, brother."

Chapter 8

My eyes jerked up and saw that same slow smile on Zack's face he usually sported when some boofhead came into the gym, wanting to take him on, but it was Mason he was staring down, not some tweaker. My eyes flicked between the two of them, seeing what I'd kinda always known but not understood why—Zack looked like Mason, though he was bigger, heavier in the body, and he was all lazy amusement where Mason fairly bristled.

"This is the dickhead who turned you down?" Zack looked down at me, inspecting all my scruffy, tear stained glory and making me feel like I was some kind of Victoria's Secret model. "He always did have difficulty knowing the difference between his arse and a hole in the ground."

I heard Mason's growls in the background as my face broke into the first real, true grin since I arrived. But I didn't look at Mason, I couldn't. Zack's eyes, warm and dark as a massive cup of coffee, as sweet as chocolate, held mine, and I didn't want to look anywhere else. I should have been asking questions, shouting something about the big reveal, but I just couldn't. He was here. He'd followed me all the way back to hell, and Zack was here.

"I don't have that problem, at all." He reached over, rubbing his thumb on my chin. "I knew some shit was holding you back, that you'd have unfinished business before we could take things further. I was OK with waiting, knew it'd only be a matter of time." He leaned down, slowly, so slowly, while Mason had something to say, but I couldn't hear it. When my eyes closed, when Zack's lips brushed mine, something shifted. An aching, clawing, keening thing—my wolf. She rubbed up inside me, pushing, trying to get at him. He pulled back slightly. "Now's that time, babe. I'm not leaving this town until you're mine."

"WHAT THE FUCK, ZACK?"

Mason's voice had our heads whipping around, but Zack paid it little mind, steering us inside the front door, assuming this was my place.

"So, brother?" I asked, arching an eyebrow.

"When I heard you talking about a Mason when you first came to town and you mentioned this place, I wondered." Zack shrugged. "I guess now I know. We aren't close, obviously."

"Obviously. You never said you had a brother?"

"What was I gonna say? We grew apart. Maybe we were never really close. Mum died, he went his way, and I went mine." He wavered a little on his feet, looking punch drunk. "I'll answer any question you like, babe, but right now?"

"I'll take you upstairs, settle you in," I said. "You must be trashed."

"I am that, but you need your rest too. Have you slept since you…?"

Got back from the hospital. This reticence to mention what we both knew was the reality, I remembered it from when Mum was sick.

"A little. I had to organise a family meeting."

As if summoned, the tribe of Spehrs spilled from the conference room into the big foyer that made up the front of the house. Everyone was very quiet, very still—the wolf's way of assessing the lay of the land.

"So you're a friend of Paige's then?" Nancy said, stepping forward. I saw where Selma got her smile from as Nance plastered one on, holding out a hand for him to shake. Zack did without letting go of me.

"I'm Zack. Friend, trainer, boss. I've fulfilled a lot of roles in Paige's life since she left. I don't see what's happening down here changing that."

"Trainer…?" Uncle Alan asked.

"Your girl's a fighter. A damn good one at that."

But they weren't listening to his responses. No, their eyes were trained on the way Zack's fingers played with the end of my plait. Fuck, I was focussed on the way he was doing that. On the ticklish feeling on my scalp, on the press of his body, on that fragile sense of wellbeing he brought with him, but mostly, those words reverberated around in my head, not letting any others in, even my family's.

I'm not leaving this town until you're mine.

Jesus, what the fuck did that mean? Like, it was plainly obvious what it meant, but…Zack and I, we kept things simple, easy. We were always there for one another, sexually if that's where we needed to be, but he'd never said anything like this before. But I knew Zack, knew that mulish look in his eyes when he was determined to do something, and right now, that was me.

"You're a fighter? Fucking—"

"That's enough, Bridget." Nance's voice was sharp, sharper than she usually allowed in front of 'company.' "It appears we have a lot more to talk about. I'll take the girls home, get them to pack a bag, and then come back here where you can explain—"

"Not today, she won't."

When Nance's eyes snapped up to meet Zack's, they were blazing.

"And who are you to be making orders in this house?"

"Here? This town? I've got nothing to say about that, but Paige? Yeah, you'll find I have a lot of words to share. She drove all night to get down here. She's been to see her dad in hospital. Anyone with half a brain can see she's maxed out emotionally and fucking exhausted to boot. Whatever pissant bullshit you got going on here can wait until she's had a decent sleep. With me."

I felt my muscles sag, my body drooping slightly, but he held me tight against him. It wasn't that I couldn't do this, couldn't stand up to my family or whatever, it was that I wanted to not need to. I needed them to remember that Dad and I, we were living breathing people as well as pivotal players in the town political landscape. I needed someone to put up boundaries and say enough, even if just for today, because I hadn't been raised to do so.

"Fine," Nance snapped. "Mason, have the maids set up rooms for both the girls. We'll be back tomorrow."

"Of course, Nancy," Mason said much more calmly, giving her a respectful nod.

"C'mon," Zack said with a tug on my hand. "Show me where the fuck the beds are around here, because I'm dead on my feet."

So I didn't stick around, saying goodbye to everyone in that long, protracted way families often do. Instead, I turned my back on them and walked up the stairs with Zack.

"This is my room," I said, pushing open the door. "You can sleep here and I'll—"

"Sleep right beside me." He yanked his shirt up over his head, stopping me in my tracks when those massive slabs of muscles were revealed. I saw them most days at work, but it said something about the sheer fucking beauty of Zack's body that it made my brain go offline each time I did.

He took a deep breath and shot me a sleepy smile. "That damn scent. It's been one of the few things that kept me going, that hot flush of receptivity." But when he walked around the bed, he just pulled me into his arms, holding me against his chest. "But I'm beat and so are you. You've been stretching yourself thin again, haven't you?"

Zack likened the uncompromising attitude I'd learned at my father's knee as treating yourself like a rubber band—you just stretched yourself and kept on stretching until the goal was achieved, your own needs be damned.

"Look, I have to—"

"You don't have to do shit," he said, pushing me towards the bed, then he went around the other side and peeled back the covers before sliding his sweatpants off.

He was hard. That often seemed to be the case when we were in a room together, though he'd shown himself more than adept at ignoring it when required. He just grinned when he caught me checking him out and then got under the covers.

"Get in the bed, Paige, before I get out and drag you in."

"Fucking bossy shifters."

He just watched me strip down to my underwear with heavily lidded eyes, as I pulled a loose T-shirt on instead of the compression top, that lazy smile getting broader as I did what he asked.

"Mm…" he said, pulling me in close when I tried to stay on my side of the bed, tangling our legs together, dwarfing me with his huge frame. "That's it. That's what I needed." A few long breaths from him had my own regulating against it, something he'd trained me to do so many years ago. "That's it, baby, slow and steady. Everything will be there, ready to be picked up when our eyes open. Just let it go for now. Just let go."

I always fought this, the soporific hum of his voice, the stroke of his hand on my back, the regular thud of his heart, because mine knew no such peace. When the quiet came, so did the rest of it—all the worries and the pain and the bullshit I fought so hard to keep at bay. Just like in the ring, if I let my guard down, the crap came in swinging.

"Listen…" Zack mumbled. "Feel… Be…"

It should have been as inscrutable as a Zen koan, but I knew what he meant. I had to focus on what was, the feel, the sound, the smells around me, not the endless hamster wheel of my worries. With him, I'd learned how to get on and off it, but coming back here made that easy to forget. He made a pleased rumble when I snuggled into him, my hand going up almost tentatively to his collarbone. He covered my hand with his, our breaths becoming longer and longer, and the tidal hiss of them tugged me down into the blackness of sleep.

. . .

"DADDY!"

My eyes flicked open, for a moment disorientated by the dense darkness around me, my gaze flicking around as my heart thundered. As if to provide further evidence to support my panic, there was a sharp rap at the door. I struggled to sit up, to reach out for the lamp and turn the light on, but a heavy weight held me down.

Zack... my mind supplied belatedly. It was Zack.

"Hey..." he rasped, but then another knock came.

"Paige, we gotta go."

Mason's voice was muffled, but we both threw back the covers and pulled our clothes on, hearing the urgency there. Mason jerked back when the door was wrenched open and took in Zack's bleary eyed state, but he forced his attention to me.

"Your dad... The hospital called."

I heard the jangle of Zack's keys as he grabbed my hand, pulling me out the door and down the stairs towards the front door.

"She comes with me," Mason growled.

"Fuck off. You can walk in the door with her and do whatever it is you gotta do, but if you think I'm letting her get beyond five feet of me while this goes down, you're dumber than I thought, brother."

"We don't have time for this," I snapped, grabbing his keys and walking out. "Dad's had a turn for the worse?"

"Yeah, we need—" Mason started.

"Get in the back. I'll drive."

"Oh no, sweetheart. I remember what you did to my gearbox last time." Zack lunged for the keys.

"Then get us there as fast as you can. I don't have time for family dramas."

We piled into the car silently, another car following behind us. That'd be some of the enforcers coming up the rear.

"Paige—" Nance said as we rushed into the hospital ward reception area, but I brushed past her, Bridget, everyone to find the room he was in. I flew down the corridor, hearing the raised voices, the frantic pace of the machines surrounding my father, and knew I'd done everything wrong.

Lone Wolf

I'd let myself be distracted, by the contenders, by Mason, by the family, even Zack. I'd let all the minutiae of the living bog me down, because that's what we did. Nance asked for my time, Mason wanted to talk to me, I wanted to see Stevie. That great spider web of relationships had surrounded me, ensnared me the minute I got into town, and kept me from this.

"Ms Spehr, I'm afraid things aren't looking good," a harried doctor told me, trying to stand between me and my father. Because they all scurried, scurried, scurried to try and keep the reigning alpha alive. Because there was no heir apparent waiting in the wings.

I'd come back home, thinking things were like they were in the city, that the only expectations on me were my own. I should've been here, parked my arse in that chair, and refused to leave until Dad either walked out of here or was carried out. That was my duty. I pushed past the doc, not willing to accept any other barriers right now, and plastered myself against the wall as the medical professionals compressed his ribcage, trying to make his heart take over and do the work, despite the high-pitched whine and the disturbing flat line on the vital signs monitor.

But it was too late. I'd known that when I heard Mason's knock, his terse words. I'd known it when I saw Dad for the first time in the hospital. I didn't understand medical procedures, but respirators, that was never a good sign. Fuck, I'd known it in that terse call in the middle of the night, but there was something else too.

When I'd walked away, when I'd refused to come back. When I'd stopped taking Dad's calls. When I'd 'moved on with my life' and allowed myself to enjoy my existence. That had to come with a price, didn't it? The doctors and nurses worked and worked, the screaming sounds of the monitors a wretched soundtrack. They worked until finally one, then another, pulled back, the reality hitting all of us. But some of their eyes darted to me, and they took up the fight again, compressing and placing those electrical paddles on his chest, shoving his body over and over in the dim hope it would come back to life.

But it wouldn't, would it? I'd been given opportunity after

opportunity to make things right, mend the breach. Shit, work with Dad to change his mind and transfer the designation of heir to one of the other girls as Zack had urged. Do something. But I hadn't wanted to, too much of the here and now keeping me busy, keeping me from thinking of him.

Well, I wanted to now, didn't I? But I was too bloody late.

"It's OK." My voice didn't sound like my own, echoing around in my head. "You did your best."

That appeared to be the absolution the people in the room needed, their breaths coming in sharp rasps as they stepped back from my father's body. Alpha Adam Spehr was dead.

I threw my head back, my throat struggling to make the noise in this form, the urge to take fur too much. I let out a long, mournful howl, one that reverberated throughout the room and down the halls as others joined my wild dirge. The door slammed open, and Zack came running in, red marks on his skin making it evident he'd had to fight past someone to get to me. I looked at him for a second before I released my hold on this form and gave in to the other.

The stink, of humans, of bleach, of death, all smothered in layers of human lies, was too much. Fleet of foot, I ran from the room, careening across the too slick floors, smashing into walls, into IV stands, into chairs before scrabbling out of this too bright, too clean, too horrible place. I paused only for a minute when I got outside, sniffing the air and listening to the stories on the breeze, and then I was off, running with a sure and steady gait.

More howls filled the night, some long and sad, some much more frightening in their intent. They announced challenge, let the pack know a hunt was on. My feet tore on the asphalt as I ran and ran and ran, the devil chasing me now, or they would be. I veered off, down familiar alleyways and long quiet streets, past houses and cars until they bled away to paddocks and sheep. They skittered at my presence, those soft creatures kept locked up and vulnerable, but I ran past them too. Ran until I stumbled into the peace of the softwood plantations, the huge stand of radiata pines covering the ground in a thick blanket of pine needles, the hush of the breeze through their leaves enough to cover my rasping breathing.

Lone Wolf

We needed to hide, that's what my beast's instincts told me, or get in one of those metal boxes man liked so much and drive until we were well beyond Lupindorf. To another pack's territory, that would stop them. Packs didn't invade other packs' turf, only lone wolves could pass through unmolested. My whine was slight, weak, as I considered just how far that was. I got few chances for my wolf to run in the city, reduced to slipping out with Zack and our workmates when the press got too great, taking off on a camping trip to allow us the opportunity to take fur. But it was too late. The howls, they grew louder, closer, the bloodlust up.

With the ancestral memories my kind carried in fur, I realised this was how it always was. Not in animals, not even in other packs, but in ours it was thus—the female of the line was the key to power, and as such, a commodity that could be taken, stolen, fought over.

So they did.

My muscles quivered as I heard them approach, announcing to all and everyone their aim. Some refuted, snarled their violent objections, but which set of paws were theirs and which were my attackers? My furred ears flicked wildly, trying desperately to predict what they'd do, where they'd come from, before my body exploded. All the pent-up adrenalin I needed to use in the fight to come flooded my system as my animal brain grasped what was going to happen.

Grandma Spehr had told us one night, when all us girls were on the brink of womanhood, of the old ways. When the daughter of the moon, Mother Moon, was set before the strongest and fastest males of the pack and chased to ground. Run until her legs gave out, pursued until her heart beat too damn fast, the males falling upon her, upon the other males with a viciousness that signalled one intent—he who was still standing at the end took control of the pack.

"This is how we know we are not truly the animals whose forms we take. What lives within us is some kind of inscrutable magic, but it is not a wolf. The females fight amongst themselves far more viciously in actual packs. Males are content to snap and snarl, bare teeth and bluster, but not the females. It is for them the vicious pleasure of sinking fangs into haunches and tearing, writing

clearly on the other female's flesh your will to power. She who emerges on top, it is she the alpha male 'chooses.'"

Grandma smiled then, her old yellowing teeth seeming too sharp in the dim light of her front room.

"This is why you must heed your alpha, ensure the path of succession is clear." All my female cousins' eyes swung around to look at me, something that just made me shrink down against the floral flounce of Gran's lounge suite cover. *"Without it, the old ways will return. Friend fighting friend, brother fighting brother, chaos and blood and terror reigning until one emerges, red of tooth and claw. But what of those he stepped over to take that position?"*

She shook her head and picked up her knitting, her fingers working the needles swiftly. "I saw a hunt when I was younger than you, saw the chaos and the pain it created. Heed my words and start casting your eyes now over the contenders. Know your own heart, so that by the time the choosing comes, you'll be happy with your mate. It's all any of us want for you girls—to find the other half of your heart and live happily in peace."

The memory racketed around in my brain, like a pebble in a shaken bucket, Gran's words repeating over and over and over until…

When I found the clearing, they came. I stumbled out into the middle of it, the light of the moon so damn bright like a spotlight, and I was in its centre. The males came after, crashing through the undergrowth or slinking from the shadows, one after the other in a ring around me. For a moment, I just panted, my lungs working like bellows to suck air back into a body deprived of it. But with oxygen and moonlight came clarity. My eyes darted around, tracking each and every time a wolf stepped from the trees and into this empty space of grass, heads lowered, legs crouched and coiled to spring.

My human form came back without thought, and the wolves took their cues from me, until I was surrounded by a ring of naked men. All but twelve.

Dark fur only faintly flecked by grey, two of them barrelled through the clearing, stopping only once they reached my feet and then spinning around, fangs bared, the ten enforcers placing themselves at all points around me, ready to attack.

"This is how it has to be, Paige," Aidan said, smirking in the low light. "You didn't make a choice, so now we get to make it for you."

I stared him down, feeling the pressure to look away, even with the distance between us, but he just snorted to himself when I didn't.

"We fight this out, tonight, and the last man standing takes you and the role of alpha."

"Fucking take it for all I care!" I snapped. "Set up the chick with the big tits you were all over in high school as alpha female. Honestly, I don't give a fuck about this place. I came home for Dad. I came home to say…" My voice was cracking, my heart was cracking, and if I let it do so here… I forced my eyes up. The musical sound of growls from the wolves at my side were all that stopped the men from getting too close, but that would only last for so long. "I came home to say goodbye, for good. We've already talked about it. Selma's prepared to step up and take my spot. Go and fight for a place by her side."

I spat a mouthful of foul bile out on the grass, unable to stand the steady trickle of it in my mouth anymore.

"That's not how it works," another man said. "I've got a mate. I love her, want to put her in your place and give her that big house in the middle of town, but I can't."

"It won't be Selma," Aidan said. "It can't be her."

"What? But—"

"He didn't tell you. Fathers don't as a rule, but they insist on those rules, don't they?" A dark-haired man stepped forward, a mocking smile on his lips. "Those wolf shifters you met in the big city." His eyes dropped down to one of the wolves at my feet. "They wouldn't know this. Their packs aren't like ours. The first of her line bestows the crown." And as he said the words, so did many of the men, my head whipping around to take in all the speakers.

A fight to submission… Me as the prize… My brain was torn by pain and exhaustion and grief, but this, this was all familiar stuff. I'd settled many a grudge match in the gym. No reason why we couldn't do the same in this instance. And doing so formally, with witnesses and rules would do the same as it did in the gym—ensure an even playing field and make sure the proceedings were fair.

I didn't want to do this. My wolves growled as I cleared my throat, trying for a clear, calm declaration and no doubt failing.

"You want this? You want to do this the old way?" A round of grunts indicated that they did. "So let's do this properly. A stage will be set, a roster of everyone who wishes to put themselves forward as alpha will be drawn up, and then it's fighting through the rounds until one wolf remains."

"You're stalling," one of them said.

"You want me to. Some of you have mates you love, some have those you've got your eye on and they aren't me. I can go through the collective wisdom of the pack, sort through the records they brought over from Germany, and see if I can find a way to make that possible for the winner. That would free me to go my own way, free you to have the mate of your dreams."

"And what if it's you?" Aidan asked, running his eyes slowly up my naked form.

"Me? Well, that's a whole other fight you have to win, but you'll have time, showboating in the ring, showing off your fighting prowess to all the single women in the pack, including me." I couldn't believe I was going to say this, but I couldn't see any other way. "Throughout the entire process, anyone who wants to see if we're compatible, I'll make time for." Several growls came from the wolves around me. "Doesn't mean I'm down to fuck, but if I feel drawn to you, we can go on a date, you can get to know me like you would any other girl."

"If everyone's in agreement?" a masculine voice said.

Mason had come back to skin, standing tall, a wall between me and the other men, then Zack and the enforcers did the same not long afterwards.

"Don't try and skew things, beta," one man said. "Everyone knows about you and the heir."

"Then you know I've knocked her back once before already. I rejected what you seek" —I jerked a little at those words, feeling them hit me physically— "so by my reckoning, I'm the safest one of all of you to ensure this process is carried out in an orderly way."

"Fair enough," Aidan said. "There's a period of mourning, the funeral, and then…" His silver eyes slid to me. "The battle begins."

Declan waited until all of the other men had faded away, leaving just me, Zack, Mason, and the enforcers standing there.

"And what about us, Mase?" he asked, but his eyes were on me, not his beta. He was trying not to stare, but those whiskey eyes were bleeding silver. Alien, animal, they felt like they stared through the darkness and took in everything I was.

Which was such a perfect illustration of pack life. I was sure Dec didn't want to be ogling me in the middle of the night right after I'd seen my dad die. I watched him frown, try to rip his eyes away, and it took Zack stepping between us and hiding me to allow that to happen.

"Are we to enforce a fight we want to participate in?" Declan forced out.

"We'll bring all the contenders together, hold a general meeting before the whole town," Mason said in the usual calm, measured tones I remembered so well. This was why I'd chosen him all those years ago. His voice was like my father's, able to settle a group of unruly shifters with a few words, while making it clear disobedience wouldn't be tolerated. "What Paige suggested, it's the best option. It gives everyone who wants a go a means to put themselves forward and prove themselves to the community. You won't be excluded from that. If there are questions about objectivity, I can bring some of the mated men in to take over your duties. But we have to remember, our alpha passed tonight."

And there it was, the truth behind all the panic and the drama, and I started to shiver in response to it, my body fighting to process everything I'd subjected it to.

"We need to get Paige into the car and some clothes," Zack said, moving closer and wrapping his arms around me, even as some of the enforcers growled. "And then she needs to get in front of a punching bag if she's to have any chance of sleeping tonight."

"What?" one of the enforcers asked.

"We've got a gym set up at the back of the alpha residence," Mason said. "You can take her there."

Chapter 9

They followed me into the training room. Because it was part of the enforcers' quarters at the back of the alpha's house. Because they were keeping an eye on me. Because I was silent all the way home in the back of the car, curled up in a ball, despite Zack's attempts to soothe me. Because I shivered and shivered, even though I'd pulled on the warm sweats that smelled of Mason.

"C'mon, baby," Zack said in a low voice, steering me into the room. "Too much, way too much today, but you gotta let all the adrenalin out before you can crash. We'll keep coming back, like we always do. Go through the movements, babe. You've got them now."

My body felt heavy, leaden when I tried to bounce on my feet and get the blood moving. It had already, rushing around, running through the forest, but Zack was insistent.

"Don't worry about them," he said when my eyes went to the guys leaning against the wall. "Listen to my voice. Start with your stretches. Legs first, then arms, then back."

This was our ritual, our moment together. Before we opened the gym, before we started dealing with the day, he'd walk me through the routine, even though I knew it by heart. He'd do it too, his body shadowing mine, his muscles on display, being forced to lengthen, soften, warm up in preparation for what we would require them to do.

"All right, let's throw a few punches. Not too hard, you're locked tight, too much fight or flight right now." It made sense and I felt it as I moved, my hands up, ready to defend against an invisible enemy, then punching out to hold them off, smack them down, those sharp brutal actions making my heart race again, but for a whole other reason. I forced my body to stay loose, mobile, active. I wanted to harden myself against the world, against the burden I'd set down for just a moment.

Dad...

That would come. There was no escaping it. The loss, the... It was a gigantic black wolf at my heels, ready to swallow me whole if I just...

"Do the work. Don't get in your own head. Focus on the movements. Give your body time to process all that stuff, and then your mind will follow." Zack's words were gentle, persistent, dragging me back to the here and now, back to him.

My body went slack and still, just staring at him for a moment, taking in the muscular bulk of his body, the hard planes of his face, the scruffy tousle of his dark hair, and those eyes—eyes I could get lost in. But the fact he was good looking, that he got me hot, was almost irrelevant. I could say the same about every guy in the room. Wolves tended to make pretty babies that grew up to be hot men. What was here in the room between Zack and me was something else.

If those arms were much thinner, wrapped with ropy muscles rather than bulky ones, it wouldn't have made a difference, they'd always be open to me. They'd be reaching out to catch me before I even knew I was falling, pulling me back against him into the safe harbour of his body. But they'd open just as easily to let me walk free, walk far, if that's what I needed. I looked into those implacable dark eyes and saw something I always knew deep down but never really articulated.

Zack would always be there for me.

I nodded, all the acknowledgement I could give him, but that twist of a smile told me he saw past that. Then we bumped our knuckles, and I walked across the floor to the heavy bag.

I touched my fists to the bag, checking my distance, making sure I wasn't too far away and swinging wide. My knees bent, my hands up, then I shoved the bag and started the shuffle.

"Just start shuffling at first," Zack had told me in my first lesson. "Don't even throw a punch. It's much harder for your opponent to hit a moving target, and you're smaller, so you need the advantage speed and mobility can give you. You might be up against a heavy hitter" —he smacked one massive fist into his palm— "but if they can't catch you, they can't hit you. Start moving, pivoting, getting your legs used to shifting your weight at fast notice." He'd demonstrated, swivelling around his bag with a kind of deadly precision I'd thought was well beyond me, but right now, I fell into the same patterns.

I didn't have to hit the bag. I didn't need to hit the contenders or even Mason, who deserved a smack in that sour mouth of his. I just needed to focus—on my body, on my breath, on my movements, in sync with the bag. I maintained the distance between us while it swung, occasionally giving it a shove with my shoulders to set it off again.

And then I needed to hit it.

I never felt a rise in aggression when I learned how to fight, and most of Zack's clients didn't. Roid heads and pumped up douche bags didn't last long at the gym, in the ring or out of it. The way he saw it, it was about knowing your body, knowing what it could and couldn't do, and seeing if you could push that. Then when faced with all the dominance bullshit that came with being a shifter, particularly an unmated female wolf shifter, you could meet just about anyone square in the eye, because you knew.

I struck out at the bag, liking the way it jumped in response. Not hard, not decisively, because I had no protection on my hands, and right now, even that wasn't likely to help. I felt them curl in my spine, all those feelings, then stiffen, swell, manifesting as a need to slam into the vinyl surface.

I followed with another few quick punches as I moved in close, pivoting around the bag, smacking my fists and my knee into it before swinging back. I bounced away on the balls of my feet, feeling the blood pump, all that damn adrenalin that was still coursing through me rising with it, making my muscles twitch faster, my reflexes snap tighter as I stepped in and kicked the bag hard. Thoughts fell away and muscle memory kicked in as I moved smooth as silk. Elbow strike, punch, knee, then kick. I danced around the bag, performing string after string of blows in rapid succession, pushing until my breath was coming in hard.

"Keep breathing," Zack said, observing from a safe distance. "Hands up."

"I think I'm done," I said, feeling the shake in my limbs. I'd pushed myself so hard, running then, fighting now.

"No, you're not. You're not done until I say." That got a growl from the crowd. "Hands up, do the work. You know how."

I looked at Zack, frowning at his words, but they were the same as they always were—calm, sure. So I raised fists that felt a whole lot heavier now and kept going. But it wasn't the same, didn't he see that? He was watching my every move, the commentary coming as always. *Watch your feet, keep moving, don't drop your guard, maintain your defence.* It was the steady background noise I'd always heard when I trained, but somehow, it'd become something else. His tone hadn't changed, but I had, my body unable to comply with his steady litany of demands, no matter how hard I pushed myself. I stumbled over my feet, went crashing into the bag.

"She's had enough!" Mason said sharply.

"I'll say when she's had enough. I know her better than you ever will," Zack snapped back, his eyes not leaving me. "It's OK, Paige. Do the work. What you need, it's there."

"Why are you doing this?" I sobbed between breaths. "I'm tired, my feet hurt, my everything hurts. I've got bruises everywhere." My attention made the pain in my sides from where I'd smacked into walls flare bright, and when I looked down the collar of my top, I saw them there, murky and sullen on my skin.

"Do the work, Paige."

"I'm hurting, Zack. I'm gonna need to lie in an Epsom bath for hours and down a box of ibuprofen as it is."

"Excuses aren't gonna help, babe, you know that. Keep moving, keep your hands up—"

"Shut up, Zack!"

"No one can touch you when you stay on your feet."

"Zack, that's enough. You may not respect pack hierarchy but —" Mason growled out, pushing forward.

I did what he said, because that's what I did, most of the time, but now, when I faced the bag down, my view was blurred by the tears in my eyes. Push, push, push, that's all anyone did. My feet and my fists slammed into the bag with wild abandon, sending it rocketing on its chain, and I stepped in and caught the backswing face on before striking again. Ever since I'd gotten here, I'd been pushed by one group or another. Do this, choose this, let them sniff you, let them fight.

Bang, bang, bang!

I was doing this all wrong. It hurt my wrists when I didn't hit the bag square on the knuckles, the slap of it against my knees and feet feeling like one to the face. My muscles screamed, and sweat poured down my face and into my eyes, masking what came.

The first sob was too loud, too harsh, announcing to the whole room what was happening, but when I heard them come forward, I kept on punching. My fists flew wide, the bag smacking into me as my knee thrust pushed me off balance, but I snapped back onto my own two feet. I kept striking at the bag, but it wasn't where it should be, careening now in patterns I couldn't follow and catching me in its wild swings.

Then I did what I'd always been told not to do—left my side wide open as I threw a wild punch, and the bag took the advantage. It slammed into my side, and a great surge of pain blossomed out, out, out, through my whole body as I staggered back.

I went down, not because of my fuck up but because my body couldn't anymore. I couldn't dodge or weave or punch. I could barely breathe. I sucked oxygen in with great shuddering breaths, but right when I needed it most, my body refused. How could I take a full breath when this was taking up all the space in my chest? I was on my knees, wavering, and that was fitting, because this, this would have me beat.

Dad…

Zack had helped me keep that at bay for the moment, but now it came rushing back twice as hard, and when he came to stand before me, I saw in his face that this was exactly what he'd planned.

"No…" I croaked.

"Yes, baby. It's what has to happen. You can't compartmentalise this, not this."

"No!" I screamed as he bent down and scooped me up. I screamed it again as he held me close. As my nails clawed his back, tearing the fabric of his T-shirt, scoring his flesh deep. Again as I thrashed in his arms.

He had me gripped tight, just as the black wolf of grief did. Both brought with them the too bright room, the hiss of the ventilator, my scream matching the high-pitched alarm from the vital signs monitor as I realised that my dad had been dead the moment I woke up from my sleep. That brief time, early in the day, that's all I got with him, just watching the machine breathe for him.

"It's OK. It's OK…" Zack said the words like a prayer now, over and over, and for once, I was glad to hear that calm shredded just like mine was. He was pleading almost, his voice growly and ragged, his hold tight until finally, finally, I went limp.

It all came rushing in, all of it—the pain, the loss, the disbelief, the total spaced out feeling of unreality, because surely this wasn't the way it worked. I needed, no, deserved another chance. But I wasn't gonna get it, and that hit me hardest. No matter what I thought or felt, this was the reality. This was the way it was going to be.

"Let's take her to the hot tub," Mason said, his voice oddly like his brother's—softer, surer. "You can hold her in there, give her muscles a soak. It's what we do after a training session."

"Show me," was all Zack would say, and then Mason did.

Chapter 10

I woke up the next day, embarrassed. Zack stirred when I did, looking down at me through bleary eyes.

"Don't," was all he would say, as if the flush of shame was spelled out on my skin. My eyes darted away and I curled down into a ball, but he wasn't having that. He pushed me flat on the bed, came forward, and kissed me, despite my squeaks about morning breath. When I relented, going loose under him, he pulled back.

"This whole thing is bullshit. You've gone through so much and more is coming. We could bail. We could get in the car, drive back to the city, leave all this shit behind." I could hear it, the hope in his voice, the need. I could imagine it too, my arm out the window, my hand feeling the waves in the air as we escaped…

"But you won't."

But I wouldn't. I'd skipped out, lived a lovely life of reprieve, and this was what happened. I didn't get a chance to say goodbye to my father, to show him… I shook my head. This was what I'd been born to do—keep the peace, ensure the future prosperity of Lupindorf, take a mate, see to bearing the next generation of female heirs.

And watch over the old alpha as he was returned to Mother Moon.

I went to sit up, that prime directive vibrating inside me, but Zack rolled on top, pinning my hands to the bed and settling between my legs before kissing me deeply. I tried to wriggle, to buck him off, but those persistent soft lips got the better of me. I wanted to surrender to them, to suck that too full bottom lip of his into my mouth. I wanted to get lost in all that hot, sweet…

A sharp knock at the door put paid to that.

"I've gotta go," I said as I pulled back.

"Not yet," Zack purred, looking down at me, at my squirming, with a wide grin. "I'm coming with you today."

"Zack—"

"I'm your fucking shadow, Paige. Remember that."

"You won't be able to—"

"Then wherever I can go, I'll be. You're not going through all of this alone."

My head fell back on the pillow. "Fine."

"Because you need to remember, no matter what happens, no matter what's going on, you are—"

"Enough," I finished for him, knowing the line but not really feeling its intent right now. But I nodded to keep Zack happy, the twist of his mouth making it plain he wasn't convinced, but he'd take what he could get. Zack was still pulling on his clothes when I opened the door to see Mason standing there, but his eyes went to his brother, not me, just watching him pull a T-shirt over his head.

"I'm sorry, Paige, but your family is here."

"I guessed that. Thanks." I opened the door wider, readying myself to go out, Zack at my back.

"You need to stay out of this, brother," Mason said when he went to follow me.

"I'm not leaving her."

"She just made a deal with all the men in town who think they can take the role of alpha, promising that they can fight to win the position and court her. If you follow her around like a little puppy, sleep with her, drown her in your scent, mark her indelibly as yours, they won't be able to miss that and the message that sends."

"Good. They fucking shouldn't." Zack moved until he was

almost toe to toe with Mason. "I'm not leaving her. I'm not walking away from her right when she needs me the most."

"What she needs is to settle this. If there's a way to change who the alpha female is, find it. Then you can do exactly as you please, but until then, keep your distance." Mason reached into his pocket and found a ring of keys and threw them to Zack. "There's a spare room in the enforcers' quarters. You can stay there until we've sorted things out."

"You cold fucking prick. I'll fight every damn one of those contenders if that's what it takes to keep Paige, then leave you the keys to the city. Or is that what this is about? What you want?" Zack snarled.

"You have no idea what I want," Mason retorted, but his eyes dropped to me rather than his brother. "Have another shower, use the gel in the bathroom and the shampoo. You need to wash every trace of his scent off if you're to pull this off."

"Fine," I ground out.

He wasn't lying, Mason. I felt the truth of his words in my bones, but how did that bastard just stand there, with eyes like ice, as he sliced me clear in two?

Because that's what Mason does, my brain supplied. *Duty and honour before all else.*

He should've accepted my offer and agreed to become the next alpha, because no one was better suited. I yanked my clothes off and tossed them on the floor before doing exactly as Mason said—scrubbing myself until I was squeaky clean. But when I got dressed in fresh clothes, Mason was waiting and Zack wasn't.

"Got rid of him, huh?" I asked, arching an eyebrow. I was going for defiant because I couldn't display the way I actually felt. "Do you get some sort of kick from crushing me? Is it like the only thing that gets you hard?" I looked down at the front of his jeans for an insulting length of time, and sure enough, when I looked back, he was fuming. I smiled when I saw his jaw flex, that tell that always made it clear when I'd pissed him off, but I felt no joy in it.

"I didn't ask him to go to upset you. I did it because—"

"You know what? Save it. It doesn't matter. You don't matter. This is just the same old Mason bullshit."

I went to push past him. If I was going to have to endure this shit, I was going to at least enjoy the dubious pleasure of flouncing off. But his hand snapped out, stopping me in the middle of my stalk, then he wrenched me back and pushed me against the wall.

"If you're disappointed that everything is still the same with me, how do you think I feel, seeing you refuse to listen to me, again? Walking off in a snit, again. Casting everything I fucking do for this family in a shitty light, no matter what it does to me, again. You know what? Last night, I felt a glimmer of fucking hope. That scene in the forest could've been a bloodbath, but you managed to redirect it and come up with a sane way forward that may actually work. When I saw you work that fucking bag, I could see the discipline and determination you've put in. Where is she now?"

He went to poke me in the shoulder, but my hand whipped up, wrapping around his wrist and twisting it until he thought better of that idea. For a moment, there was just the tremble of our muscles, the sharp slice of our gazes, as we fought for dominance.

"She's hurting, Mason." I hated the ragged tone of my voice, even as it gave greater credence to my words. "And you just took the one person who can make me feel better away."

Well, that transformed his face. I should've been glad, because I had a ringside seat for catching a real genuine expression on Mason's face, something I didn't think I'd ever seen. It warped into a sneer, his lips curling, his eyes glittering.

"Is that how he got his hooks into you? Made you strong and hard and fit, but left that fatal flaw in your armour? Whatever you achieve, no matter what you do, you still need Zack to make it all right again."

"Fuck…" I broke our holds with ease now, since there was no real desire in Mason to keep me pinned. "That's how you live your life? No one gets under your 'armour'? Needing no one for support?" I shook my head. "I used to be so angry with you for turning me down like that, but now? I just feel sorry for you."

His claws dug into the wall, I could hear the gouges he made, but I ducked out from under his arms, walked down the hall and then the stairs, and made a beeline for the conference room where my family waited.

"PAIGE..." Aunty Nance said with tear filled eyes, walking towards me, arms outstretched.

"Yes, Paige," Alan said. "What the hell happened last night? The rumour mill has gone mad. Saying you're organising some kind of tournament?"

"No." I sat down in the chair at the head of the table, my father's chair. I could feel the way the foam had been moulded to fit his body, not mine, and somehow, me sitting in the gap he'd made seemed fitting. "We're not doing that now. We're not talking about any of that until the funeral is over. I'll go to Dad's side of the family, talk to them about how they want to proceed and make the arrangements, then I'll sit vigil for him tonight. Mason will organise a town meeting to discuss the proposal for handling the succession."

He'd arrived at the door, face like a thunder cloud, but he nodded respectfully when I mentioned his name.

"We'll hold a meeting before that, but I won't be disrespecting my father's memory by squabbling over who gets to be alpha before he's in the ground, am I clear?"

I was, but they didn't want to accept it. I could see it in the shifting eyes and their restless movements in their chairs, but I didn't wait around for them to object.

"Who do I need to take with me to Nan's place?" I asked Mason stiffly as I walked to the door.

"I'll drive and have several of the enforcers with us. That should be sufficient. Even the hottest of heads know not to mess with a vigil. My car is parked around the back."

He pulled out his phone, tapping out a message as we strode through the house to the rear carpark, several men coming from the enforcers' quarters at the back of the house.

"Hey, you OK?" Declan asked, moving in closer, reaching out to put a hand on my shoulder, but a growl from Mason stopped him.

I smiled, a fragile forced thing, but I'd take whatever kindness I could find right now. I needed it to get me through this. I completed the gesture, taking his hand, feeling that weird mix of familiar and unfamiliar when I did. In year eleven, these hands went a whole lotta places, but while the freckled skin was the same, now they were much larger, the skin tougher, a scattering of reddish hair across the back of it. I rubbed my thumb across it, just focussing on the way the hair sprung back when it passed before nodding.

"No, and I won't be for some time," I replied belatedly. "But thanks for asking."

I saw the intake of breath, the expansion of that broad chest as he went to say something else, ask something else. I couldn't pick up their scent like they could mine, but I saw it, in those keen eyes, ones that had caressed my body thoroughly last night. "After," I said, not giving anything else away, watching to see if he understood. Declan nodded, blinking and looking a little abashed, but he recovered by grabbing my hand and holding it tight before drawing me over to the now open car door.

"It'll get better," he said in a low voice as we settled into the back seat. "It won't feel like it for a while, but it does."

Chapter 11

It was only when I pulled up to Nan's place that it felt real. I watched Mason get out of the car first, go to meet Nan and my paternal aunties standing at the gate. He'd obviously let them know I was here. I stared at the purplish hydrangeas poking about the cute little white picket fence, the riotous geraniums growing in the gap between it and the footpath, and was hit instantly with all the memories of playing in the front garden.

"Ready?" Declan asked. He tried to smile, but it didn't work and that wasn't good. He'd always had a ready grin, his role as class clown a big reason why I'd been drawn to him. But those whiskey-coloured eyes dropped down to my lips, his brow creasing for a moment before he opened the door and ushered me out.

"Nan—" I started, trying to keep my voice even as I got to the gate, but she surged forward, surrounding me with surprisingly strong arms and a cloud of lavender scent, her body soft as a pillow when I sank into it.

"There's our girl." Her hand stroking the top of my head held the echo of all the times she had before, soothing me through tears and tantrums, tying who I'd become as a person to her. "She'll be staying here until it's done."

"April, she—" Mason said.

"I know. Everyone knows. Damn gossips in this town are having a field day, but there'll be none of that, not until my Adam has… Not until he's been taken back by Mother Moon. I won't stand for anything else, Mason Klein. You're a good man. You stood by my son for many years, but I won't budge on this."

"Of course. I'll station some of the men around the house."

"You'll pick someone other than yourself and stay here until it's done. The house is big enough, and you need to see him to his final resting place as much as any."

A long sigh, and then there would have been a nod. Nan might not have been of the alpha's line, but she was plenty strong enough to assert herself over most people.

"C'mon then. I've got the kettle on and it's time for tea."

"LOOK AT YOU, ALL GROWN UP!" Aunty Lyn held me at arm's length, looking me over with a smile. "What did they do to you in that big city? You look like you could take on the world."

"She's too skinny, is what she is," Nan said, bustling around the kitchen, and as if in agreeance with her, my stomach rumbled noisily. "Sit down, sit down. I'll put some toast, eggs, and bacon on for breakfast."

"Nan…"

"Don't you Nan me." My grandmother spun around, fixing me with those steely blue eyes of hers. Dad's eyes. Either way, no one could gainsay them, her will beating down on mine. "They don't look after you in the big house. All alpha this and succession that. You tell me differently, and I might believe you."

Aunty Rose slipped in, taking a seat at the big kitchen table on the other side of me, grabbing my hand and squeezing it as I shook my head. I felt disloyal, the age-old prohibition of not sharing what went on inside the estate pushing at me, but this was my family. While I wasn't counted as much by the rest of town, Dad's family had more than made up for that, always embracing me wholeheartedly and often picking up the pieces the others left.

"That's what I thought. Adam wouldn't want you neglecting yourself." I glanced at the aunties, saw that they noted the faint tremble in Nan's jaw too, but didn't say anything. "It isn't fair, my love, what happened, the way it happened, but that's the pain of those who are left behind. We get to endure that peculiar kind of agony, of seeing to our body and our mind's needs, right when our hearts hurt the most."

She nodded to the table, to Declan and Mason and the other men he'd brought with him as they all took a seat. Nan had a massive open plan kitchen-dining room for this reason, because unlike the cool of the conference room in the alpha residence, this was the heart of her house. I'd sat here playing cards and board games with my family, my aunties and uncles and cousins all clustered around. Other times it was munching on Nan's homemade biscuits as the adults talked about stuff none of us kids could understand, but we listened anyway. A lot of what I'd learned about politics, about leadership and how to do it well, I'd picked up here.

"You better let her feed you," Rose said with her characteristically husky voice. "It's how she communicates. I love you, eat this. You need help, eat that."

"You're in trouble, swallow this. God, cod liver oil," Lyn said with a shake of her head.

"Well, you'll get bacon and eggs today if you behave," Nan said, firing up the hotplates.

"Mum, the doctor has said I need to cut back on the cholesterol."

"What would that boy know? I still remember him running bare arse naked as a baby when his mother and I were pregnant with our next ones." Nan laid out slab after slab of meat on the grill. But when she turned around, her face was solemn. "What we have ahead, the vigil, this will be hard on all of us. He…" Nan's only concession to emotion was a sharp shake of her head. "He went too soon. Every mother feels that way, but to bury your child…" Her eyes dropped down to scorch holes in the well cared for linoleum. "It isn't fair. Hard to believe that this is the Mother's will, especially for Paige…"

I shrank a little in my chair at their collective gaze being directed at me, until Nan's frown had me straightening again.

"You'll need your strength, all of you. Mason, you'll help select those of Adam's boys who'll carry the casket?"

"Of course, April. Declan and Micah here are willing."

"I'd be honoured," Dec said as she transferred food to plates.

"For a feed of that bacon, I'd do just about anything," the other man said, peering at the plates as they were ferried over. I didn't know Micah well. He hadn't been an enforcer before I left school, but he looked across the table, all tawny brown skin and reddish hair but with startling grey eyes that winked at me before he was a picture of the polite guest as Nan slid him a plate with a chuckle.

"Nan, I can't eat that much," I protested as I was served the lion's share.

"Course you can. Meyer women are known for their appetites." Meyer was Dad's last name, but he'd changed it to Spehr like all alphas did. A couple of choked responses had us looking down the table, where Declan and Micah were eating oh so respectfully.

Once everyone's plates were groaning with food, toast buttered and dispensed, tea poured, Nan finally sat down.

"Your father was worried he didn't have long," she said, resting her elbows on the table and clasping her hands. "We spoke about it before…" She let out a long sigh. "The details are all organised. The funeral home out on Jetty Road has him, and we'll conduct a viewing tomorrow, but tonight, we'll go to the chapel and sit for my son, your brother," she nodded to my aunties, "your father, your alpha. Any and all who wish to mark his passing are welcome to come, but all of this…unpleasantness will be left at the door."

My teeth dug into my bottom lip, but Nan reached across and squeezed my hand.

"He loved you, Paige, so very much. He showed me the clips on the YouTube of your fights, sent me links to articles when you were featured. Hold that in your heart tonight, sweetheart. That's what he would have wanted you to remember."

I met Nan's eyes and saw none of the usual dominance there. This wasn't her commanding me to eat or look after myself better.

Instead, she was as she had been when I was a kid—a strong, reassuring presence. I swallowed hard. Shouldn't it have been the other way around? She was getting old. It felt like I could see the fragility of her bones through her flesh, the once robust figure looking like it was wasting away. But her smile was strong, and so was her hand when she reached out and cupped my chin.

"Eat up, and then a sleep before the night comes. It'll be a long one."

THERE'S a peculiar kind of strangeness that comes from revisiting your childhood bedroom. It was much more so here than my actual room in the alpha residence, probably because the room I always slept in at Nan's was frozen in the 1970s still, the décor hopelessly outdated, even when I was young. The faded curtains with their lurid floral patterns, the quilted satin bedspread, always clean and warm, having kept many a child happy at night. The little narrow beds, enough to house whichever kids were staying over at the time.

"We made sure everything was freshened up and washed." Rose leaned on the doorframe.

"Probably gonna be a little squishy, now you're all grown up," Lynn said. "But try and sleep. You're probably too young to remember your mum's vigil." She reached out and smoothed a stray strand of hair away from my face. "It's hard, love. It's just you, the chapel, Mother Moon, and him."

"We didn't know…that Adam was sick," Rose said. "If we'd known…"

I nodded. It went without saying, didn't it? But I thanked them for it anyway.

"Excuse me, ladies. If I could just have a minute with Paige?"

They both turned to see Mason had appeared in the hallway.

"We'll come and get you when you need to get ready. Rest, even if you can't sleep," Lyn said, squeezing my hand before pulling away.

. . .

WE WAITED until they'd disappeared off into the house to speak.

"Your grandmother's put me in here with you."

"In here!?" I clapped a hand over my mouth, as if that'd hold back the yelp I'd just let out. For some reason, I could see my Nan's eyes clear as a bell in my mind, and they winked at me, just once. That meddling…

"There are separate beds?" He ducked his head in through the door. "Single beds. Well, beggars and all that. Look, I'm the last one you want in here, and if it's that big a deal, I'll take the couch and Declan or Micah can come in here."

It was weird, seeing that familiar mask of anger transform into… I shifted my weight from foot to foot, the way I would to prepare for a fight. I remembered this look. His eyes shone with challenge, daring me to make a big deal of it. We would have separate beds, sleep in the same room like a couple of siblings. Fuck, even his mouth twisted slightly into a… Was it? Was that an actual smile? I stepped back abruptly, gesturing for him to come in.

He shrugged off the leather jacket he was wearing. You know those ones that are cut close, that just seem to exist to further emphasise the breadth of a man's shoulders? Keys, wallet, were all chucked on one of the beds. The one where my cousin, Kelly, usually slept. Gun, belt. Wait, what?

"Why do you have a gun?"

"We all do," he said, shooting me a sidelong look, then reached behind to pull his shirt up over his head. He said something else, some kind of explanation by the tone of his voice, but while my focus had sharpened exponentially, it wasn't on what he was saying.

I'd dreamed of this moment so many fucking times, and the fact I was getting it the day after my dad died was one of those cosmic jokes. I still felt empty, hollow, and my head ached, but then there was this. I'd cried my heart out on that chest when Declan and I decided it wasn't going to work, when I didn't get the grades I'd hoped for, and sometimes just when being the heir got too much. He'd held me with those arms too, the ones with the wolves running up the forearms. When he sat down on the bed to pull his boots off, it all got a bit much, because this had happened before as well.

Maybe it was my scent, maybe it was the frozen silence, but those dark eyes rolled up to meet mine, and he paused mid shoe removal.

The light in my room had been similar to this, even though it was a different time of day. Nan kept her house shrouded in gloom, preferring the low light for the homey, cocoon like feel. Then, it'd been late in the afternoon, just before my birthday party. I'd been stuffing around in my room, pacing the floor half naked, knowing what was coming. We weren't married off at eighteen, not unless we wanted to be. Usually, the heir indicated who her choice was before the pack, and they had time to get used to the idea. Then a protracted courtship began to make sure the youthful decision was the right one. The heir and her mate were slowly eased into pack leadership, taking more and more cues from the existing alpha pair, until finally, they stepped back and the next generation took over.

Dad had put it down to Mum dying young. Me not growing up with a strong female role model—though what the hell he thought his own mother and sisters were, I had no idea, let alone Nance. How else could I have chosen so wrongly? I'd been tossing around outfits on the bed that night, looking at combination after combination, only in a pair of sleep shorts and a sports bra, when he knocked.

It was that which really had me on edge. We'd shared so many moments, Mason and I. I felt them like a weight on my chest. All those glancing touches, those long looks, that secret smile that seemed to appear just for me. I'd asked him to come up and see me. Heirs talked privately to those they wanted to take as mates, to feel them out, make sure the feelings were shared. I knew his wolf liked me a whole lot, being able to feel that keenly, but the man?

Back in Nan's room, I jerked off my top and sweatpants, leaving me standing there in just a sports bra and girl boxers when he finally saw it. His shoe dropped to the floor, but we didn't acknowledge it, eyes boring into each other. That faint smile, that look of challenge, it was all stripped away to reveal this.

"Paige…"

"You whisper my name. You did it then too. How often do you catch yourself doing that, Mason?" I said, my voice a low, deadly growl. His eyes went wide at that, deprived of his professional mask. I liked that a lot. I wanted something, anything other than that distant, shitty mask all the time.

"I—"

"You do it all the time, don't you? Sometimes I'd swear I could hear it on the wind. You don't want to, but you do."

"You don't understand what you're asking."

"Nope, I don't. I really, really don't. There is literally nothing I understand about you or about that night."

"There's nothing to understand, Paige. It's done. I turned you down, you left."

"And that's the last time I saw Dad."

His teeth ground together, those long, sensitive fingers gripping each other, as if that was the only place they could find support.

"You blame me."

The words were bald, hard, hanging in the air between us, sucking up all the oxygen until we were both gasping.

If Zack'd been here, he would've been redirecting me away from this, trying to get me to attack the issues with Mason in manageable bites, rather than this, now. He'd be worried I was maxing myself out again, putting what I needed to one side again, and just throwing myself in, despite what it was doing to me. My heart thudded so hard, so fast, if I half closed my eyes, I could see the forest around me again.

But I wasn't the hunted this time, he was.

"You should." He met my gaze head-on, flat, empty, no hint of dominance. This was the stare of a wolf pinned to the ground, surrendering. "I tried to resign, told Alpha Spehr that I was moving on to another town, another pack, but he wouldn't hear of it."

"He chose you over me."

He shook his head. "He told me that this was right, that this is what you needed to do. To see life beyond the little microcosm of Lupindorf, to get more experience, to be free."

"So what did that have to do with you sticking around? Why couldn't you transfer?"

"Because when you came back, he said you'd need me."

It was odd how words could pack the same power as a punch to the head. I jerked back, stiffened, feeling the slap of them against my skin, even though he hadn't moved an inch. Fuck, I'd rather he came at me with his fists, as I knew how to put him on his arse if he did. My body thrummed with a need to do just that—to smash that fucking face with all its perfect angles and perfect stubble and perfect full lips that I could still feel the ghost of.

"And what do I need you for, Klein?"

His chin tipped back a little, revealing an expanse of tanned brown neck. For a human, this might appear like an act of rebellion, but for a wolf shifter? Mine growled within me, shifting back and forth at the submissive display. She wanted to shove his head back, fully bare that throat to me, and then sink her fangs in, just a little, to force him to show the respect he'd never seemed to be able to after that night.

So I did.

The wind was shoved out of him with an *oof* as I landed on him, forcing him back onto the bed, one hand on his jaw, the other on his chest as I hunched over him. A low, vicious growl started in my belly, growing louder and louder until…

"That's it." His soft voice came out strangled, my fangs on his throat making it difficult, but speak he did. "That's it, Paige."

He wanted this, that had my wolf balking, scenting the air as if that would give us a hint at the mysteries of Mason Klein. But we couldn't seem to let go, not just yet. All of it came rushing up, as it would over and over, I was sure. The pain of my eighteenth, of the rejection, sure, but that was old and well worn. Plastered over top of it, much thicker, much more intense, was the pain of what I'd lost, leaving town, not coming back fast enough. Not seeing…

The first sob was ugly sounding, coming through outstretched jaws, so I forced my fangs back as my tears hit Mason's skin. But when I went to pull back, his arms went around me. Foreign and familiar, I remembered their weight, their strength, the way they pulled me down against him, holding me nestled against the wall of his chest. My wolf fought this, our jaws flexing, snapping, ready to rend and tear, sure there was yet more threat here. But my body

Lone Wolf

uncoiled in tiny increments as he just kept stroking my hair, crooning nonsense words to me, until finally, I relaxed.

HE WAS GONE by the time the aunts woke me. Of course he was. I stepped free of the blankets under their impassive gaze, then they reached for me before I went to pull my clothes on. They shook their heads, leading me by the hand, down the hallway, past the guys who were stripping down and walking out the back door. They would have a kiddie pool of lake water set up there, but we would use the bathroom. My nan looked at me with a beatific smile when I entered, clad only in a simple white cotton gown.
"And now the purification begins."

Chapter 12

As we drove to the chapel, people lined the streets. They stood there, eyes down, silent witnesses to our passage.

"We bathe our sister, our daughter in the waters of the lake," Nan said, *collecting a dipper of water from the bath, no doubt collected from Blue Lake, and poured it over Rose's head. We watched it trail over her skin before Nan bent down to do it again.*

The crowds got thicker the closer we got to the chapel. I was wedged now between Mason and Micah, only able to see the people when I peered past either man.

"Let the water of the mother wash pain and fear away. Let it wash away worldly concerns. Let it open our hearts so we can accept her light in."

I felt the weight of Mason's leg against mine, of Micah's. Each man shot me a sidelong look or two when I got in the car, pressed against their bulk, but something had happened when it became my turn.

I'd stepped into the bath, stripped naked, walking in as I'd come into this world. Nan recited the words, poured the water, and something...shifted. It'd been so long since I'd done this. Moon worship was something some city shifters did, some transmuted and added to the more conventional human Christian religion, focussing on Mother Mary, and others just left it behind.

That'd been what I did, ready to shed any and all of my history when I left town. I hadn't really noticed the loss of the sacred until right now. It was just water from the brilliant blue lake that had formed in a limestone cave outside of town, but as it slid over my skin, I felt it, that shift into a quieter, softer, denser space. Nan's words resonated through my body, but my mind refused to engage too much with them. It stilled, for the first time in so damn long, no mindfulness or meditation needed to make it so. Or rather this was a meditation, dressed up in a ritual maybe? It didn't matter. I stepped out of the bath, was wrapped in towels as I had wrapped each one of my aunts, while Nan performed the ritual for herself, water forcing the white cotton of her gown to stick to her skin as she forced out the words.

We turned as one, heard the shake in her voice, saw it in her hands. Tears joined the trailing water as she poured it over her head, her body. Again and again, she bathed herself in the water, seeming to need more from it than we did, until finally, the dipper dropped, her gown was unbuttoned and left to float in the water, and she stepped out as well.

I looked down at where Mason's dark jean-clad thigh pressed against my white cotton covered one. We were her priestesses, every woman was, so we wore her gowns, this one embroidered many generations ago by another Meyer, another woman whose blood beat in my veins. She'd used a scratchy silver thread on the fabric to mark out the Mother's phases, showing us how she turned her face against the world, only to bring it back again.

Micah's hand shifted on his knee, jerking my attention to him. I watched him with cool, clear eyes, saw those grey eyes burning bright against that tanned skin, the furtive lick of lips that had gotten too dry as those eyes dipped down to look at mine. My head twitched slightly, as if to capture that moment more clearly, to see what he'd do next. The thick muscles of his throat worked, his chest sucking in air as something built inside him, this stranger, this man.

"Paige, we're here."

Mason's voice was soft, solicitous, but it jerked my attention like a dog on a lead, my eyes swinging around to see the chapel, all white stone, graceful arabesques, and pitched roofs, gothic ornamentation spilling across its face. Mason took my hand when I stepped out, Declan moving closer to do the same, but my eyes stayed on the big circular window at the apex. This is where she would come in, Mother Moon, where she would bathe us, bathe Dad in her light. Which was why I didn't see him.

He leaned against the chapel wall, Zack, a wall himself of masculine energy. I noted the contrast between the two of them, and it made a kind of sense. He'd have to have gotten here early, damn early, to get such a choice position, but he was all lazy confidence right now. Those dark eyes, the echo of the other ones watching me right now. Brothers, twins, if I closed my eyes slightly, I could see them overlapped—Zack against the wall, Mason standing just in front of me, a question in his eyes. But what question was that? I wanted to open my mouth, say something, anything, but my lips remained glued together, a hand sliding into mine breaking the hold they had on me. I looked up to see Declan standing beside me, squeezing it. He drew me past the two of them and inside, where I needed to be.

It was beautiful, I guessed, but sometimes pretty things hurt so much. He looked so much more like my dad laid out on the white marble dais, a similarly embroidered piece of cotton covering him like a sheet, like he was just asleep. Because that's what they did, these magicians of embalmment. Before they washed him down with the waters of the lake, they removed all evidence of medical trauma, then cleaned and prepped what was left of my father to create this perfect facsimile.

I walked down the steps, Declan's hand a warm weight in mine, feeling like I, we, floated along. My aunts, my female cousins and my grandmother all fanned out, creating a ring around Dad, waiting for me to take my place at his head. I let go of Declan, feeling light, too light, as I moved closer, as if he anchored me to the here and now, so where was I at this minute? I knelt down on the cushion on the left-hand side of Dad, Nan across from me on the right. She spared me one long look and then nodded.

I'd been weirded out the first time I went to a human wedding. The Christian rite was so…talky. So many speeches, so many words to communicate the sacred. That was not our way. The kind of still quiet I sought when I did meditation fell so much more easily over me. That's what this was for, I remembered that from when Mum died.

Human life was so full of stuff. I'd fallen into its rhythms when I went to the city, and it had worked for me for some time, but this... I looked at my father, really looked at my father for the first time in so long. My eyes took in the way his hair had begun to thin, to recede, the deep chestnut colour threaded through with much more grey now. I saw all the lines on his face, drawn deeper by his mobile expressions—always smiling, laughing, frowning, growling. That was one thing the funeral director couldn't capture, revealing only the passage all those many emotions had left. A nose broken when young, fighting on the footy field, a short beard, almost all silver. Strong, broad shoulders that I'd felt blotted out the sun when I was a kid, arms that had reached out to stop me from blundering, that gestured for something to be done and it was so, that moved when he spoke, as if to communicate the meaning, that wrapped around me, swung me up, pulled me close until I drew back.

A single tear fought free. It wasn't great to cry early. The vigil was so long, the sun slowly dropping in the big round windows, going down, dying as my father had, to give way for her. But where there was one tear, there was another and another. They slid down and acted as a herald almost to the others.

Choked back sobs came from within the chapel, from without. The people outside wouldn't sit the full vigil, but they marked the alpha's passing with the required respect. That wasn't why I was here. I couldn't give a rat's arse about his role, his standing in this town.

Daddy...

The point of the quiet, the dress, the dais, the chapel was this—the stuff of life, human or otherwise, was put to one side. You couldn't distract yourself, couldn't let all the many, many things that were going on in your life get between you and your grief.

The pain rose as the moon did, and I tried to push past it, not let it break me, like I did in the gym, keep on breathing, keep on going. But I underestimated the weight of this, this final severing of the parent-child relationship. I couldn't say I was all alone in the world, but I wasn't anyone's kid anymore, didn't have anyone checking in, keeping tabs, being part of my life, having seen it in its entirety since it began.

I didn't want this.

I didn't want to sit there, kneeling, looking at my dead dad and thinking thoughts. I wanted this to be bullshit, one big ruse to drag me home, where he would open his eyes, smile, and wink at having tricked me so completely. I wanted my tears to dry on my cheeks as I saw him rise and sit on the side of the dais, grinning down at me like he did when I woke him up in the morning, busting in with childishly created breakfasts of Vegemite toast. I wanted this to be a life lesson—don't assume you have endless time left because you might not. I would be the most apt of students.

I would. I'd learn this lesson, if he just…

This wasn't fucking fair. My teeth locked down so hard, I could almost hear them crack, anything to hold back the screams inside me. I wanted to shatter this fucking place with my cries, have it ringing out through the whole place until the stones themselves crumbled.

How could they not? How could they stay so solid and impervious, when all this pain poured out within it? People cried, sobbed, whimpered over and over and over, a relentless fucking wave. My eyes snapped open. I hadn't realised they were closed, and I stared up at the moon now streaming through the circular window, bathing all of us in that white light.

It was pitiless, endless, this illusion of Mother Moon as this gentle nurturing goddess fucking bullshit, because where the hell was my peace? I saw it now, with much wiser eyes, eighteen and packing my bag, shoving my gear into it, but my focus was on him. The worry, the fear, the pain as he watched me get ready to walk out on him, the wrench inside him at my harsh words, my snapping responses. Him walking in, trying to pull me close, but me… My fangs lengthened, my hands going to claws as I watched myself push him away. He spoke in a steady stream of reassurance, of concern, of a need to fix this, fix me.

But I wouldn't be fixed.

Every step I took away from him was a slap to my face, as it had been to him at the time. He'd watched me run down the stairs, getting farther and farther away, the twin pains of wanting to stop me with every breath coupled with the knowledge he knew he couldn't.

I needed this.

Fuck, that slayed me, cut a great swathe through my heart as I saw my Dad accept my actions, even though it killed him, knowing exactly what was going to happen. That I'd grow apart, on my own, to my own dictates. That I'd stop being a child and become a woman, and he'd miss it all.

Because that was the true depth of the parent relationship, something I'd never fully understood until now. He sacrificed everything—that anal need to know what I was doing at all times, the constant checking in, the steering and training me for the role that was to come, that connection between heir and alpha. That connection.

I saw all the times he called and I didn't pick up or return his calls, the stiff conversations when I did. My wriggling, writhing need to break free of the cocoon, right when he wanted to wrap me tighter inside it. But he held it back, so fucking much. The rush of pride each time he found mention of me on the internet, his dedicated collection of every scrap of information, because that's all I'd given him, no matter what he needed—scraps.

My focus stayed on the shaking hand holding onto the bannister, knowing I'd find the marks of his claws there when I got home. They'd dug in deep to hold him back as I walked out the door.

At some point, my vision blurred, my eyes gone with tears. Whether it was hours or minutes later, I couldn't tell. The chapel was always a timeless place. I cried because no matter what I wished or had done, this was the reality. That was the purpose of vigil in the end—acceptance. She might be our mother, but like any parent, sometimes she had to witness the pain of her children as they fought to accept what they must. There was no fighting, no logic, no way through this but to reconcile themselves to what is. I blinked my eyes until they were clear enough, stared at my father's face, bathed in moonlight, and said my goodbyes.

"PICK HER UP."

Hands were on me, jostling me from my frozen position, my body numb, my circulation sluggish, as if everything inside me slowed down once the real grieving began.

"It's going to hurt her. She's been awfully still. Rub her arms and her legs, get the blood going."

"Is she… Will that be OK? I can get Zack."

"Your brother is asleep outside the chapel, and you are the ones that Adam charged to care for her. The longer you wait, the more it will hurt her."

Hands, so many hands all over my body, I wanted to shove away, but I couldn't control mine enough to do so. My body, my heart had become numb, sinking deeper and deeper into grief. Away from the chapel, the moon, the world, life, just down, down, down.

But they fought to bring me back, something that drew a strangled cry, because it hurt just like my limbs did as they rubbed the circulation back. A sharp prickling at first, then followed by a heavy, dense pain that just grew and grew and grew. Scrambled, ragged noises clawed their way up and out of my throat despite my attempts to keep them down.

"She's… We…"

"It's painful coming back. It hurts so much to choose to keep on living when someone you love has died. They take some of that with them, that determination, when they go, but we must remind her of all that remains here, waiting for her. Rub her skin, stretch her limbs, work those muscles—"

"No!"

My eyes flicked open, and I saw all of them, clean, clear, and all too crisp. Nan stood over me, my aunties and cousins clustered close and looking down at a sprawled out me, but it was them I glared at —my father's men, here to carry him to his grave. Their hands worked on me not him, massaging my skin, drawing my attention back to it, stroking my body, my head, my hair. They all stared at me, Declan, Micah, Mason, but it was his gaze that grabbed mine and held it.

"Yes," Mason said with a definite snap. "You can't stay here anymore. It's hurting you. You've done your vigil."

"No! No!" I fought my way out, lashing out with those ungainly, uncoordinated kicks I always scorned in new fighters, scrabbling free before clawing my way to the dais. "No!" I shouted at the moon as it faded, the dark sky going purple, then blue as the Mother turned away from her children and the sun was reborn. "No…" That was more of a howl, a horrible drawn-out wail of a thing, a sound so fucking alien, I couldn't believe it came from me. It didn't stop when Mason's arms went around me, when hands pulled me back from Dad, holding me tight, the living, when all I wanted to do was hold on to the dead.

Scents clashed in my nose, arms wrapped around me, their hair and skin and muscle and bone all thrust itself into my consciousness, right when I didn't want them to.

"Paige Marie Spehr!"

Nan's voice cracked across my face like a bare-handed slap. She moved closer until she was standing before me, frowning, then looking me over with compassion.

"Darling, it's time."

"No, Nan, no!"

"Yes, darling." I heard her own calm tone waver, but her nod was decisive. "Adam's boys will carry him to where he needs to go, at his side one more time. Don't take that from them, Paige. I know you don't want that."

Which of course ripped the suffocating caul of self-involved misery from my eyes and made me see the chapel in total for the first time since we walked in here. Everyone was waiting, hurting, needing for this to end so they could go home and grieve on their own, and I was just dragging this out, because why? I felt a flush of shame, but Nan just shook her head.

"It's OK. You can let her go now. She's back, and you have your burden to pick up."

I felt them pull away, every withdrawal of touch somehow feeling like another smaller loss, but I wrapped my arms around myself as I watched each man take a corner of the stretcher Dad had been laid out on. Mason, Declan, Micah, and Callum who had made up the fourth, walked out of the chapel with the body in tow, and we followed behind.

"Paige?"

Zack looked rumpled and exhausted, but he approached me as I stepped out onto the cold stone steps, Nan nodding when I took his hand. She led the trail of mourners down the street the short distance it took to get to the burial grounds.

Half the town was clustered around the grave site, though they were kept well back by temporary barriers, which made me wonder who had been here to set them up. As if sensing my thoughts, Mason looked back at me for a moment before they lowered Dad's body into the grave.

"Are you OK? You were in there so long. You've not had any—"

I pressed my fingers to Zack's lips, stopping the flow of terse whispers as my father's beta stepped up to deliver the eulogy.

"We're here today to commit back to the earth our alpha, Adam Meyer Spehr. I'm not one of you, I wasn't born in Lupindorf. Rather, I came here as a young man seeking…" His hands flexed on the empty air. "I don't know what I was looking for, but Adam seemed to know. I wasn't much when I crawled into town. Skinny, been in fur too long, half feral. I'm sure there was plenty that thought a bullet in the brain would have been a blessing, but not Adam. He was early in his leadership then, but still, he had the unerring ability to see the good in people."

My hand went to my lips now, wanting to hold it all back, and Zack's arm snaked around my shoulder and held me tight.

"He gave me a feed, took me into his house. His alpha female, Lucy, Paige's mum, she wasn't too pleased. Just took me to the enforcers' quarters and told me to have two showers. One to just get the dirt off, then another to get off the stink. But he just nodded when I came out, put a plate full of food in front of me, and told me to eat."

He took a long breath, then looked out onto the group of people around him.

"I tried to argue with him, thank him for the shower and the clean clothes and everything and get the hell out of Dodge. It's what I wanted to do. I hadn't been around people for a while by that point and Paige was just a kid, so Lucy was none too pleased about me being around. But Adam?" He nodded to himself. "Maybe there were faster men or tougher men, but there were none stronger. He just looked at me with those steely eyes of his. Anyone who's grown up here while he was alpha would know what I'm talking about." A smattering of amused chuckles. "He just looked at me and said, 'Mate, be the man I can see you are inside, and you'll have no problems with me.'"

It was then that Mason's face transformed, became something so damn hauntingly beautiful, my lungs sucked in air with the shock of it.

"So I was. You couldn't help it with Adam. You wanted to be better, because it made him happy, because he believed you could. I saw it over and over with the young blokes he brought in as enforcers. They'd be antsy and wanting to prove themselves, or jumpy and wondering how they fit in the hierarchy, and he'd just walk out, all cool, calm, and collected, and then they were too. He helped men forge bonds that last lifetimes, find strength they didn't know they had, become something more than they'd ever have thought possible, and then find them willing to walk over hot coals just to serve him. We lost a good man…" His eyes shone in the early morning light. "No, a great man, the other day, but the Mother, there's some children she holds tighter than others, wanting them back with her because they're too bloody good for this world, and I think that was Adam."

He bent his head, clasping his hands before him, and we all did the same.

"We return to you, Mother, your son Adam Meyer Spehr. We conduct him to your care, know you'll hold him within your heart, lead him to the pack lands beyond, watch him run free for eternity, a child of the moon."

My tears ran freely, dripping on the ground, so when it came my turn, I stumbled. There were a few gasps from the crowd, but I bent down, grabbed a solid handful of earth, and then tossed it down on the body below. Nan stepped forward next, doing the same, as did my aunties, then all the women on the Meyer side. Nance and the other Spehrs did the same, then the enforcers, each one placing a handful of dirt in the hole. Then, when we all stepped back, Mase, as Dad's beta, grabbed the shovel and scooped up the remaining dirt, the silence broken only by the sound of digging and transferring soil until it was done.

I felt hollowed out and empty, like a bell when I saw the mounded earth, the white marble headstone. I wavered a little on my feet, the lack of sleep and food coming crashing down on me, forcing me into submission.

"There's a lot to talk about, since we don't have a clear line of succession," Mason said, moving closer to the barriers. "But I ask you to respect the family's need for time to grieve tonight. Tomorrow night, a town meeting will be called, contenders will be identified, and a process hammered out for going forward. All of this will be done in an orderly fashion. We will avoid the bloodshed and the bullshit other packs go through when succession is not clear, because we fucking owe it to Adam."

I'd never really heard Mason use his alpha whip, but he did right now, forcing the whole damn town in submission. Fuck, he was totally the right guy for alpha. If only… I shook my head. Maybe there'd be a way that he could take it without taking me. I shouldn't be the thing that stopped him from becoming what Dad obviously thought he could be.

"I'll make sure everyone knows about it. We'll move forward on this, together."

AND THEN THAT WAS IT. People slowly moved away, including my Spehr family, then the Meyers as well. I stood by my nan, blank and empty, when they hugged me, wished me well. I gripped them tight when they did, trying to make clear that despite my absence, my lack of response right now, I still loved them, that I absorbed every stroke of my face, my hair, the kind comments, like a parched plant did the morning rain. Then Nan turned to me and Zack.

She watched him put his arm around me, pull me into his chest, the way my eyes closed for just a moment, absorbing him too.

"You love her."

It wasn't a question, it was a statement, as Nan's often were, and it wasn't to me, though I stiffened in response.

"I do." Zack's rumbly answer vibrated through me from head to toe.

"He loves her too." My muscles tightened and I went to turn away, but Zack kept me pinned where I was. "At least a few of them do."

"Why wouldn't they? You've seen her grow up. You know who she is. What someone else feels isn't a threat to me, not even how she feels."

Something ached inside me, getting harder, more painful at his words, at the slow slide of his hand down my back.

"So you're strong then? Good, you'll need to be. I've no loyalty to any one of you, no vested interest in seeing any man take the role of alpha, but Paige? You'll find I'm very interested indeed in anyone who wishes to be a part of my granddaughter's life."

"Then I'd be honoured to come around, introduce myself, and earn your approval. Paige'll tell you, I don't back down from challenges, and I'm glad she has people looking out for her best interest."

"A roast lunch, then," Nan said decisively. "It's been too long since she's had my roast potatoes." I groaned, my stomach rumbling, almost able to taste those crunchy, fluffy, herby, buttery spuds. "You'll be doing that at the end of one of my meals too. You've gotten too skinny, Paige."

"Yes, Nan."

"Go on then, love. Eat something, sleep, let your body process the vigil. You'll come out stronger, Paige, I know it. See you soon, Zack."

"Did I tell her my name?" he muttered to me.

"Nothing gets past Nan," I replied, pulling back, seeing my father's… No, they were mine until the succession had been finalised. Seeing my enforcers waiting, ready to take us home. I nodded, feeling chilled now, standing around in a flimsy gown, so home we went.

Chapter 13

How did I feel on the way back home? It was hard to say. Zack steered me over to the car, seeming to understand that I needed to go with the enforcers, even if that's not what he wanted.

"She's gonna need to crash when she gets home. She won't want to, but she'll need to," he told Mason, still holding me in his arms.

"We've all been through a vigil before, Zack. We know," Mason replied.

"But this is different now, for her. This is her first one on her own. I need to... I want to hold her while she sleeps. She's got plenty of time to shower off my scent before the meeting."

All twelve sets of eyes went to me, Mason's, Zack's, and the rest of the enforcers'. Declan was going to say something, and Micah watched me closely, so closely, I wondered at what he was thinking, but Mason spoke for all of them when he finally nodded.

"Last time, brother. You want to take the spot by her side going forward, you compete with everyone else. She rides with us though."

"Done."

This pricked at me a little, the big boys making the decisions for me, but I wasn't up for much more. I just came along quietly when Mason reached out for my hand. He led me to the car, wedged me between him and Micah again, and I just lay back against the car seat, a limp mess.

"Is he gonna be the next alpha?" Declan asked, looking back at me from the rear vision mirror, waiting for an answer before starting the car.

"Dec, not now," Mason growled out.

"Nah, it's a valid question," I said, rubbing my hands over a face still sticky with tears. "You know if I could, I'd relinquish the position to any of you. Mason, Callum… Honestly, if you were good enough to protect Dad, you're good enough to run this town."

"It's not just the town."

Micah stared at me with those curiously pale eyes that seemed to hold a whole lot of intensity, dropping down again to look at my…

"No, it's not, and that's the problem. I tried to solve this when I was eighteen. Honestly, I tried…" My voice broke on the words. Zack was right—this was too much too soon. "I'm sorry."

I couldn't think of anything else to say, didn't even know what I was apologising for right at this moment, but right now, it felt right.

"We'll work it out," Declan said, then started the car.

HE WAS WAITING in my room when I returned, Zack. He'd stripped down already, just a towel wrapped around his waist, and he went to whip my gown over my head when he saw me.

"Family heirloom, Zack," I protested, taking over, removing it and then folding it neatly so it could be dry cleaned later. But when he took my hand and tugged me into the bathroom, I went willingly.

There was no heat in his gaze, in his touch, when he started the water. The last time I was in here, I'd jerked off to a memory of his brother, but right now, there was something chaste about Zack. He lathered the soap, washed my limbs, made the water scour all evidence of my tears away until I was just me again.

A me hanging by a thread. Lack of sleep induced an almost drunken state. I was too clumsy, too floppy, too biddable, so when he pushed me towards the bed, I went willingly, falling down onto it.

The blankets were a welcome weight, as was he when he got in beside me, cradling me within his arms. I started to shiver, his body heat stifling even while I felt cold, so cold. He held me tight, weathering my shakes until sleep rose up and swallowed me down.

I WOKE UP FEELING SMOTHERED.

I thrashed initially, dreaming a landslide of mud was swallowing me whole, sucking down my limbs, pinning beneath its immovable—

My eyes flicked open, and I saw where I was, what was happening. Zack was cuddly during sleep, my common complaint that he liked to pin me to the bed when we did so together.

Need to know where you are, that you're safe, even then, he'd replied with a grin the last time I told him off about it. So I was adept at wiggling out from under him without waking him, slipping out of the bed, pulling on my pyjamas, and padding out of the room.

My throat was dry, my head hurt, and my stomach felt like it was turning in on itself from hunger, so I ran down the stairs, only to find I had a visitor.

"Hey," Stevie said, holding up a bottle of tequila in each hand. "Didn't expect to see you up yet. Brought some supplies for your harem."

"They're not my harem."

"Only if you don't want them to be. Pack princess and all. I think you'd be surprised at who was nursing a crush. But not the right one, maybe?"

I shook my head. While I'd always considered Stevie my friend, her bar was the epicentre of town gossip, so finding more was as natural as breathing. I snorted, but when I went to retort, my stomach spoke for me, growling loudly.

"Got food too. Those boys need something to line their bellies before they drink the amount I think they're gonna drink. You in?"

She tilted her head back slightly, that glitter of a challenge the same one she'd always used right before we were gonna do something dumb. But right now, dumb sounded like a damn fine idea.

"This is a wake."

"Yeah, I guess it is."

Her voice was quiet, but she made no excuses. Stevie never did. She just eyed me sideways, reading me like she did everyone.

"Yeah, I'm in."

"Good girl," she said with a cheeky grin. "C'mon, I got the boys unloading most of the heavy stuff."

I WOULD ALWAYS NOTICE my father's absence in weird ways I'm sure, but right now, I did because I was walking into the enforcers' quarters for one and in my PJs for the other. Dad had been *really* strict about me keeping clear of the boys.

"I know some of them are your friends, Paige, and I want you to be able to trust them, lean on them, but until you've chosen your mate…" His voice trailed away, just a little hopeful I'd interrupt him with my decision. *"Then you need to keep a respectable distance."*

"You act like this is some kind of Regency romance and they'll turn into ravening rapists at the sign of a well-turned ankle," I'd said.

"No, but any man who looks at you also sees a way into this chair. Enforcers are ambitious, they need to be. They're our best and brightest."

Yeah, well, they weren't so bright right now.

Music pumped loud from the stereo system, playing something raucous and aggressive. Smoke filled the air, a couple of the guys were at the pool table, and the rest were ferrying in slabs of beer or bottles of spirits, along with trays of food. Well, until they saw us. It was seriously like one of those needle scratch moments you see on TV, when everyone turned around.

"Well, well," Stevie said, brandishing her bottles. "The gang's all here."

Mason turned around, a lazy smile on his face, already a little soft around the edges from drinking by the look of it, and with that, I caught a glimpse of the Mase they knew. The stick was well and truly removed from his arse, until he saw me.

"Paige, you can't—"

"Save it," I said, noting everyone was watching the two of us, our stances, our stares as we each took the other's measure. I walked over to the table, picked up a couple of grimy shot glasses, and held them out to Stevie.

"Fuck, have clean ones at least," Micah said, moving in and reaching to take those from me, handing me fresh ones. Three, I noted. I jerked an eyebrow up, and then my friend cracked the bottle.

"This shit's been sitting in an oak barrel for over three years. Don't need no lime, no salt, no shit. It's as smooth as a baby's bum," she pronounced, filling each glass and passing the other two to me. I gave Micah the side-eye before giving the third to him. "To Adam," she said, holding up her drink.

My hand went up and so did everyone else's as the music was killed for the moment, and when I looked around, I saw what Mason had talked about—that bond. There were no reluctant or resentful faces in the place, each other glad for the opportunity to honour my father. Belatedly, I realised they were waiting on me, so I said, "To Dad," putting the shot glass to my mouth and drinking the tequila down. The toast was taken up around the room, every person taking a drink before the noise all started again.

"C'mon," Stevie said. "Let's get some food in you. I've got a bottle of my best Patrón with your name on it, girl, but you gotta get something into your stomach."

"Paige, I'm glad you came down, and thanks, Stevie, for putting this on." Mason had arrived, following us into the kitchen, where big aluminium foil trays of food were being uncovered.

"But," Stevie said with a smirk. "I'm sensing a but."

"There's always a butt," I winked back, taking an exaggerated look at the very well formed, jean-clad butts in front of us. Declan spun around, catching us in the act, a slow smirk matching ours in minutes.

"But until the succession process is locked down, being here is a liability. You'd be seen favouring the enforcers—"

"Oh my god, Mason, do you ever stop?" There it was, that same mulish expression, right back where it belonged. "It's one fucking day. One day. Can I not have something to fucking eat and drink with some friends and spend some time commemorating the life of someone I loved with other people who loved him?" I watched his resolve falter a little, but that didn't mean anything with Mason. He was such a hard-headed prick. "Actually, why am I asking permission?"

"Ooh…" Stevie said in a low voice, snickering when I shot her a look. She'd arbitrated a lot of Paige vs Mason fights in the past.

"Unless anyone else has objections to me being here?" I turned around and saw we had the focus of everyone in the room, but they weren't looking anywhere near as pissed. These were typical Aussie blokes, for all they were wolves, so some were checking out my tits, some were checking out my arse, and the rest just wanted to get fucking drunk and anyone who was a friend of the beer was a friend of theirs.

"Paige—"

"The only words I wanna hear from you are 'Yes, Paige, have some of this delicious BBQ chook and salads that Stevie has so kindly put on' or…" I grinned, the feeling odd after yesterday, yet as familiar as breathing. "Or get in the ring, motherfucker."

"What!?" Declan spluttered. Well, him and most of the blokes in the room, the others just cheered wildly in that time-honoured Australian tradition when someone was about to do something dumb while drinking. Stevie took my glass and a couple more she found on the kitchen sink, poured out shots in a line of deep golden tequila, and passed me two.

"Get in the ring?" Mason asked, crossing his arms while I fought very hard not to notice the way those big biceps popped when he did so. "So what, if I can get in the first hit, you'll go upstairs and back to my brother?"

"If I can put you on your arse, you have to butt the hell out until the succession is sorted and either you're alpha or someone else is," I shot back.

"Oh, this is gonna be good. Food first, girl. You need to fuel up to fight," Stevie said, moving to grab a bread roll and piling it high with meat and salad. "You can fight, can't you?"

"Yeah, I can fight." I took the food from her and had a big bite.

Damn, fresh bread, rotisserie chicken and salad—Aussie BBQ heaven. Mason watched me munch that down with a curious mix of concern and amusement.

"Zack's obviously shown you a thing or two, and you're fit. Doesn't mean much in a real fight."

"Aw, are you mansplaining fighting to me?" I asked. I was being a cheeky little shit, but that felt good right now. I'd only just begun the grieving process, but I wanted to take a little pitstop before I moved onto the next step. Eat, drink, have some fun, try to shore myself up, get ready for what was coming.

I remembered this look. His eyes shone as his jaw tightened, but not in preparation for his usual frown. This was his attempt to smother the laugh that was coming. He always did that, like laughing out loud would lead to licentiousness or something. I scarfed down the food, took a swig of Declan's beer to his initial dismay then laughter, and then took off out of the room.

"Giving up already, princess?" Mase called out.

"Just getting dressed in something better to kick your arse."

"HEY..." Zack said sleepily as I rummaged around in my bag for some tights. I had some good thick Lycra ones which were perfect for this kinda thing. "Whatcha doing?"

"Gonna put your brother on his butt so I can sit up drinking with the enforcers."

"Yeah?" He flopped back onto the bed, letting out a long sigh. "Keep your hands up, move faster than he can, and sweep the fucking leg."

"You going all Cobra Kai on me?"

"Old footy injury in the right knee. You'll have him down in seconds."

"You coming down?"

"Nah, I'm fucked. Haven't had enough sleep lately. Neither have you. You'll crash after this, you know."

"I know."

He gave me one long appreciative look as I stretched my legs, feeling the range of the activewear before pulling my T-shirt off and replacing it with a sports bra.

"Well, you'll have his attention, anyway. Distracting him with boobs? Good plan."

I stopped still, straightened, and then crawled onto the bed, his hands reaching out for me as soon I got close. He kissed me long and slow, until I wondered what the hell I was fighting for.

"You're talking about your brother checking out my tits."

"Noticed that, did you? I can't get jealous, Paige. I won't let myself." He ran a finger down my cheekbone. "I'm not sure in what capacity I'm gonna get to have a relationship with you, so I'm staying open to the possibilities."

"What possibilities? You and…" I stopped talking. I couldn't make those words out, I just couldn't. Shifter men were growly, pushy, and possessive. Sharing was not part of their vocabulary.

But if it was…

Stevie and I, we'd talked about it some nights at the pub. I'd been underage, of course, but she turned a blind eye to the alpha's daughter. Better she knew where I was drinking, and it sure as hell wouldn't be at some house party with boys. The short-term impact alcohol had on shifter's systems made parents more relaxed about it.

"So what if you didn't have to choose?" she'd asked me, pushing a coffee my way.

"That's not how it works. They'd…" I shook my head. It wasn't even worth thinking about.

"C'mon, live a little, even if it's just in your mind. People have all sorts of relationships now. You could have a throuple going with a couple of those enforcers."

"Is that what you want?"

I never saw Stevie with anyone, ever. She was a beautiful woman, caught the eye of many a guy, but if they tried flirting, she just smiled and laughed at them.

"What I want is irrelevant. What you want is gonna change this town, one way or the other."

"So this is about predicting what the new regime will be?" I shrugged. We both knew who I wanted to choose, but I couldn't articulate it. To say it out loud was to make it a real possibility, and I wasn't ready for that yet.

"Dream big. It's just words. These guys, they tell you that you have to do this and that. An eighteen-year-old working out who her mate is and then making him leader of the whole town? Never heard anything like it outside of this place."

It was hard to remember Stevie hadn't always owned the bar. While her face was smooth and unlined, there was something ageless about her, like she was perpetually twenty-three.

"Who'd you take, if you had the choice? If you could walk down the stairs, past your dad and your aunty and all that bloody family, stroll into the enforcers' rooms and just take your pick…"

"You like that idea," Zack said with a sly smile. "You do."

"Stop sniffing me," I said, pushing myself off him with a punch to his shoulder. "Scent isn't everything. What I want is to kick your brother's arse."

"Then do it, baby, and then when you're done with drinking, come back to me."

Chapter 14

The party had decamped to the training room, booze, food, and music all brought along. The speakers were blaring Guns and Roses' "Get in the Ring," which just made me laugh. I went through my usual warmup routine, but that was somewhat distracted by Mason stripping off his jacket, then his shirt.

"Don't let the eye candy keep you off your game. You're striking a blow for the sisterhood, girl," Stevie said from my side of the room.

I shook my head, tried valiantly to keep my eyes to myself, and then worked on my head game. To the sound of an eighties synth rock track, I saw a montage of me striking out at Mason, forcing him back, slipping under his more powerful but slower hits, running rings around him, and then putting him on his arse. I held onto that when I walked to the centre of the room.

"So how you wanna do this?" Mason asked, looking down at me with a smirk. This was all just a formality for him—I'd do what he wanted once he showed me who was boss. Fucking wolf shifters, always the same.

"First one to get a hit in?"

"You said you were gonna put me on my arse."

I shrugged, seeing that delicious reality clear in my mind. "Works for me." I shifted into a fighting stance, something that made Mason snort.

"So bets!" Declan said brightly, grabbing a cap from somewhere and holding it out. "C'mon fellas, we've gotta show some support for our girl here. Paige puts Mason down, five to one."

"Yeah, I'll take those odds," Micah said, pulling out his wallet.

"Yeah, me, but I'm banking on Mase."

The other guys all clustered around, working out their bets, when Mason turned to me.

"You ready?" was all the warning I got before he took a swing.

It was my time to snicker as I ducked easily. He had a lot of power and relied on it, like most shifters. Zack and I had to work with them to unlearn that overreliance on sheer brute strength in the gym. I slid under his arm, moving like lightning with all the explosive power I'd worked hard to develop, smacked a couple of good hits to his ribs, and then was away before he'd even wheeled around.

"So you're fast," he said with a wince.

"Gotta be."

I replied, kept the banter up, but I wasn't really focussed on the words. I just needed him distracted while I wore him down, and then I'd consider using the dirty trick Zack had suggested. This wasn't a bout, it was for beer, and almost every Australian would be prepared to do battle for that.

I kept dancing around him, something that made him snort with frustration. Point one for Paige. Then he forced himself to move in earnest, fists up, trying to follow my movements. I needed to keep him doing that, willing to bet he didn't have my cardio strength. He took a swipe, then another, but I dodged out of the way, forcing him to waste his energy.

"C'mon, Paige! Bring the fucker down!" Declan shouted. Mason stopped to growl at that, so I chanced a move in on his right side, kicking out and slamming my foot into his right thigh.

"Jesus!" he yelped, and sure enough, his knee faltered for a moment, dropping down before he righted himself. But when he turned to face me, I saw it was no more Mr Nice Wolf. "So you wanna play, do you?"

"Have been since we started," I said, raising my fists as I grinned.

This might not have been well thought out.

He was a whole lot faster when pissed, and I saw the glimmer in his eyes as he charged. Another few much tighter, much more controlled strikes, not leaving his ribs bare this time. This was good, I told myself. The more speed he put on now, thinking he had a short, decisive win in his sights, the less he'd be able to bring later. I ducked, ducked, blocked, something that had his eyes widening. Stupid boys, thinking they were the only ones who could take a hit. What he'd done hit him just before I did, his fists dropping, his hands up, as if to ward off the consequences of his actions, but I just came on hard. Bang, bang, two punches to the gut that, for all his perception of my weakness, had the air rushing out of him, his body doubling over as he tried to protect his now sore midriff. I raised my elbow, striking down on his shoulder blade, avoiding his spine. I didn't want to immobilise him. He dropped lower.

"Fuck yeah!" Declan shouted. "Finish him!"

Finish him? Oh yeah, the leg. I shot a cheeky grin at the crowd, saw all the boys were up off their feet, waving money and beers around, Stevie just pouring out more tequila in anticipation of a victory. I shook my head and went to stand at a safe distance away from the now sore Mason, sitting there on his hands and knees.

"Ready to relent? Don't make a big deal of me staying for the wake, and I'll stop."

"I can't."

There was something serious there, something that was ready to tug at me, have me asking why, but I shook it off. Not now, not yet. I had all the time in the world for serious. I just wanted this—one break, just one. I didn't know how he didn't see that.

But maybe he did. There was regret in his gaze, which gave me pause. I'd never expected to see that on Mason Klein's face, ever. Which was probably how he caught me off guard.

"If they charge you, there isn't a lot you can do to block that. You don't have the weight or the muscle, but you do have physics. Show her."

One of the female masters that frequented the gym stood there, small and wiry in the face of Beast, one of the biggest, though gentlest guys we had in the gym.

"You sure about this?" he asked us.

"I can take you, big boy, don't you worry," she'd replied.

I'd watched in alarm as he'd shrugged, then barrelled towards her, all of his massive bulk gathering momentum.

Which she used against him.

She ducked under his grasping arms, not even trying to stop him from grabbing her, dropped down low, and wrapped hands around his arm and thigh before righting herself and sending him flipping over her shoulder.

We all walked over to where poor old Beast lay on the mats, looking dazed.

"Told you I could take you," the master said with a wink, then turned to show me how.

It was harder, he was much lower to the ground, but a fighter moves to meet their opponent, so I slammed down onto my knees, ducking under the torso that was launching itself at me, and threw him as best as I could.

"Oh, ow!" I said, getting to my feet and rubbing my back. That was deafened by the whoops coming from the crowd, the guys rushing in, but I wasn't focussed on that. I stalked over, putting my foot on his right knee when he went to get up.

"So, I get to stay?"

He shook his head, looking to one side before meeting my eyes, and there was something a little different there, reinforced by the slow smile.

"A few drinks."

"I won. I do what I want."

"Then you go back to Zack."

"I won. I do what I want."

"Fine, will someone get me a beer?"

Chapter 15

"Your dad would shit, seeing what you just did," Declan said, steering me over to the table. Several had been set up in a long line in the living area near the kitchen, probably where they ate their meals. "But you just made me one hundred and fifty bucks." He swept out a chair, making a show of brushing it off. "For milady."

"So you still love acting like a dickhead?" I asked, cocking an eyebrow but taking a seat anyway. My body was almost vibrating with the leftover adrenalin, and I needed to dial it back again.

"Of course. Laughing's the same mechanism as an orgasm." He took a seat on my left, putting his elbows on the table and leaning in. "If you can get them doing one, it ups your chances of getting them to do the other."

"This is what you got from Mrs Rogers' biology class?"

"Not all I got, was it?" He moved in slightly, eyes going heavily lidded, his teeth scoring his bottom lip as he just watched me until I remembered what he was on about.

"Oh!"

"Your girl," he said to Stevie when she sat down, "liked to torment me when we were kids. She was my first real serious girlfriend. Well, the one who let me touch her boobies."

"He really did call them boobies, even when we were making out," I said with a shake of my head. "What the hell was I thinking?"

"A whole lotta squirmy, hot thoughts, if memory serves. But perhaps in revenge for said unfortunate naming conventions, Paige used to like to…push my boundaries a bit. I was a walking hard-on, like most blokes my age, so perpetual wood was my curse to bear, and then came Paige." His eyes sought mine, just holding them for a second, taking me back years in an instant to sitting with the cool kids with him by my side. "She smelled so fucking good and was funny and awesome, and then she decided I was the same and picked me out of all the blokes in school to be her boyfriend."

Those eyes on mine again, holding them well past what was polite, just watching me with that warm gaze, softened by the ever-present smile.

"You asked me, remember?" I said, filling the silence.

"Only because I knew by then you'd say yes. Anyway…" His eyes went down the table, his mouth twisting in a smile. "She worked out pretty quick how…responsive I was."

"So you had premature ejaculation issues back then as well, did ya, mate?" said one of the guys down the table. He had longish mid brown hair he kept tucked behind his ears.

"That's not what your mum said the other night, Will." Declan grinned when the guy stuck his finger up in response. "So anyway, seeing as I was cracking a fat on the regular, your girl figured she could manipulate that for her amusement."

Every eye down the table turned to me, my hand going to the beer bottle and raising it to take a looong drink, just to deflect that attention for a second.

"Do we really need to tell this story?" I muttered.

"Yeah, we really do. So we're sitting in year eleven biology, and Mrs Rogers is talking about reproduction. It's all urethra this and gonads that, and Paige decides to do a little…hands on exploration herself. We had to wear these fucking stupid grey shorts that didn't hide a lot on a good day."

"Not that you have much anyway, Dec."

"Fuck off, Jason. And sitting on a stool, my girl has access to pretty much everything she likes under the table. So she's doing that thing that drove me nuts, just running her fingers along my inner thigh because the damn shorts were so short. And my teenage brain is just like 'touch my cock, touch my cock,' but at the same time, is completely fucking transfixed by the feel of her fingers so damn close yet not close enough."

Why did I think this revenge was a long time in coming? He took a swig of beer, winking to me as he did.

"So my dick's like fighting to get out of my shorts. Down the leg, out the waistband. It's like the thing's fucking prehensile and semi sentient. It just wants her. Then the fucking teacher starts showing slides of diagrams of boners. I do not need this right now, having become very much reacquainted with the phenomena, and as the bloody teacher uses this pointer stick thing to point out the different parts of the male anatomy, bloody Paige is doing the same beneath the table." An explosion of laughter from the table had my eyes trained on the table. "I'm fit to fucking burst. Like I wanna fuck off to the toilets and choke the chicken until my nuts stop fucking boiling, but that'd mean walking out of class, announcing to one and all what I had raging in my pants."

"Like anyone would wanna look at your dick, you wanker," someone shot out from the end of the table.

"So there I am, caught on the horns of a mighty dilemma—keep letting her stroke my dick through my shorts like every cell in my body wants or push her away and think about dead kittens or something. But I want it, want to feel her little hand wrapped around my cock. I want her stroking it long and slow, like she always did."

Jesus, he always did have a way with words, Declan. I hadn't thought too much about that day, but as he described it, all of it came back. The bright lights, squeaky linoleum, Mrs Rodgers droning on, and him, smelling all spicy and male like he did, filling my nose, which made sliding my hand up his thigh seem like a good idea. And he was right—back then, I'd felt a kind of power, being able to turn a man rigid at will. Probably anyone could have put their hand on his leg and gotten the same response, but right then, I'd been power-tripping on the fact it was me.

He looked across at me, grinning, something that faltered a little when he met my eyes. For a second, just a second, we weren't in our twenties, we hadn't broken up, and we were right back there, in the classroom, the hand sitting decorously on my knee itching to reach out and do exactly what he'd described. The moment dragged on and on, neither of us moving, neither of us looking away, until someone shouted out something offensive.

"Shut the fuck up, Dec," I said, packing those memories back up and putting them where they were supposed to be, in the past. "Just shut up. Get this man a beer. Fuck, a ball gag will do. Anything to shut him up."

"Now you know what we go through on most days, love," Will said with a smirk. "All right, keep going. I'm looking forward to hearing how the alpha's daughter made you disgrace yourself in the classroom."

"Wouldn't be the first time," someone else said. "So does this story end explosively?"

It didn't, but it got close. Now I kinda rolled my eyes, but teenage Paige had felt oh so naughty. I gulped, trying to swallow the lump in my throat, remembering exactly what I'd done. I'd palmed him in the middle of class. Well, as much as I could. Dad had hassled me about not giving my virginity away to just anyone, but to be honest, it was Declan's considerable size that had deterred me. I'd heard plenty of stories of how it hurt that first time, and he was… But I'd loved how responsive he was, that I could take this big, tall, smart-arsed guy and reduce him to fucking putty in my hand. Putty whose breath came in short, sharp pants, something he'd tried to hide as I'd closed my fingers round as much of him as I could, someone whose hips had bucked up slightly, as if begging me for more. Someone who—

I looked into Declan's eyes, remembering how that class ended and suddenly feeling really exposed. That was the problem with going home—all the people that knew you, that walked around with a mosaic of memories of who you were and, in this case, what you'd done. He stared into my eyes, mouth curving into a lazy smile before sucking off the beer from his bottom lip. There it lay, a challenge, a gauntlet thrown down. Would he reveal all to the table or…?

"Nah, the bell went, and I used my books as a shield. Ducked into the boys because it was lunchtime, and took me about three strokes before I came so hard, it felt like it was gonna blow the top of my head off."

"Well, that's two strokes more than you usually get, isn't it, Dec?"

But that wasn't what had happened. I'd been teasing him all lesson, and when the bell went, he'd grabbed my hand, his grip like iron as he hauled us out of class and down the hall, way, way away from where both of us were supposed to be. I'd had maths and he'd had…

He looked behind us, the farther we got away from the main student body, ducking down a hallway until we reached the disabled toilet.

"Dec, we can't."

"We have to."

He looked at me with eyes of molten bronze, then opened the door and dragged me in. His lips were on mine, hard and hungry, and I felt an answering one rise in response. I was young, still trying to work out who I was sexually, but right now, I liked this. Declan was always so fucking competent—fixing my flat tyre, doing tricks with his BMX, on the footy field. But me, I'd managed to undo all of that right now and replaced cool, chill Declan with this beast.

His hand slid up my skirt, finding the seam of my underwear unerringly and hooking those nimble fingers underneath.

"You're wet…" He pulled back for a moment, resting his forehead on mine, just panting and examining my face, as if he couldn't believe what he was feeling, but not for long. His fingers speared inside, making me gasp, but he swallowed that down, sucking and biting my lips.

"Fuck…" he growled as the lewd sounds of my wet cunt filled the room. "I want in you so fucking much."

"We can't… Not yet."

"I know, love. We have to wait, see what your dad says, but fuck… I need you so much."

My hand went to his shorts' waistband, and he pulled away, unbuttoning them and yanking down the fly. He drew that thick rigid cock out, giving it a few strokes, like he couldn't keep his hand off it.

Off me.

My foot was lifted and placed on the lid of the toilet, spreading me open for him, and he surged in, pressing against the damp cotton of my underwear, only backing off when I wrapped my hand around him, a long hiss escaping his lips as I swivelled my hand up and down.

"Fuck..." he ground out, one hand whipping out to steady himself against the wall, but the other? Two fingers pushed inside me, too fast, too hard, making me yelp at the stretch, but then he moved, his thumb brushing inexorably across my clit.

"Dec...!"

We moved as one unit, stroking, tugging, thrusting, as his cock twitched in my hand and I twitched around his. I'd made myself come before, but it had been nothing like this. He surrounded me, filled me, swallowed me down, wrapping me up in this hot, gasping cocoon of sensation.

"That's it, baby," he crooned as my pants grew faster and faster. "Come for me, Paige. Come on my fingers."

I was helpless to do anything else, holding his cock in a death grip that just made him thrust harder, one, two, three...

I should have been concerned at the sudden splash of liquid on my school skirt, at the second bell going on the PA system, at the fact we were using a toilet restricted for people who actually needed it. But for a moment, there was only my fingers digging into his shoulders as my body went rigid, then a rolling wave of the sweetest, sharpest bliss rolled through me, so bright, my vision went white for a moment. My mouth pressed against his shoulder, the muscle hard and impervious as I panted out my pleasure, my whole body shaking with the aftershocks.

Declan looked bloody radiant in the bright artificial light, an expression of complete male satisfaction on his face. But his head ducked down, capturing my lips, kissing me much slower, much more thoroughly now.

"Good, baby?"

He wanted validation, some sort of clue, but my brain was completely scrambled, struggling to find words, actions, anything. His smile curved up at that as he pulled me in close and just held me with that kind of sweetness you didn't realise doesn't always last past your teenage years.

Of course when we pulled apart, we saw what kind of mess we'd made, cleaning up the floor and each other before creeping out of the toilets into the empty hallway.

"And what are you doing, roaming the halls, Mr Werner?"

We'd spun around to see Mr Kennedy, the assistant principal, standing there, arms behind his back, looking the two of us over with a critical eye. The wet spots on our uniforms, our harried expressions all declared our guilt.

"Paige was feeling sick, sir. I rushed her to the toilet, held her hair back, but…"

"Did you, indeed? Then Ms Spehr needs to go to the sick bay, and you need to get to your English class, unless I'm mistaken?"

"Of course, sir. I'll just walk Paige to the—"

"I'll escort Ms Spehr. You run along."

I came back to the room with a start, the chatter having started again while I had a walk down memory lane, someone else getting teased mercilessly.

"You did that on purpose," I hissed quietly to Declan.

He grinned, tipped his beer at me, then shrugged.

"Seems to me there's some people reminding you of the way things were around here, and I figured I'd throw my hat in the ring too. We were good together, Paige."

"We were teenagers, then we broke up."

"Course we did." He leaned back in his chair, aware, I was sure, of what that lazy posture did to all the muscles on display under his T-shirt. "No matter what backward fucking rules this place runs on, I wasn't ready to settle down at eighteen and neither were you. Your dad spoke to me about that, y'know."

"What?"

"Didn't say he didn't think I had the chops for alpha, but didn't want you locked down too early. Said it hadn't been good for your mum and he didn't want that for you."

"Is that why…"

The words dried in my throat. When we'd split up, Declan had broken my heart in the way only teenage boyfriends could. We'd made the decision mutually, talking it through and seeing only that as an option. He knew I liked him, but he also knew he wasn't the only one. As if sensing my thoughts, we both looked down the table to where Mason sat at the head, staring back at us. His fingers traced circles in the condensation on the tabletop.

"That's why we broke up? Seems like the same obstacles are still there."

"Only if you still see them as obstacles, I guess." His eyes slid slowly over me, taking his damn time, making it clear exactly what he was doing, and with a twitch of his hips, making me wonder if he was in the exact same state as he had been back in class. "I can show you where the loos are here, if you need me to."

"So just like that?" I asked, eyebrow cocked. "There's a guy waiting for me upstairs, naked, in my bed."

"And there are guys down here waiting for you too, the naked part is, of course, optional."

"You were never like this, didn't come on this strong."

"Because I was a kid back then." He reached out, taking the hand that lay slack on the table and holding it in his, his skin scalding hot. But I didn't want to pull away, did I?

People talked about grief doing funny things to your head. One minute, you were lost in pain, the next, you forgot everything and were caught up in the here and now. Grieving seemed to put you in two worlds, the living and the dead, and you were the uneasy conduit between them. Declan's skin, the firm stroke of his fingers, anchored me firmly in the right now.

"You're trying to help, trying to stop me from grieving too hard."

"I'm always here to help, Paige, you know that. But mostly?" I saw a faint frown form and then fade away. "Mostly, I want to touch you as much as I want my next beer. You still smell like you always did, sweet, floral, drowning me in your scent, making my fucking mouth water. We were just kids fucking around, working out what we wanted. Well, I know what I want now."

The deadly serious tone of his made my eyes jerk up. Where was my sweet eyed joker right now?

"I don't give a shit about the bloke you brought home, the other guys around this table, Mason, any of them. Tell me in what capacity I can get back into your life, and I'm there, even if it's just as a friend." I searched his face, hearing the wistful note in his voice. "The friend who strokes his cock every night, thinking about your tits."

My fist balled, and I punched him in the arm, right as he burst out laughing. Had he been playing me, or was any of that serious? You never knew with Declan. He downed the rest of his beer and then put the bottle on the table.

"I gotta see a man about a dog, but think about what I said, please."

Just before he got up, he dropped his hand under the table, sliding up my thigh to give the top of it a squeeze. He chuckled when I jumped, and then he was gone before I could belt him again.

"So, having fun catching up?" Stevie asked me, turning away from Will, who she'd been talking to.

"Yeah. Fun."

"We need more girls if the only thrills I'm gonna get tonight is hearing Dec talking about almost getting a hand job in class," Will said with a frown.

I picked up my phone off the table and thumbed through my contacts.

"I'll call my cousins."

Chapter 16

Somehow, this all ended in dancing.

Music was pumping, half my cousins over the age of eighteen had rocked up, and the room was full of drunken, shouting, dancing people.

"You need to get in there," Stevie said, passing me a couple of shots before drinking down her own with a slight wince. "And I've gotta get back. I'm opening in the morning, so no rest for the wicked." She wrapped an arm around my shoulder as we polished off our drinks. "Don't let the Lupindorf shit get to you, not tonight. There's plenty of time for all that bullshit tomorrow."

"The town meeting," I said, feeling my gut drop.

"The town meeting," she agreed. "When you got out of here, got out from under the label of alpha's daughter or heir or decider of the town's fate, you must've had time where you could just be selfish, did whatever you wanted to do?"

"Yeah…" My eyes hit the floor. Those days where you rolled out of bed on your day off and you just did whatever. Chilled in front of the TV or went for a run. Hung out with Zack or went and had breakfast at a café. Long, lazy days to rest and recuperate.

"Channel that tonight, because after this…"

"After this, shit gets serious." I turned to her, my head feeling slightly too big for my shoulders, swimming a little when I turned to face her. "Hey, you know all the town gossip. Any way I could relinquish the title as heir, give it to one of the cousins?"

"Not Selma," she said, pulling a face.

"Or maybe scrapping the heir thing altogether. Make the town a democracy like the rest of the country."

"You'd want that?" She just stared at me for a moment, then shook herself. "Um…not that I know of, but there's some stuff I could take a look at. I'll let you know." She gave me a quick hug, then pulled away, putting the Patrón bottle in my hand. "I'll see you at the meeting."

And with that, she was gone.

"What're you doing hanging out here with all the hot guys over there?" someone asked as I took a mouthful straight from the bottle, and when I looked back, my cousin Bridget was sauntering over. She took the Patrón and gave it a look before having a swig as well. "Is this the way it's gonna be in the alpha house going forward? Because I, for one, welcome our new overlord." She winced. "Mum's not letting us move in. Said you wouldn't be 'a suitable influence right now.'"

"You just wanna get your grind on with the enforcers."

"Can you blame me? I dunno how you did it, having a goddamned harem just down the stairs and out the back, where Daddy warned you to never go. I woulda snuck out, no lie. I'd just wanna dive on into that sea of man flesh and let myself drown."

I smirked and took the bottle back.

"I did a few times, going to see Mason. Dad always caught me though." In my mind's eye, I could see him coming out from behind the staircase, stopping me on my way up. "He'd sit me down and give me lectures about messing around with grown men. 'You might see him as a friend, Paige…'"

And with that, I was sitting in his office, wriggling in my chair as he spoke sternly to me. *"But he sees you as a woman, with all that entails. I know the two of you are close. I want you to feel like you can trust and rely on my beta, but, sweetheart, you're too old to sit on his lap and cry out all your problems."*

I knew that, Dad knew that, and Mason knew that, because he said much the same thing, but not before Mason heard me cry my heart out over Declan. Not before he held me tight, stroked my hair, the big hand on my back edging lower until it froze still. Then he'd pushed me off him, gently of course, but not before I felt a similar rush of power that I'd felt with Declan.

Declan was a boy, Mason was a man, but the fact that both of them could…respond to me in that same way? I felt my tears drying, my eyes growing hot as I catalogued all the differences between men and boys, and all the ways they were the same.

"He was smart, Dad. Knew that flying off the handle, banning me from seeing Mason would just prick my teenage pride. Instead, he made it a social justice issue. Mason was a man, he wanted to do what men and women did, and I wasn't ready for that. I needed to preserve some distance up until such time as I was ready."

"And when you worked out you were? What happened that night? Mum always brushed it under the carpet, never wanted to talk about it, and I…I didn't think it was something I could just ring up and say 'hey, what went down?'"

I looked into my cousin's warm brown eyes, smiling at the riot of auburn curls, that broad, mobile mouth uncharacteristically thin right now. I reached out and smoothed the wrinkle in her brow.

"I realised I was ready, that Mason was the one. I asked to see him before the party, just as I was supposed to. Dad had given his approval, but it was tentative, I realise that now. Back then, I could see it—this great and glorious future. I'd finally be with Mason…" My eyes slid to where the man himself sat in a chair on the perimeter of things, drinking his beer. "I'd ask him to be my mate and he would love me and we'd spend the whole of my party being celebrated and then that night—"

"You'd get to ride the baloney pony into the sunset?" I spluttered at that. Bridge always did have a way with words. "Don't worry, we thought that was the way it was going to go too. What happened? You both seemed so close, especially after you broke up with Dec. You hadn't been seeing anyone for over a year, were always talking and joking."

I frowned, my view of that much more carefree man overlaid over the one we both saw now.

"Um…come in," I said, gesturing stiffly, acutely aware of the freaking chaos in my room, but Mason didn't see that. His eyes were slightly too wide as he took in my half nakedness. My eyes dropped down, seeing the sports bra and shorts, and I yelped, then strode over to the wardrobe, pulling out an oversized tee and then yanking it over my head.

"Your father said you wanted to see me?"

"Ah…yeah. Take a seat." I went to brush past him, pull out my desk chair for him, but a hand on my arm stopped me. Just that one touch. I felt the warmth of his fingers reflected all the way down to my toes, and when my eyes slid up, I thought he felt it too.

Why else would he be frozen to the spot? Why would his breath rasp, his eyes be locked on mine? Why would I feel that tension in his arm? Why would his gaze drop to my lips and stay there, like the world's secrets could be found upon them?

But he mastered himself, Mason. I'd seen glimpses of this before, and each time, he locked them up behind that wall, but watching him do that now made my nerves falter for a moment. Maybe he…? What if…? *I swallowed hard, straightened my spine and then said—*

"I'll stand," he said, pulling away. Damn, that hurt. Couldn't he see what he was doing? No, I needed to be calm, say my piece, and then accept his decision. I'd spent my life—

He settled against the wall, arms across his chest, forming a barrier between me and him.

"OK…" My hands dropped down to play with the hem of my shirt. "You know it's my eighteenth birthday today."

"We've been hauling booze and food in all day, Paige. It better be, or we're gonna be eating pasta salad for a long time."

I heard his amused snort, his tone, but when I looked up, that died away. I'd felt so strong, so powerful with Declan. He'd seemed weirdly glad for my atten-

tion, despite the fact so many girls were throwing themselves at him. But he was a boy, and Mason wasn't.

It felt odd somehow, getting ready to talk to him, not as Daddy's little girl, not as the pack princess, but as a woman. Aunty Nance had talked me through the rite, made clear what I needed to do, so I squared my shoulders, took a deep breath and said the words.

"Then you know what I'm expected to do. I have to choose a mate, Mason, someone who'll become leader of this pack one day. Someone dominant enough, someone reliable, someone the community likes, someone who can keep us on the path Dad and Granddad set us on. There's a lot of men who fit that bill. This is a good town, we have a strong pack, but, Mason…"

Today, looking back, I saw the fear, the reluctance, but back then, I'd been too much in my own head, forging ahead before my nerve deserted me.

"I have to choose someone to help continue that, and I…" My throat was bone-dry, as if that would be enough to stifle the words which were to come. "I want that to be you."

Being brought up with my role as heir beaten into me from a young age, I'd imagined the moment I chose my mate over and over. I'd made my dollies kiss after Barbie chose Ken. I'd practised with my cousins, perhaps where Bryant got his ideas from. Every time I watched a romantic storyline on TV or in a movie as a tween, then a teenager, I'd seen me and…? He'd been vague in detail at first, then he was tall, had broad shoulders like Daddy, dark hair, then…

Then when Declan and I broke up, he was Mason.

I'd seen him over and over in my dreams, when I asked him to be my mate and he surged forward, grabbing my arms and pulling me to him in a brutal kiss that communicated all the hot simmering desire I thought I'd seen in those dark eyes. When he did move, when his hands wrapped around my arms, when his fingers bit deep into my flesh, when he held me, first at arm's length, looking at me like I hung the moon and the stars, when those dark eyes burned as I burned for him, my heart swelled and kept on swelling.

This was it, the destiny I'd spent my life walking towards, and now it was here.

His lips were gentle at first, I hadn't expected that, his arms trembling with the effort of holding himself back. He just brushed mine with his, emboldened when I gasped, when they parted, a whistle of air all that alerted me to what was about to happen.

He picked me up and shoved me against the wall in a way no one had ever dared, parting my feet with his and surging forward, pushing his body into mine until part of me fist-bumped internally. He was wild for me. He was fucking rigid for me. His hips bucked upwards, pressing something long and hard right where I needed it, his hands pinning my wrists to the wall as his mouth burned for me. His kisses stung, a nip piercing my lip, blood welling, but I craned my neck, trying to follow them, keep his taste in my mouth when they trailed down my jaw, then my neck.

Yes…yes… I thought. That's where the mark would go, when he claimed me, made me his. He'd sink his teeth in right when he sank his—

"No!"

It took me a moment to feel it, the gap between the two of us, the heat of his grip still on my skin after he snatched his hands away. I blinked, trying to clear my vision, expecting to see my love, my mate, looking upon me with that mixture of desire and need the adult mates always seemed to wear.

What I hadn't expected was the back of his hand to his mouth, like I'd hurt it, tainted his lips somehow. Like he'd been scrubbing away my taste.

"Mase?"

"Don't take another step," *he'd said, but he hadn't meant it. There was no real exertion of dominance in his voice, so I kept on coming. He rectified that. He pinned me to the spot, had me frozen, powerless in my own bedroom, forcing me to look at the man I thought I loved gaze at me with a mixture of fear, anger, and revulsion.* "I can't, Paige. I need you to understand this. You'll find the right guy and forget all about me. I'm too bloody old anyway."

That was the problem with being pinned by someone more dominant than you—I couldn't move, couldn't run down the stairs, couldn't escape this. The command didn't stop the tears from forming in my eyes, then burning as they fell on my cheeks.

"I'm not the one for you." *He was talking to himself more than me, I now realised.* "You just think I am because of proximity, because…" *He shook his head definitively.* "I'll always be there for you. Always. Remember that. I'll always help you when you—"

"Help me now."

I'd injected so much into those three words. Help me understand. Help me to work out what the hell had just happened, how I'd gotten this so wrong. Help stop the never-ending pain that rose in my chest right now, threatening to obliterate me. Help me by freeing me.

He knew. He saw. He gave me that particularly horrendous pitying look a man gives a woman when she confesses feelings he doesn't share.

"I can't, Paige!"

He'd snapped his response and stormed out of my room, his hold on me fading once he left, slamming my door behind him. My fingers had gone to my lips, feeling the split, the scratches his stubble had left that gave lie to his assertion, and then I'd turned to the pile of clothes, shoved them to the floor, and found my bag.

"HOW COME two of the hottest chicks in this place are standing in here, looking so serious?" Will asked, sauntering close, Micah at his side. "We're celebrating today because the pain starts when we wake."

Bridget giggled, taking his outstretched hand and letting him twirl her close, dipping her in time with the music before waltzing her out onto the floor.

"I don't dance," I said, nodding to the crush of bodies beyond. "Fighting, yes, but dancing, I've got two left feet."

"Do you want to though?"

Micah had an odd quiet stillness to him, like his words only came out when they really needed to, never just small talk to fill the gaps.

"I…" My eyes slid over to that chair, to that man, to the guy who walked around with a sharp knife in his hand, dripping with my heart's blood, he just didn't know it. "I want that release." I nodded to the dancers. "Will's got it right—it's gonna hurt so much tomorrow." It hurt right now, all of it. My voice wavered, the great subterranean beast inside me rising, rising, but I kept it down for now. "I want to forget, just for tonight, but I also want to remember him and everything he did."

"I can do that," he replied, moving in so close that I stiffened, but he just shot me a sidelong smile before he poured the rest of the Patrón into a couple of dirty beer glasses, then he held his up as I held mine. "Your dad was a good man. Every guy here will miss him. It's gonna hurt, getting used to the fact he's gone, but it doesn't take away from that. Remember the way he was with people, the way he helped, supported, was everyone's dad."

Because he couldn't be mine, I thought. But I put the drink to my lips and downed it when Micah did, and then he drew me to him, bringing my body against his in a way that dancing made OK.

"Put your arms around my neck," he said, a little challenge in those grey eyes. I did, feeling the sizzle of strange skin, the broad muscles there on his shoulders.

"Your hair is really soft," I said, letting my fingers play with the loose strands for a second before realising that was completely inappropriate.

"Argan oil conditioner," he replied with a smirk. "Now, I'm gonna put my hands here…" He put them around my waist, those long fingers sliding down to my butt. "And then your body follows mine." He swayed back and forth, and I moved with him, letting my muscles go loose. I frowned for a second, then smiled, liking the heavy buzz in my limbs, the partial surrender of control of my body.

"OK, so where does the forgetting part come from?"

"Here," he said, swinging me out, past the tables and the chairs, out of the kitchen and into the throng in a series of whirling movements. I laughed, feeling that same childish joy that came from doing whizzies, as I'd called them as a kid. Micah smiled too, but there was something more intent there. "Now, to really forget, you have to give up all those thoughts and feelings and stuff clamouring in your head."

"Zack makes me do that when we're doing mindfulness activities. I have to bring my consciousness to the here and now, what I can see, hear, feel…"

His grin spread slowly when I realised what I could see and feel most right now. I swallowed hard, the tequila buzzing in my head temporarily.

"That's all a man asks for." He swung us out into the crowd, into the mass of gyrating bodies where ours moved at a much slower rate. "Just feel the music," his hand slid lower, "and feel me."

I didn't know what I was doing. My mum and my aunt had all tried to instil some kind of grace and decorum, giving me ballroom dancing lessons with my cousins when young. But I'd hated them, and my tutor had deplored of both forcing me to do them and getting a graceful result. My family had relented after three long years of stumbling, foot stomping, grumbling crap. So now, it felt oddly exhilarating to be moving with any sort of coordination, though mostly it was just following where he wanted our bodies to go.

"That's it," he said as his hands went to my hips, pressing me in closer, forcing them to shift as his did in long thrusting motions that were in time with the throbbing beat of the song. I felt a curious lightness in my body, lost in movement and the sensation of Micah's body. He wrapped his arms tight before dipping me low, pulling a startled yelp out that quickly turned into laughter when he righted me, swaying again, his mouth grinning along with me, getting closer.

"I was gonna ask to cut in, but I think I just wanna join up."

Declan's voice was a low buzz in my ear, my eyebrows creasing for a minute as I felt two long hard bodies against mine now. I just had to follow, the both of them shifting me back and forth in more complex swivels and shimmies of hips, not letting anything but the music and them register. Hands moved, trailing over my skin, underscoring that as well, making me notice the arms that—

"What the fuck are you doing?"

The roared question was followed swiftly by a hard shove that had my dance partners, everyone's partners scattering.

"Dancing, Mase," Declan snapped, recovering his balance and then approaching the other man with eyes that bristled with anger.

"You're feeling her up like a fucking whore. Both of you are!"

"She's not a whore," Micah said with a low growl. "And lemme just say that's a shitty outdated term. I asked her if she wanted to dance, and she said yes. She just wanted to let loose for a bit. Everyone's clothes were on, but the question to be asked, of course, is what fucking business is it of yours?"

"She's Adam's daughter."

"She's a grown adult," I said drily. When I turned, Micah and Declan looked like they were about to say the same, and I smiled at them in thanks. But seriously, I'd been dealing with the particularly toxic brand of Mason Klein's bullshit for some time. "She kicked your arse. She can do whatever the fuck she wants, up to and including stripping off naked in this room and taking all comers if she sees fit."

"What?"

Mason snapped out the word, but to be fair, so did plenty of the other guys, just in different tones. Female sexual agency wasn't exactly a concept that had filtered through to Lupindorf, apparently.

"I didn't ask to have the golden vagina that will make you the true king of this pack if you dip your sword into it," I said, drawing a cackle from behind me. Bridget, I was willing to bet. "But let me make this super clear—I dance with whoever I want because I'm a grown woman with all the rights and liberties associated."

"You're showing the town—" Mase growled out.

I shoved my finger into his chest and liked the way the muscle didn't relent, liked more how he staggered back slightly.

"I touch anyone I want, because I'm a grown woman with all the rights and liberties associated."

"This isn't what your dad would want. He'd be horrified and you know it."

Sometimes when you were dealing with conflict, it took a while for the other person to see your point of view. I'd dealt with that plenty in the gym, so I had this.

I shoved Mason hard, watching his arms flail as he reeled backwards, and I kept on coming as he recovered.

"My dad doesn't own my vagina. This town doesn't own my vagina. No one owns it but me."

"And what a nice one it is too."

Our eyes jerked up to see Zack standing there, leaning against the doorway. He looked like the ultimate gym porn thirst trap in just a well-worn pair of grey sweats hanging low on his hips, almost outlining the clear V there.

"Still with the archaic bullshit, brother?" He strolled over, clapping Mase on the shoulder, but the other man just shrugged him off. "Feminism was a movement in the seventies. You might want to look it up sometime. Has all these radical ideas in it about women owning their own bodies."

"You don't get it. You just float on by, like none of this matters. Because it doesn't to you. If this gets tough, if she gets tough, you'll be off again, leaving me to pick up the pieces, as always," Mason snarled.

"Fuck…" Zack shook his head. "Like I can see you're drunk and everything, but you really have no idea who I am, why she…" He pursed his lips, looking down, then over at me. "Whaddya reckon, baby? Ready for bed?"

And just like that, I was. I didn't have the energy for this anymore. My head was spinning slightly, my body leaden, and collapsing onto the soft surface of my bed sounded like heaven.

"Thanks," I said to Micah and Declan, "that was fun. You cleared my head for a bit."

I got slow, cocky smiles at that, Micah crossing his arms to reveal a pair of very impressive guns the tequila hadn't made possible to notice until now. Damn, past me had missed out.

"Bridget?"

"Yeah?" she said, untangling herself from Will's arms.

"Make sure the cousins all have somewhere to sleep upstairs and don't tell Aunty or the uncles I let you do this."

"Dude, snitches get stitches." She cast an eye over our younger cousins. "You don't even have to ask."

"Then I'm for bed. Someone wants to make me bacon and eggs for breakfast tomorrow or do a Macca's run? I'll pretty much hand the reins of this town to you there and then." There were some mumbled replies at that. "Or use whatever funds we have to get Stevie to cater it. I don't care."

When I turned back, Zack was watching me with that patient amused stare he usually had. That's what I liked about him. Some girls bitched about predictability, but not me. I loved that the leash was off with him, that he'd never threaten the guys I was dancing with, but he'd be there when I was done, as he was now. He reached out and took my hand, pulling me after him away from the enforcers' quarters, into the night and then back into the house.

The problem was Mase came too.

"He made me do it, y'know," he announced, but it wasn't that which had me turning around, pulling away from Zack. I didn't think I liked drunk Mase much. Emotion I'd never seen before on his face was all there on the surface. He looked…destroyed. Because of Dad, because he'd died, because we hadn't had enough sleep and too much alcohol and were gonna pay for it tomorrow. But those dark eyes lifted, skewering me through so thoroughly, I felt actual physical pain in response.

"Your father, Adam, he took me to one side—"

Stab, stab, stab.

"Mase, now's not the time," Zack growled out, but I held him off with a raised hand.

"I knew what was coming. I fucking craved it. When you walked away from that boy, Declan, and came to me, I knew what I'd always known—that you were my mate."

My blood dripping on the finely polished marble floor, scarlet red.

"My dad, he told me, you know. Klein men know. He knew my mum was his when they were both still in primary school, but he watched and waited until…"

"Mase!" Zack shouted.

"Every time I held you, I knew it deep inside. Every time I brushed away your tears, listened to your hopes and fears. Every time you came to me, I knew."

My chest aching as his claw like fingers work their way past the bones of my ribcage, shattering them, reaching in deeper to get what they wanted.

"I loved your father like he was my own. I waited for you to be ready, would still be waiting, if that's what it took."

"No," I ground out, shaking my head for emphasis. "No, you said—"

"He took me aside the night of your birthday, what I thought was going to be the happiest day of our lives, and he said, 'When she asks you to be her mate, take your place by her side, you have to say no. You'd make a damn fine alpha and a good partner to my daughter, but if you love her, you'll say no.'"

I couldn't see or feel anything but the single tear running down the side of his face, following it until it dropped on the floor.

His hand holding my bleeding heart, still pumping, within it.

"I love you, so I said no. That's why I said no."

Chapter 17

In the life of an heir, your time is not your own, but sometimes you have to make it so.

I hadn't responded to Mason, said anything, couldn't even look at him. Zack knew what was going on, having seen me max out plenty of times before, so he put a hand on my shoulder and steered me upstairs. Mason called out for me, his voice getting harsher and more pained, but I couldn't. My lips were welded shut, my mind blank, my body limp when Zack put me to bed.

But of course, Mason followed us up with the peculiar selfishness alcohol sometimes brings.

"We need to talk about this. You can't stop that," he shot at Zack.

"Probably, but she can't right now. She drove all night to get here, then saw her dad die, then sat up all night to mark his passing. You're gonna have to move the town meeting."

"I can't!"

"She won't be up for a day or two. She pushes and pushes herself until she can't anymore, and then she collapses when her body forces her to rest and recuperate. If you loved her, you'd know this."

"She didn't do that when she was living here, ever."

"Well, she does now. Sober up, get your shit together, and alert the town. I'll fight the lot of them if that's what it takes."

"And we'll fight beside you." A long sigh. "Fine. I'll have someone bring up her food in the morning."

Then there was a heavy weight against my back, then blessed nothingness.

SLEEP WAS AN OCEAN, and I dived deep into it. Occasionally I'd surface, feel Zack's body against mine or his hand in my hair, stroking it, but I'd push myself back down into oblivion, trying not to resurface for some time.

"Paige, you need to eat. You haven't eaten much lately and—"

I caught snippets of conversations, some directed at me, some not. They didn't make a whole lot of sense in the format I got them, so I paid them little mind. I just closed my eyes and dreamt of great dark oceans that swallowed me down, dragging me lower and lower into their endless depths.

It was nice down there. No noise, no sounds, no feelings, no thoughts. Just seamless dark peace. For a long time, I just listened to the sound of my own breath and stared into the void.

But the human tendency to neglect our bodies does not work with shifters. We were two souled, and the other part of mine could feel the ways we were weakening, staying down here. It was OK for a time, to try and process the pain we'd been forced to endure, but there comes a point where the medicine causes more bad than good. My body shifted into wolf form and then trotted out of the bedroom on legs stiff from disuse, going down the stairs and following the smell of food.

"Hey, Paige…"

We knew this human as family. She laughed a lot and we enjoyed being around her, but right now, she did not look happy at all. We shied away, unable to entertain human emotional complexities when our body clamoured for food.

"Paige…"

The same noise said over and over by more man things, but we ignored them, moving to the table groaning with food. That was what we needed, not their bleating. We jumped up, putting our front paws on the table and angled our head to snatch a chunk of meat, but a sound behind us had us wheeling around.

"There you are, sweetheart," the low rumble said. *Mate*, that was our first thought, then meat. He lowered a huge plate piled high with it down to the ground, and this was right, true. Mates provided food. We licked his hand once, then fell to scarfing down the meat as fast as we could. We felt her shifting, moving, protesting, wanting to put all of her many teeming thoughts between us and what we needed, refusing to take the satisfaction that comes from being cared for by your mate. We did not hold onto this form for long normally, but we growled, defending our turf, even from ourselves, and when she finally quietened, we filled our belly to the point of groaning, then let go.

WHEN I CAME BACK to myself, the first thing I felt was my stomach was full almost to the point of pain. The second was I was standing naked in the kitchen, most of the enforcers and my family sitting around the dining table in the adjoining room. Zack went to pull his shirt off, but Mason went to the kitchen door and retrieved the old robe hanging there for just this purpose. It smelled of Dad. The third was the silence as everyone just stared.

"How long?" I asked, my voice creaky from disuse.

"Two days and a bit," Zack replied, putting down the spatula he was holding and walking over to me. He held me at arm's length, taking me in, and then pulled me close, wrapping his arms around me. I felt like crying then, my wolfish instincts still fresh, still pressing. My teeth ached to mark him, to make him mine as I knew he was.

But as I looked past him to the table beyond, I realised to my wolf, he was only one of a few. I sighed, not ready to take on that burden yet.

"Paige, now that you're awake, we—" Nancy said.

"Stop," I said.

"You've had a tough—"

"Stop." I injected a whole lot more dominance in that command now, and when I looked down the table, I saw they all had frozen. The only thing anyone did was breathe. "It appears I'm the heir until I can find some way around this. The men are not prepared to accept another in my place. I'll be spending the day looking through Dad's papers, seeing what I can find, if there's some kind of loophole." I looked up to my cousin Selma. "If you're still amenable, I'm happy to work night and day to try and find a way to transfer the role to you."

I let my hold on everyone go, heard the gasps and the sighs of surprise, the rising protests, but when I let my gaze trail over everyone, they fell silent again.

"I'm amenable," Selma said belatedly, "if I have family support."

"I'll let you guys sort that out yourselves. I smell like death, so I'm going to go have a shower, and then I'll be in Dad's office. Set up the town hall meeting for tonight. I'll be ready to talk to everyone then."

"So no discussion beforehand?" Nance asked, getting to her feet. "No preparation? You can't expect us to walk into this meeting blind!"

"No," I said, "and yes, I do."

Mumbling began before I even left the room, but I went to the fridge and pulled out a massive bottle of OJ, chugging about a quarter of it before taking it with me as I did exactly as I said.

HE CAME to me as I washed, my mate, opening the door, stripping off, revealing a body aching for mine. He opened the shower cubicle door and then filled it with him, hanging back for a moment, but that never lasted. There was so much to be said, to be explored. We'd never talked about him and Mason. Had he known I was fleeing his brother when I met him in the city? But as often was the case with Zack, when I stared into those dark eyes, words died but understanding bloomed. He smiled, just a small, crooked facsimile of his usual grin, and I reached out and touched it with my fingers, like I could memorise its shape, because it would be difficult to do so going forward, with all the restrictions coming.

And then my other hand dropped lower.

There it was, what we both knew and tacitly ignored, the big swelling in his cock, his knot. It'd developed not long after the first time we had sex, and while we'd both stared at it, we'd never said anything about it ever.

His head jerked up, and his breath sucked in abruptly as I encircled his thick length, something that only increased when I jacked my hand up and down.

"Fuck, Paige… We don't…"

There were no full sentences. There couldn't be right now. There wasn't enough room in this cubicle for them and us, so I chose us. He trembled under my grip until his control was shredded, until he pulled my hand away, shoved me against the glass wall, and then dropped down to his knees.

"No, Zack."

"Yes." He looked up at me, those eyes way too canny. "This feels like goodbye, and if it is, I want you bursting all over my face, filling my mouth with the taste of you before I fuck you."

"Not goodbye." I stroked his face. I would walk the fuck away from this place and let it burn if that's what it took to keep my mate, but it wouldn't be that simple.

Because he wasn't the only one.

"Then whatever this is, you come first."

And with that, he opened me wide as he did my heart, slinging my leg over his shoulder and then diving in.

Zack was often a careful, methodical lover who took great pains to wring every damn pleasure out of my body before attending to his, but there was none of that right now. He was unleashed and off the chain, devouring me, and my fingers clawed at the walls as I rode his face. Teeth, lips, tongue battered my most sensitive flesh, the sensations coming on too fast, too strong, but I couldn't do anything but ride them out.

I came when he pushed his fingers into me, thrusting hard, stretching me for what was to come, and I was still twitching when he hauled me up and wrapped my legs around his waist before lowering me down onto him. I hung upon the cubicle wall, nails scratching the glass as he worked his way in, always a stretch at first, then stopping for just a second when he was buried deep.

He looked in pain then, my love, my mate, his face torn up with some complex emotion, but before I got to explore that, he moved. Slowly, that thick dick dragged where I needed the most, creating a terrible friction that just made me squirm. Then his thumb dropped to my clit, massaging it in glacially slow circles, ignoring my protests of sensitivity and powering through.

Then he got faster, deeper, unable to hold back for long, needing what I needed—the connection. I threw my arms around his neck, hugged him to me as he fucked into me, driving harder and harder.

My heart ached as my teeth did, looking down at the small section of skin I could see on his neck not covered by his wet hair. I needed it, to latch on, drive my fangs in as his cock did, close the loop. *Not yet, not yet...* I told my wolf breathlessly, but she thrashed inside me, her instincts pushing hard. She attacked me with teeth and claws, leaving my already bleeding heart in tatters, fighting her way free, shifting my eyes first, then my fangs right as...

"Fuck, Paige..." he gasped, jetting his cum inside me, my own body responding in kind, but it felt like a distant thing that happened to someone else. My wolf howled her dirge, at this missed opportunity. She knew, she knew we were making a mistake.

One I intended to rectify.

Just give me a little more time. There's a way out of this, I'm sure.

All I got in return was a snarl and then a swish of her tail as she disappeared into my depths.

I found his lips as I was lowered to the floor, nipping, tasting, wanting what he wanted, something to take with him.

"I love you, babe," he said between them, not waiting for an answering response. "So fucking much."

I wanted to say the same, to share all that was within my heart, and I was glad I was wet because my tears just looked like water droplets when they came. I rested my head on his shoulder and held him close and made a silent vow before I was forced to get him out of the shower and wash all trace of him off me.

I'd grown up with a purpose, to find a mate and make him the next alpha of this pack, and I'd failed at that, but that was OK. I'd found a new one, many new ones since, but this one beat hard and deep inside me. I was going to find those I shared my heart with, and then I was going to work out a way to keep them, irrespective of what the good people of Lupindorf thought. I respected my mother and my father's legacy, but now I needed to find my own.

Chapter 18

I filed in with my family to a packed auditorium filled with the townspeople of Lupindorf. Not all of them, obviously. We'd organised for the meeting to be livestreamed for those who couldn't or didn't want to make it. Mostly, it was contenders and their families, business owners, and people who had a vested interest in the transfer of power. There were several seats on the dais, but two were significant.

Both were beautifully carved from well-seasoned oak, brought across when our families came over from Prussia, escaping the changes being made as Germany became unified. One was the alpha female's and now mine, and the other was my father's or my mate's. Which was perhaps why there were gasps of surprise when I sat down on it.

I'd thought it through on the way over, sitting in a car surrounded by my enforcers. Micah sat on my right again, watching me with those ghost-like eyes of his, studying me like a sacred text for clues or an indication of what I was thinking, I guessed. I hadn't expected him to take my hand and give it a squeeze though.

Maybe he'd done it for comfort, maybe to get my attention, make him stand out from the rest of the enforcers. It worked. I'd just stared at him, so surprised by that small act of kindness, I couldn't think of a response except to squeeze back. Mason watched us in the rear vision mirror so closely, it was a wonder we made it in one piece.

"SO A DECISION HAS BEEN MADE ALREADY? You're our new alpha?" Aidan called out when I took my father's seat. A chorus of titters followed his comment. Of all the possible contenders, he was likely to be the most problematic. My eyes took in the neatly pressed plaid shirt with the pearl buttons, the clean jeans. He'd made an effort before coming to this meeting, for me. That was how I was going to get through this—I was going to work out what they wanted, what they were doing, just as my family had trained me to do, and then I would do what I wanted with that information.

"No. I know it's customary for one of my male relatives to negotiate for me in the absence of my father." Alan and Bill shifted in their seats, no doubt pissed they'd been sidelined in all of this. "But 2020 and all that, I've decided to advocate for myself."

That got some mutters and snorts. Lupindorf—ignoring feminism since 1845.

"To fill everyone in and hopefully reassure you, I had fully intended to do as I'd been raised—to take a mate at eighteen, and then the two of us would work with my father to learn all there was about governing the pack for its benefit. I had someone selected, and as is customary, I approached them before my birthday party to make sure they were OK with being selected as my mate."

I had the attention of everyone in the great hall, their eyes trained on me. In the five years I'd been absent, there had to have been countless discussions about just this.

"That was Mason Klein." Gasps, mumbles, mutters rising to outright discussions, voices growing sharper and clearer until I held out my hand for silence. "I thought until recently that he did not share my feelings, that I had been mistaken in my choice, and in an attempt to work out what was next for my life, I left for the city. I built a life there, a good life, until I was called back home." For a moment, I could see it—my flat, the gym, the city… I shook my head and charged on. "Speaking to Mason recently, I've discovered that what I believed was not true, that he rejected my offer due to my father's urging."

Definitely a bigger response then.

"So you'll take Mason as your mate and he'll become alpha?" Mr Collins was head of the local chamber of commerce, and from memory, just wanted business as usual. This would be a popular choice. Mason was beta, waiting in the wings, in theory, to take my father's place. If I was attracted to him, if I I—

I pushed that to one side, because there were more than a few obstacles to that.

"The question is, of course, why he didn't want the man he trusted as beta to take his place, to become his daughter's mate? Perhaps we're secretly half siblings." That got some chuckles. "There's also the possibility Mason does not want the role."

"I do."

I jumped slightly at the rapid interjection. I knew what I was doing, putting everyone on the spot, but especially Mason, but damn, I was about due some public declarations. But knowing that and hearing those words, looking across the stage and seeing the man who broke my heart look back at me with longing in his eyes was a whole other thing. For a moment, the crowd, no one else existed. For several heartbeats, there was just Mason.

And there was just Zack in the shower and just Micah in the car. My wolf couldn't understand my issue with this. Zack was worthy, Micah, Declan, Mason might be. Hell, maybe half the contenders might be. Surely it was up to them to prove themselves, not for me to worry about.

Yeah, right.

"Well, that's settled then," Mr Collins said, clapping his hands together.

"No, it's not," one of the guys from the forest said. "The heir agreed to a contest for the position as alpha. We could have settled things then, taken the heir, and set ourselves up as leader like they did in the old days. Instead, we held back, respected her need for time to grieve the old alpha, and waited. I dunno about the rest of you, but I'm done waiting."

With the implied threat that they could all fight this out here and now and come up with a much quicker, though bloodier solution. I sighed.

"I did, and you will get your chance. That's why I'm here. We'll take nominations" —voices rose again— "but you'll need community support." That turned the tone to a disgruntled one. I waved my hand. "Without it, you're not going to get very far. You can't just install yourself as alpha and expect to be followed. If the community doesn't back you, you'll just make a fool of yourself trying, or worse, hurt people trying to insist they do. Today, we'll take nominations from anyone who thinks they should be alpha. They'll stay up on the town noticeboard for over a week, and then we'll have a vote. Those with the most support will go forward into the next round. We'll work with the local gym to set up a standard MMA ring, and a set of rules and scoring strategies will be circulated to the contenders so they know what they're getting themselves in for. He who comes out on top becomes alpha."

"But what about you?" Aidan said. I didn't think he'd even noticed me at school, being so much younger than him at the time, but those hazel eyes seemed to cut across the crowd and straight into me. "Any legacy any of us create as alpha depends on having a daughter with you."

"What a romantic proposition," I said, letting the sharp bite of anger that I felt rise. "Being a broodmare to your ambitions." A chorus of '*ooohs*' at that. "I haven't made a commitment to any one man. I'm interested in finding out who I have a connection with and who I don't."

That seemed to placate people for a minute, but I was saving the best for last.

"But if you think I'm just going to take whoever wins this contest as mate, be a good little alpha female, bend over for the new alpha, and produce more daughters to keep this dysfunctional cycle going, you've got another thing coming. I don't have to do this, any of this. You don't have to do this. Some of the contenders already have mates. They could become the alpha female. You could win the contest and find a girl you like, and she can become it."

"No." The answer was decisive, coming from several sources in the crowd, all young men. "It has to be you."

"Why?" I snapped. "This doesn't make sense. Apart from hereditary privilege, there's nothing special about me."

"Of course," Mr Collins said. "We'll work with the heir to find a way forward, a peaceful way that preserves the prosperity of the town."

"My Selma has volunteered to take the place as heir if Paige chooses to step down," Nancy started to say, Mr Collins nodding along.

And then one of the men said something very revealing.

"No," he said, "you're the alpha female. It has to be you."

My heart beat loudly in my ears, drowning out some of the chatter and turning the rest into meaningless noise. What he said, the way he said it… I was already the alpha female. The role didn't pass to me when I chose my mate, and in choosing a man, I transferred that power to him. I held that thought tight, my first real clue as to what the hell was going on in this town. But I needed to pack it up and hold it safe for later.

"Very well, then we go through the nomination process," I said.

"Any who wish to nominate themselves will do so using this form," Mason said. I'd filled him in on the basics of my plan, and what a terse conversation that had been. "Once the nominations have been collected, you will have five minutes to have your say on why you think you're the best candidate."

He put the pencils and nomination sheets down on the stage, and I thought that'd be it. He'd said he and the enforcers would keep the process orderly, and that was all I'd expected of him. But he picked up the first sheet and a pencil, looking over at me when he did so, then he let his eyes linger for longer than polite, just openly staring. The other guys ambled in, taking the forms, then most of the enforcers, including Declan and Micah, and lastly?

Zack was keeping his distance, as directed by his brother, but he pushed away from the wall he was leaning on at the back of the room, whispers going up as he walked up the centre aisle. There were some growls from other men at the sight of the newcomer, but he just did what he always did when guys got caught up in dominance displays. He stared them down with eyes just a touch silvery, not breaking his stride for a second, and then grabbed himself a nomination. He looked up at me on the stage, gave me a wink, and then went to fill it out.

This didn't make sense. I'd seen and participated in elections in the city, seen that most candidates were older, established men who had a track record of success, but all the men stepping forward were younger—twenties, thirties, or early forties at the latest. I needed to investigate this further, look at the historical records. How old was Granddad, my great grandfather, and so on when they'd been chosen by my forebears?

SOMEHOW, I was a contestant on the worst dating show ever.

Mason had collected up all the ballots, because I'd realised this morning until an alpha was designated, he was my beta now. He'd walked over, put the sheaf of paper in my hands, watching me closely as our fingers grazed for a second, and then pulled back to stand by my chair. I hadn't expected that, but it was where the beta stood.

"Um…can we have Riley Lang to the stage?"

I squinted a little as he approached. That was the problem with growing up in a small town, I had to work out where I knew everyone from. But as that tall frame unfolded, a longish sweep of blond hair and dark blue eyes that still twinkled with mischief, I knew who he was—one of Declan's partners in crime.

There was something weird seeing the same expressions, the same movements you catalogued on childhood friends on the bodies of adults. I saw the boy who did trick shots on the basketball court, using his incredible height and skill to wow the lot of us, when he walked up to the stage and then jumped up on to it, all cocky swagger, until he got to me.

I caught the moment his smile faltered, just fell. His eyes silvered, he blinked, then swallowed hard.

"So, Riley, your speech?"

"Yeah, right." I saw the effort it took for him to turn around and face the crowd and wondered what the hell that was about. I wasn't hideous, but I wasn't exactly 'derail a guy's train of thought' attractive. "Look, you guys know me, know my family. We've been here for more generations than I can count. Well, like most people here, I guess." His eyes slid sideways to look at me, for what? "You know the Lang's are reliable, hardworking, and I'd bring the same to the alpha role. We own a lot of the farmland out on the east side of town, for those not familiar, so bringing that knowledge of farming I think would…"

His words trailed away as I observed his body language. Turned towards me, he was listing for me his virtues, not to the crowd, though they were the ones who would rule him in or out. He was stumbling in places, seeming to lose steam each time he met my eyes, sometimes leaving sentences hanging in the air, unfinished, until finally whatever was going on with him stopped him cold.

He looked…surprised, eyes wide, almost unfocussed as he took a step towards me, then another to the rising sound of Mason's growl. When he kept on coming, Mason moved to block him, a large hand going to the other man's shoulder.

"You're getting in the way," Riley snarled, his voice more his wolf than his. "She's right there!"

"What the fuck…" I hissed.

"And you're gonna sit your arse down. Now, Riley."

The man came back to himself with a snap at the sound of Mason's tone, his will beating down on the other man. Riley looked almost distraught, looking at the stage, me, Mason, the crowd, seeming to wonder how he got here. When he loped back to his seat, it wasn't so confidently. A stiff, uncomfortable silence reigned as he sat down, and I broke it by calling the next name.

SOMETHING WAS UP.

Mason stood at the left arm of my chair now, a boundary between me and the contenders. Some didn't like that at all, their spines curving, their fangs flashing as they fought to keep control of their beasts. Some mangled their speeches, one even just using the opportunity to shout his claim to me to the crowd. Silver eyes were the default.

But why?

I leaned back hard against my chair, tucking my legs up under me, remembering that run through the forest, the male wolves at my heels.

I needed to know what was going on.

Then I called Aidan up to deliver his speech.

He got to his feet with a shit-eating grin that had Mason growling before he even reached the stage. Like Riley, he leapt up onto it with a fluid grace, moving to the front of my chair rather than the side, trying to circumvent Mason, who wasn't having that.

"Step back, Aidan."

Where the other guys had postured, Aidan smiled, a glorious golden thing that made doing anything but what he wanted seem patently absurd. He looked to the crowd as if to say 'can you believe this guy?'

"Thanks for letting me speak, Paige," he said, ignoring my beta and turning to face the hall, all that cocky arrogance washing away. "I just want to say what a privilege it is to be given a platform to talk to you all. This hasn't been the way we've done things before. Look, I know some of you are a little underwhelmed by the fate of the town leadership being placed in the hands of one girl. Where else in Australia does an eighteen-year-old have this much power, amirite? But we've all seen Paige develop from this beautiful girl to the accomplished woman before you. She's had to deal with some tough stuff, the problems with the succession are obviously not hers, and I think this is a real opportunity for Lupindorf."

I'd been watching the crowd during the speeches and saw people turning off. Arms crossed, expressions tight, or just frankly losing interest, eyes dropping down to phones, but he turned that around. He wasn't dressed in a suit, making him look like he was putting on airs, but had a relaxed kind of confidence that seemed to put people at ease.

The confidence of a leader.

Mason seemed to sense the threat, shifting closer and closer until he was almost standing over me, as if even laying eyes on the man was too much.

"Mason," I hissed. He shot me a quick look, but his focus went right back to Aidan. "Beta," I said, quietly but firmly, dominance leaking into my voice, "step back."

Mason wasn't my mate, and I couldn't be seen hiding behind his skirts, no matter what he wished. He was here to make sure things ran smoothly, not to push out those he didn't like.

Aidan turned around at that, almost shyly surprised by my words, his face lighting up when he saw Mason obey my command. He paused, his smile faltering until I saw something much more honest rise. He looked at me with the kind of smothered longing I knew all too well, but seeing it on his face was completely alien. He'd never shown me the slightest bit of notice at school. Up until now, I would have been sure he had no idea I existed. So why the look? I fought the urge to frown and waved a hand.

"Continue, Aidan."

He let out a little snort as he scraped his hand through his dark blond hair, ruffling it until it stood up in spikes.

"I had this whole speech, but it's gone now." He gestured to the air. "I…I think we'd be good together, Paige, if you just gimme a chance. You probably don't remember me, but I remember you. I just want you to get to know me, see if we can…" His eyes darted out to the crowd, as if only just remembering they were there.

"Shit…this is embarrassing." I watched his jaw flex, and then he shook his head. "Vote for me or don't. I've got no say in that." Those hazel eyes slid my way. "But I hope damn hard you do."

A spell was broken when he turned away, jumping off the stage and walking back to his seat, hands shoved into his pockets.

"Paige?" Mason prompted.

I shook my head, looking down at the paper in my hand.

"Lorcan Roth?"

I was still trying to pull myself together when Ovulation Boy got to his feet, chin up, slouching slightly as he ambled up, a slight smile on his face. What I meant by that was studies had shown that when women were ovulating, they liked bad boys—strong angular faces, piercing eyes, deep voices. The guy who looked like he was gonna rearrange your guts. That was Lorcan. Sure, he was hot, as was each guy who'd put himself forward, but on him, it looked different.

Black hair that had been mussed, mossy green eyes that seemed to take everything in and find it all so amusing, if those full lips quirking were any indication. And tattoos. Where the hell was he getting a full sleeve tattoo in Lupindorf? I saw wolves and the moon and a woman in white all worked into the elaborate patterns before disappearing up his T-shirt sleeve. Black T-shirt, black jeans, and boots? Teenage me would have been creaming her knickers at the sight of him. Adult me was seriously considering it.

"So, is this where I spruik my worth to the town?" he asked, standing just below me, not bothering to get on the stage. He regarded the town hall with a sly smile. "I don't have much to recommend myself. Pretty much everyone here knows that. Nice little system you've got, trying to civilise all of this, but it's not gonna work."

He looked up at me, eyes deep green, meeting mine without a flinch, even when I forced a little dominance.

"I just want what every unmated bloke has wanted since you came back to town." His eyes slid insultingly slowly across my body. "A chance to see if all the dreams we've been having, of you naked beneath us, making kittenish little squeaks as we fuck your—"

"Lorcan!" Mason snarled.

"I'll fight every damn one of them for just one taste," he said, his smile widening. "And I've been fighting my whole life for what I want. Haven't wanted anything as much as you before though…" His smile faltered, and suddenly, he looked so much younger, more vulnerable as a result, a muscle jumping in his cheek before he forced it back. "Your call, princess."

He didn't expect anything from this, I could see it in the mocking twist of his lips. He made this a joke because if he didn't…

"I'm done for today," I said, getting to my feet. I thought of giving excuses, justifying what I was going to do, as women often did, but then stopped myself. "Mason, bring Lorcan to the house if he's amenable."

"Wait, what?" came cries from the crowd, several of the contenders standing up in response to this.

"Paige, what's going on?" Aidan asked.

"You want me to get to know you, to give you a chance? Well, I'm starting with him. My beta will be present the entire time, so you can be reassured nothing untoward will happen. I just want to ask him a few questions."

Because out of all of them, he couldn't or wouldn't play the game. He'd said more than anyone else in this town, and I needed that bald honesty right now.

"Mason?"

"Of course," he replied finally. "Lorcan, you can ride with the enforcers in the other car."

"Oh, I look forward to it," he said, then sauntered out.

Chapter 19

"In the alpha's office with the beta looking on?" Lorcan asked as he walked into the room. "Kinky, but I do like a girl who's adventurous."

"Sit down. Shut up," I said, sitting in Dad's chair, Mason's mouth snapping shut when he'd gone to say the exact same thing. So Lorcan did, putting his feet up on the desk, hands behind his head.

"So what can I do for you?"

"Drop the shitty eighties bad boy thing for one. Like, Judd Nelson called and wants his…everything back. I need some answers, and you seem to be really, really blunt with them, which could work in your favour."

"And what do I get for helping you? Please tell me a celebratory blow job, please."

"Does this work with like, anyone?" I shook my head. "I get you're a dick and all, but either dial this shit back or fuck off."

Lorcan's mouth snapped shut for a few whole minutes, then he smiled and nodded.

"All right, princess, whaddya wanna know?"

"Tell me about what you hinted at, what happened when I got to town. Not the dreams specifically, but…"

"You want to know how we've been affected. You didn't know?" His smile grew sly. "This is why they have you mated by the time you're eighteen."

"What?" I said the word, but my brain jumped to the same conclusion. My eyes roamed the room, saw both of the men struggle to hold onto that thought, because heat began to flare hard in their eyes. They were in a closed room, there was just the three of us and—

"Whatever you're thinking, you don't want to do that."

My voice was a sharp whip crack and sufficient to clear their heads. Lorcan settled back in his chair, feet on the floor now, fingers forming a steeple.

"Oh, but I do." For a second, that brittle veneer slipped, his voice becoming raw. He tossed his hair out of his eyes, the smile gone now, his eyes shining silver as he stared at me. I could see the predator in him, looking at me, sure he'd like just one bite.

"Pretty sure all of us knew the minute you got into town. I was sleeping off a bender, hungover as fuck, and then all I knew was I woke up fucking rigid. Like 'come on my sheets like a fucking kid' hard. And I ached. My chest ached, my dick ached. I wasn't sure if I was horny or having a heart attack. I stroked one off—"

"Is this relevant?" Mason asked.

"And blew my load with a most embarrassing swiftness, but then I was fucking hard again. I took my time with that, then again, then again. Lady, if you ever want to branch out into pharmaceuticals…"

"Keep to the story, Lorcan."

"I am, aren't I? You coulda asked any one of those blokes on the slips of paper that would've given you answers in nice decorous little bites, but you asked me." His fingers worried the seam of his jeans. "I kept jerking off, one, two, three times. Over and over, but my dick just kept rising. It felt so good when I came, like better than anything I've ever felt, and I've been to some sex clubs in the city—" I circled a finger in the air, letting him know he could move on from here.

"But it hurt too. Like, coming so hard, it felt like everything in your balls was emptied, only to go again, but that wasn't the worst of it."

Dark green eyes slid up to meet mine.

"Somehow, I knew it'd be so much better if you were there. That this fucking awful emptiness wouldn't rise once I was done. That my room wouldn't suddenly feel completely barren. That if I held your hand, twisted it to reveal your wrist, kissed the skin where your veins throbbed under the skin—"

He rose from his chair, hypnotic as a snake, while the skin of my wrist itched for just that, feeling the ghost of his lips, so full and soft, and he started to move closer.

"Siddown!" Mason snarled, moving over and forcing the other man to obey.

Lorcan's eyes fell shut for just a moment, as if in defeat, surrender, and when they opened again, they were heavily lidded.

"Let me do it," he said finally.

"What?"

"You don't know what's going on. You're pumping me for answers because you figured I'd give it to you straight, and I will. Any time you want, babe." He'd been all earnest, but slipping into cheesy lines seemed as natural to him as breathing. "Let me kiss the inside of your wrist like I dreamed, all Regency romance like. At worst, it'll be a little press of the flesh. At best, it'll tell us something."

"Tell us what?" I asked, cradling my arm to my chest, something that made Lorcan snort.

"I've got a theory I wanna test. So?"

"Paige, you don't need to do this," Mason said. "You don't need to do anything with him."

"I know that." The words were harsh but I said them softly, then met Lorcan's challenging gaze. "Don't fuck this up. I'm fairly sure Mason's just looking for an opportunity to tear your head off and shit down your neck. Touch your lips to the inside of my wrist. Nothing else, are we clear?"

He nodded, all smug smiles, as he got to his feet and walking over, laughing when I held my arm out like one would to a doctor when they were checking your blood pressure. Mason followed hot on his heels, seeming to loom over the both of us. Lorcan milked this for all it was worth, first placing gentle fingers around my arm, holding me still, then shooting me a sidelong look, holding my eyes as his lips dropped down.

You would have gotten less of a reaction from me if he'd slapped me across the face, my body tensing as sensation exploded out. A small rational outpost in my brain just detected the faint press of his mouth to my skin, but the rest? It went into overdrive as something entirely alien rose inside me, hot and hungry. My spare hand snapped out, digging into that soft mess of hair, grabbing a handful and holding him where he was, a low groan escaping his throat.

"Paige?" Lorcan asked.

I stared into those bright silver eyes and saw it, all of it. Sweeping me up in a hot tide, a girl ran through the forest, her white gown flapping in the wind as she went. My nipples pulled so tight, they ached, and I just wanted more of that hurt. Slick gushed between my legs, making Lorcan's pupils dilate, his fangs drop down. I heard the long drawn-out howls as if far in the distance, muffled somewhat by her pants, saw her desperate glances over her shoulder.

I was their paws, striking the ground, swinging their bodies forward. I was the scent of pine needles, the whip of the wind. I was her stumbling steps. I was their answering hunger as they noted the moment their prey began to falter, the bloodlust in them flaring in me. I was the memory of the taste of blood, bursting hot and coppery in your mouth, your fangs. I was the trail of slick seeping from her thighs, the burn in the muscles to keep moving

And most of all, I was the moon, hanging high, a silent witness to her daughter's demise, burning with a cold light.

Burn. That's what I felt when I came slamming back to the office, my grip in Lorcan's hair loosening, my fingers rubbing the soft strands between the pads, then caressing the side of that severely angular face. He grinned then, a predator's smile full of long white teeth, and with the cold white light coming in through the window behind me, he looked startlingly beautiful.

"Well, aren't you pretty?" I said, my voice not my voice.

"Pretty fucking hard is what I am." His words were ground out between clenched teeth, but he made no attempt to move away. "I knot for you. I didn't want to say, didn't want to… You'll find almost all of the contenders do, if my theory is right. Check if you like."

This was tossed off cheekily, but the mood evaporated as I caressed his face, him leaning into it.

"I'm not looking at your dick, Lorcan."

When his eyes opened, they were green again, and something heartbroken flared there for a moment before being quickly smothered. He pulled back away from me in more ways than one, but all that need went with it.

"You feel it now, don't you? That if you slipped your hands down those tight little jeans, just a couple of flicks of your clit…"

This should have been where Mason reprimanded him, pulled him back, forced him back to his seat or out of the room for the disrespect. But he didn't. The two men stood there, Mason's eyes gleaming silver, watching me.

"I wonder how many times you could come? Girls are always so much better at recovery than we are. Maybe you wouldn't be able to stop. Maybe that's what this is? Your body is lit by the same fire as ours is, without the same limitations. You could take the lot of us, one after the other after the other. Just one long stream of pleasure as we—"

"Stop."

As I said the word, it felt like someone had put a cool face cloth to my forehead or something. I was still simmering, just as he said, but I was clear-eyed for the moment.

"You've been very helpful, Lorcan. Thank you."

He knew he was being dismissed so he straightened up, stepping backwards.

"Sure I can't help you out?" He held two fingers in a V shape and then put them to his lips, flickering his tongue between them.

"Girls don't like to be seen with me, but they do seem to like what I do to them."

A part of me that had never seen the light of day considered that, pushing him beneath the desk, making him eat my cunt as Mason watched me come apart. The idea had so many facets to it— the decadence of using my position to do something like that, the viciousness of the strike against Mason for holding out on me. But I wasn't like that.

Was I?

"No one's doing anything today," I said, proud of the even, reasonable tone I used. "Good luck with your nomination. If you're successful, I'll see you in the ring."

He snorted, then shook his head at that. "My family is dirt in this town, so that's not gonna happen." He turned to go, eyes burning bright, before looking back at me. "But you picked me out of all of those fellas, figured I could be useful to you. I can be. I'll never bullshit you, love, and something tells me you've got a whole lotta questions. Maybe need to put some things to the test." He nodded to himself, the smirk back. "Mason knows where to find me if you need me, for anything. Absolutely anything."

And then he wandered out, proud as a cat, and I was left with my fingers digging into the arms of the office chair, anything to stop me from reaching out for one or both of them.

"Is it true?" I asked Mason, scanning that hard face.

"That I knot for you? It came when you were eighteen. Like Lorcan said, I woke up the morning of your birthday, dreaming of you on and around me. I could smell your scent in my nose as my eyes opened, so close, I could've sworn you just walked out of the room. My knot had swelled, and I knew it was for you." He looked away for a moment. "Went to see your father, see what he wanted me to do, leave town or…" He shook his head. "That would've been easier than what he asked. But I owed him my life."

"You haven't had anyone else," I said, the realisation just coming to me. "There's only been—"

"You. Only you, Paige."

Oh, how I would've wanted those eyes on me five years ago,

burning now with an unearthly fire that just built up the one inside me. This was what I'd deserved, someone whose entire being was focussed on me. Looking like he'd crawl over broken glass to get to me, he took a slow step forward.

Which is why I ran.

I was up and out of my seat, out the door to the sound of my shouted name, running up the stairs with him hot on my heels. I nearly made it too, my hand on the doorknob to my bedroom when his wrapped around my wrist, jerking me to him. Then I was shoved up against my wall, just like last time, my ankles kicked open, and in he came. When he settled against my body, I felt like I was coming home. My hand went to the nape of his neck, digging my fingers in, needing to feel him, Mason, more than my next breath. This wouldn't last, something else would come between us, I knew that, so I was greedy for the sensation of him under my fingertips. He moved in closer, holding himself back by a string, waiting for my permission.

"I kissed your brother this morning. I fucked him in my shower, felt his knot pressing hard against my cunt, wanting in."

His pants turned hoarse, his brows creasing. I was hurting him this time, just as he had hurt me, but he couldn't go into this all swept away by heat and then hate me for it when it faded.

"My wolf sees him as her mate, sees multiple people as that. I don't know why. No other wolf shifter I've met has ever admitted to that."

"And me?"

I saw the man I'd fallen in love with at eighteen brace himself for my answer, but he didn't pull away.

"She's waiting to see who proves himself."

"I can work with that."

And then his mouth came down. Just as gentle, just as sweet as it had been five years ago, a brief brush that quickly became all too hungry. He groaned into me, pushed into me, his body, his lips, his tongue, clawing to get more. And I gave as good as I got, meeting him for every kiss, sucking his bottom lip, tangling my tongue with his. I hissed against his lips when I slid shaking fingers up under his shirt, unable to move for a second, because this was Mason.

I'd laid curled up against this chest, a growing awareness of how hard and muscular it was coming to me as I got older. But touching it? I'd shoved that need away ruthlessly when he'd rejected me, so now? My breath couldn't seem to come fast enough as I pushed them up under his shirt.

"Yes…" He nodded in encouragement, then shocked me by pulling his T-shirt off over his head.

I didn't know what he thought, me just standing there and staring. Like I'd seen him shirtless often enough. Man, had I seen him shirtless. It'd been an assault to my teenage hormones, catching glimpses of hot, half-naked shifter men working in the backyard for Dad, but Mason? I reached out hesitantly to touch pecs and abs I'd dreamed about, fantasised…

He grabbed my hand and laid it against his chest, holding it there so I could feel him. This should've been the moment the illusions were dispelled, where he just felt warm and hard, like any other dude, but it wasn't. I looked up into his eyes, saw them, him, shining through. Everything my father had made him hold back was here now, he was here now.

But why? My brain complained, but I couldn't let that get between us. I moved in this time, fitting my lips to his, swallowing the rush of his breath, then him.

I glutted myself on Mason, letting my fingers roam, trail, touch, and grasp. His muscles were like iron, tensing as he held himself still, allowing me take my fill. I outlined his collarbone with my lips, traced his nipple with my nails, marked the path of his happy trail with my fingertips until his hand snapped out, stopping me from going further.

"No?" I asked.

"Yes, fuck yes, a thousand times yes." He bit the words off, making sure I understood. "I want you on that bed, naked and spreadeagled, ready for me to cover every inch with my tongue."

"But?"

"Paige, honey? Are you here? What happened at the town meeting?"

Aunty Nance's voice floated up the stairway.

"Shit, my family."

"Always your family." He surged in, claiming one last kiss before pulling his shirt on and moving towards my bathroom. "I just need…a minute."

"Right, yeah." I smoothed my hair down, sure my lips told a very clear story of what I'd been up to, but I swung out the door and met Nance halfway.

"Oh, there you are. Are you OK? You left early."

"I had some research I really needed to do, and I think we need to talk."

"Sure, what's going on?"

Her face was open and pleasant, her smile sweet as she asked the question.

"What do you know about the heir designation? Like why the Spehr family? Why the firstborn daughter?"

"Well, I guess that's the way it's always been," she said with a shrug.

"So there's no reason why all the contenders are acting so oddly?" I pushed at her slightly, letting my dominance leach into the words, and was rewarded for my efforts.

The mask dropped, if only for a few heartbeats, her brows jerking down, her eyes flashing as she looked off to one side, dealing with some foe I couldn't see. But she was still bristling when she met my eyes, her mouth thinning down to a straight line.

"You've got the touch, haven't you? Jesus bloody Christ, what was Adam thinking letting you go?" She shook her head tersely, then her arms were crossed as she regarded me with a steely gaze. "Well, there's no swapping Selma for you, more's the pity. When there's no touch, the heirs are interchangeable and there was no sign you had my sister's affliction."

"Um…what the actual fuck, Nance?"

"Since when did you talk like that, Paige Spehr? I told your father you should have been fostered with my girls. Growing up with good girls like mine might have mitigated this."

"So what? I'm a bad girl?" I fought the urge to laugh out loud. Nance was always kinda prissy, but really?

"The reason why we retain this position, why it's always our family that chooses the alpha? The women of this line, the eldest daughters anyway, they carry a 'gift.'" She said the word like one would dog shit. "Most normal shifters find their fated mate and that's it for them. They get married, have children, live a respectable, happy life."

One, up until right this very second, I thought I was going to have.

"And me?"

Her eyes were flint hard when they looked into mine.

"You can't break mate bonds or anything like that, but your touch, your scent, your presence, if you're strong with it, will send the single male population of this town into a frenzy. Back in the old country, our fathers set those of us girls with the touch before the men and gave them a head start to run into the nearby forests."

I was the thud of paws, the whistle of wind, the scent of pine needles.

"The unmated men ran them down, caught the girls, dragged them to the ground."

"And?" I asked the question, but I didn't want to know the answer.

"And then those that caught her became her mates, whether she wanted them or not. They rutted with her in the dirt, one after the other, then ruled her and the village."

Her eyes flicked up, going impossibly harder when she saw Mason had moved to the top of the stairs. Her jaw locked down tight, her teeth grinding before she turned on her heel.

"I need to inform Alan and Bill."

"Wait."

My voice was a lariat of steel, and it whipped out and caught my aunt mid step, only her hand on the bannister saving her from falling forward.

"You'll say nothing, do nothing about this without my express permission. Do we understand each other?" I walked downstairs until I could look into her eyes, seeing the anger, the hatred, the disgust that raged there, making me wonder how long that had been simmering. "Do you understand me?"

"Yes."

I'd basically pulled the word from her, but I didn't care. I needed time to work out what the hell this all meant, and I wasn't having Nance running around throwing a spanner in the works.

Nance has ambitions where your mother never did. You have to learn to manage her, love, Dad had always said. *If Mother Moon had been kinder, she would have made your aunt the heir, not Mum.*

"You can go," I said, regal as a queen, because arrogance was the only coin Nance responded to. Mason moved into the space she left as she strode from the house, slamming the backdoor when she went, and he paused to check in with me before sliding in close.

Feeling him against me, smelling his scent, feeling Mason had, for most of my life, been something that settled me, so I felt about ten years old when I rested my head against his shoulder, feeling his hand on my back.

"I need all the enforcers in the room, then I need to see Nan."

"Consider it done."

Chapter 20

So this is what a lamb led to slaughter feels like.

I doubted the wisdom of my decision the minute I walked into the enforcers' quarters. There it was, scrubbed clean of the mess we'd made the other night. Sure, it had a few dishes in the sink, a stray T-shirt hanging off the back of a chair, but it was pretty neat and tidy. That wasn't really what had my attention. It was them, filing in, one tall, muscular body after another.

The unmated men ran them down, caught the girls, dragged them to the ground.

They moved slowly, but still they prowled like the feral beasts they were. All the smiles and the laughs were gone, replaced by silver eyed intensity. They stopped in a rough line a reasonable distance away, sparing a few sidelong looks at those around them, but then everything was directed back at me.

An almost hysterical giggle rose in the back of my throat, but I swallowed it down. I didn't need to do that. A fighter assesses a threat and then works out a way to deal with it. That's what I needed right now, to know if they were threat or asset.

"You asked to see us?" Mason asked.

"I did. It's your jobs, the beta, the enforcers, to keep me safe until the alpha is chosen, right?"

"It is."

The men moved restively at that, as if there was an enemy yet to be identified that they needed to meet.

"What I need to work out is if you can."

"No one will touch you without your permission," Micah growled, his eyes glowing so bright against that tawny skin. "No one."

"That's what I needed to hear."

That's what I needed to test.

I walked over, watching the men's body language, the way they shifted and jostled slightly, and I knew why. It seemed ridiculous, arrogant to assume it was for my attention, but I knew it was, which threw up all sorts of red flags. They weren't like this beforehand. Dec had his flirty little memory share, Micah sent me spinning around the room to the music, but this… This wasn't right.

You can't fight every battle on your own, Zack had always told me, especially when I was being pigheaded again. Well, Nance had painted me a pretty devastating picture. A frenzy she'd called it. I needed to know if these guys were soldiers in the fight or wolves at my door.

I moved closer and closer, feeling like I was walking into an actual wolf pack, watching them watch me until I came to a stop, just in front of Micah. His nostrils worked, dragging me into his lungs, scenting me, his eyes shining like the moon. His muscles twitched, his hand rising then forced down.

"Paige?" Mason said, but I held up a hand, then reached out for Micah.

"I need to know if you can resist this. Can you do that for me?" He nodded quickly. "And if any of the others try to touch me?" His mouth transformed, fangs bared, a godawful snarl rising in his chest. "Good instincts. Don't hurt them, but don't let them touch me, OK?"

There was something insanely intimate about this, putting my fingers to the top button of Micah's plaid shirt and undoing it. A hard muscled chest appeared as I worked, the skin a deep brown, and I could see his ribs work as his breath came faster and faster.

"Tell me if this gets too much."

I sounded cool, clinical, yet this was anything but. The guys had moved now, circling so they could watch me work, turning the big open space into a tight claustrophobic one.

"I'm going to put a hand on your chest, and I need you to talk to me, tell me what's going on with you. I need the rest of you to stay back." I didn't inject dominance into my words because I hoped I wouldn't need to. If that was what it took to keep them in line, I'd be better off not having them around. "Does everyone understand me?"

I felt the moment that Mason appeared by my shoulder, not touching, not that close, but watching what I did.

"You want to make sure we can protect you through this."

"If what Nance says is true, every single straight guy in the place is gonna go nuts. We might need to turn the house into a citadel, and I need to know who I can trust."

"You can trust us. We're sworn to protect you."

I glanced around, looking at all the intent gazes taking in everything I did. I knew Mason wanted to trust his men, but I needed to know, because to me, it felt like things were on a knife-edge.

"So is this OK, Micah?"

His nod was jerky, his eyes unblinking as they stared at me. I stared back, caught the moment I made connection with him, saw the heat bloom in his eyes.

A flare that rushed up my arm and through my body, turning me molten, and it appeared it was the same for him. His eyes rolled back for a second, his breath coming in short, sharp pants. I could feel it, this slow-moving infinite loop of need, flowing between us.

"Talk to me," I said, pushing him slightly. "I need to know what's going on."

"Hard. Fuck, I ache for you... I can smell you, your need. I have to—I want to reach out and—" His hand whipped out and a spate of snarls went up around the pack, but it just covered mine, feeling shockingly warm and...

My eyes jerked up, looking into his and searching for what I sensed. It was a confusing tumble of need, desire, heat, and so much else. It felt like I held Micah in my hand, a great swirling mass of intense feelings I'd spend a lifetime teasing out.

"If every guy that fits the criteria feels like you do, they're not gonna play nice. I need help, I need protection." This could've been an order, but instead, it came out a plea. "I need people who'll fight with me."

"I'm yours." Fuck, whatever this was, it was brutal. It tore down people's defences and made them… "You know that."

I was shocked by the vulnerability on his face, and so was Micah. His eyes fluttered, as if realising what a gigantic faux pas he'd just made, but when he met my eyes, none of it had gone. Whatever was in him burned bright and true, and for some reason, he'd felt he needed to mask that. He couldn't right now, something that made me frown a little, wanting to know why. But I couldn't ask questions, not when a beautiful near stranger had basically put his heart in my hands. My thumb moved of its own accord, stroking across his chest in tiny sweeps, and he shuddered in response. Then I pulled it back, his still wrapped around mine, twisting until we held hands.

"Thank you."

That was such a lame response. I didn't want that. I wanted to pull him in close, taste his breath and then his mouth, keep on peeling off those clothes until there was nothing between me and him.

Which is what alerted me to the fact this might not be a one-sided thing. Nance had given me this weird non-con scene in her description, but that's not what this felt like. It was like the fun, hot feeling of the other night when we were dancing had been turned up to eleven. The fun part had been lost in the mix, but what had replaced it was intense. He squeezed my hand again, that same simple human gesture of 'hey, you're OK' that had me smiling, even as I felt my eyes ache slightly from unshed tears.

They said you truly became an adult when you realised your parents are just fallible people. My dad had known this would happen, had prevented me from taking a mate, knew me well enough that I'd leave and go live in the city. Why? He never mentioned a word of this in emails or phone calls, though how did one ask your only daughter if she's turned the local single guys into her sex slaves? I sighed, and the breath felt like it had to fight its way to get out.

"Can we sit down? If we're going to do this, you need to know what's happening. I also need to find out what Dad already shared with you."

"You heard the lady," Mason said with a short bark.

MICAH SAT by me when we did, still holding my hand, something I had to reluctantly relinquish when everyone's focus remained on it. The silver in the men's eyes faded at that.

"Did Dad ever talk to you guys about the heir, about me?"

My hands rested on the table, clasped together, and as I scanned the men, it was like their personalities came back online. Will settled back in his chair.

"Told us that you'd be back, that we needed to protect you most of all. That you were special."

"And not to touch you unless you said it was OK, or he'd cut our balls off." Declan laughed, staring into space, like he could see it. "He talked about cutting our balls off a lot."

"We just figured it was the usual pack princess thing," another guy said. "I'm Brett, by the way."

"Hey." I waved a hand limply.

"But that, that's not normally the way these things go. I came to this pack a few years ago, after you left. Couldn't get along with my alpha, but while they're protective of their daughters—plenty of alphas come from the pool of enforcers—I've never seen any girl able to reduce a man to that. Sorry for being blunt, but when you touched Micah, I felt like my nuts were boiling in my sack and that I wanted to rip his head off all at the same time."

"Is that what all of you felt? Like you wanted to remove Micah as a threat?"

The grumbles from around the table didn't make that super clear, but as often was the case, Declan piped up and added a whole lot of clarity to the issue.

"Only if you didn't share."

"What?" I looked down the table, that intense mood rising again, the smiles fading, the looks piercing. "So if I'd said, 'hey, fellas, let's all get naked and—'"

"Don't finish that sentence," Mason ground out. "Just don't."

I sat back, blinking for a second, but my mind was racing ahead, wanting, needing answers.

"So, is that something you guys have done in the past, shared girls?" I thought about my cousins coming here and dancing. "Is it like team bonding orgies or something?"

"Never," Will replied, shaking his head for emphasis. "I love these guys, but seeing their junk? I've got no interest in seeing Micah's Goofy face."

"Nor me your lily-white arse. Saw enough of that when you didn't leave the sock on the door knob that time," Micah shot back.

"Hey, Miss Penelope was hot to trot, and I wasn't standing around thinking about you when she shoved her hand down my pants."

"Nah, little Will was making the decisions again."

"Not so little—"

"So me proposing a threesome with you two right now wouldn't change your position."

The two men froze, they all froze at that, and yup, the shiny eyes of doom rose again. Fuck, there was something seriously weird going on here.

"Of course it would."

Everyone turned around to see Zack leaning in the doorway. God knows how long he'd been there. He walked over, every eye on him, and then came to stand behind me, my eyes falling half closed when I felt his hand on my shoulder.

I didn't know I needed that. I should've called him once I worked out what was going on, but being around Zack was terribly seductive. He was always ready to jump in and fix everything if I just asked, something I couldn't let him do. But when my eyes opened, I heard his words more clearly.

"Why of course it would?"

"Because, my love, you're a nix."

"NO!" Mason's reaction was explosive. He was up and out of his seat in seconds, backing away.

"Of course she is, brother. Think about it, about how they all reacted on the stage. They got within her radius, and the pull was too great. Unless they were already mated, she turned them into mumbling fools. It's why they chased her through the forest after her father died, why they went away so quietly when they could've just fought it all out that night."

Mason looked like I'd gutted his pet dog in front of him and then laughed, his eyes going to me, then to Zack in this endless flicking loop. And I saw it, some of my aunt's expression in his eyes. Fear mostly, but then something that had my blood running cold. Anger, pure unadulterated anger that throbbed inside him like a heartbeat.

"Guys, this is Zack, Mason's brother and my boss back in the city," I said by way of introductions.

"The guy you had waiting for you upstairs," Declan said, not entirely friendly.

"Yeah, we're not going into that right now. So awesome big reveal, Zack. Mind telling me what the fuck that means?"

"It's a stupid bloody word," he said, settling down in Mason's chair. "Used in the old country to describe a fae-mermaid type creature that lures men and women to their deaths with their beautiful songs. The truth gets kinda mixed up with the retelling of course."

Those dark eyes came to settle on me, similar in shape and colour to Mason's, but oh so different in expression. There was something still and calm there, like he'd been waiting forever for this day.

"A nix is a special kind of wolf, one with much greater powers than the usual. We all contain within us the ability to find our true mates, but them? They find many. In pre-Christian times, they were barbarian queens with legions of lovers who fought at their side. She calls all eligible suitors to her, then pits one against the other to find the most worthy."

There was something oddly ageless about Zack's tone, like his voice was not his own but that of history reaching from beyond the grave.

"And now?" I asked, my eyes focussed on the table, not wanting to hear the answer and knowing I needed to.

"And now they have their natures schooled and trained, coerced and corralled, forced into a shape that society can tolerate. She is made less by their inability to cope with what she is."

"You knew. This whole time, you knew."

"You stumbled into my gym leaking power, and only the agreements I have with my clients prevented a riot. It's why I trained you, babe. To overcome bigger foes than you. To build your discipline. To contain your powers. To honour your limitations, not push past the point where your innate control would falter."

At his words, the lessons he'd imparted about recognising tiredness, hunger, all came back.

I turned my head to look at him. "Why? How do you know this?"

"Shut up, Zack. Shut the fuck up," Mason growled out.

"Because it's what our mother was."

Chapter 21

"Where the hell are you going?" Zack asked Mason.

"I'm looking for the gun safe keys. We're gonna need to turn this place into Fort bloody Knox if she's at all powerful."

"You know how powerful she is. You feel her pull."

"No, no, this is not fucking happening again. She'll do the right thing, make a choice."

"Of course she will, but it won't be just one. You knew that. Deep in your heart, you knew. When her father asked you to reject her, why were you so willing? Your only true mate, and you've lived what? A loveless existence, all out of loyalty for one man. Who knows the feel of a nix's power better than we do? You rejected her because you rejected what she is."

"No." Mason shook his head over and over, like that would change anything.

I felt a sinking sensation. This should've been when the tears and the recriminations came, but that might be for later. I'd cried so much already. Instead, I just felt something cold and hard in me that may have been what Zack called this nix thing but I called something else—anger.

"You two obviously have a lot of family trauma to process, and I don't want to get in the middle of it. Really, I don't. Forgive me for being selfish, but I need everything you know about what a nix is, and then I need a whole lot more. Declan, did Dad ever talk to you about this?"

"Never. What is it? I've only ever heard it down at the pub when… Is it some thing that makes you polyamorous? Like a curse?"

"A blessing," Zack replied. "But we're schooled very hard to assume otherwise. What do you think when you look at her? That you ache for her to reach out and touch you?" Declan shifted uncomfortably, but then nodded. "And if she touched you and another of your brothers? If she touched you and me? Does your need diminish? Would you ache less for her?"

Did everyone wait on his answer with bated breath too? It was hard to say, but I knew I did. Those whiskey eyes slid to me, searching my face, but for what? Then he shook his head.

"I'd be glad that she still thought I was worth touching. We were too young when we were together. I know we needed to break up but…" He swallowed hard. "I regretted letting her go, even when I knew I had to. But I wouldn't make that mistake again." The knife of his words cut me so cleanly, the sting took a while to register. "If it meant dealing with other blokes on the scene? Well, I'd just have to find a way to make that work, wouldn't I? If this is part of her… Well, you can't have half a woman, can you? If you care, you care for all of her."

"The problem is so many will feel the same. She's stronger than Mum, isn't she?" Mason asked Zack.

"You can tell for yourself."

"Isn't she?" he pressed.

Zack nodded slowly.

"Then I'm glad you called this meeting, Paige, as we have a massive security risk to plan for. What you're emitting is a call, a chemical signature that lures all potential candidates for mate close. It's intense and overcomes normal inhibitions—inhibitions that protect you. Men will grow more desperate the longer the call goes out. It can…" Mason's eyes went wide and glassy. "It can result in people doing things they wouldn't normally do. I wish Adam had confided in me. We could've planned and been better prepared." He shook his head decisively. "Nevertheless, we move forward with what we have, help you find your mates quickly and cleanly."

"But not you," I said, the words feeling like millstones falling from my lips. I knew the answer, read it on his face before he even opened his mouth. A mouth that had kissed me so damn thoroughly.

"Not me. It's why Adam told me to say no, I can see that now. He needed someone to keep his head, keep you protected."

"And you can't do that if you love her?" Zack said.

"What I feel isn't relevant. Zack, I need you to take her out of here. Take her upstairs, keep her quiet and sated. I need the guys to focus on what I'm going to tell them."

Mason was trying to be all sensible, but it won him no friends as steady growls came from the enforcers.

"And we can't protect her by her side?" Micah said. "You said yourself she needs to take multiple mates. So what, you're discounting us?"

"You kept us from the gauntlet showing when she got back to town," Will snapped.

"Yeah, and they're the blokes worst affected by this, who we need to keep out of here," Mason shot back. "I'm not standing in the way of anyone's romantic goals. If she wants you, takes you as her mate, that's between the two of you and the other blokes she takes. But there's guys out there who are gonna insist on being considered, who, the longer this goes on, are gonna stop taking no for an answer."

I watched the man I'd wanted to choose as my mate fight a war within himself, with combatants I didn't know, about things I hadn't experienced. He wasn't just talking about me, he was talking about her too.

"I want an hour of your time, that's it. Then we work out a security roster, factoring in those who want to pursue things with Paige. We need to look at who's got gun licenses that are in date and what you can—"

"Do I get a say in this?" I interjected, and Zack smiled when my words cut through the chatter. "What if I don't want to take a mate? What if I don't want to choose the next alpha? Fuck, what if I don't want to stay in Lupindorf anymore? Maybe I want to go home to my flat and my job at the gym. To my life!" My voice rang through the silent space. "Maybe I don't want to be a fucking nix!"

"I'll fight every bloke here for every single point but the last one," Zack said, "and you can too. You know that. You know how strong, how capable you are."

Because he'd reminded me of it every day until I believed it.

"You're going to need to be. But your call has begun. If you want me to ring some people at home and set up something to protect you until you're ready to make a decision, it's done. You know Margaret and the ladies would take shifts at the gym to give you backup."

Margaret was the tiny martial artist master who'd shown me how to throw.

I nodded, sucking my breath in, then out again. Zack had trained me to recognise when I was starting to push myself too far, too hard, and I was feeling it now. My heart racketed around in my chest, like a frightened bird rather than a sophisticated blood pump. My limbs shook with adrenalin. My heart and my adrenals were pumping potent hormones into my bloodstream, dilating pupils, contracting muscles, readying my body for fight or flight.

"I need to run," I said, which provoked a low growl from the guys.

Paws slamming down into the dirt, propelling those powerful bodies further. teeth flashing, tongues lolling.

"That's...not wise," Mason ground out.

"Why? Because you'll want to chase me?" I got to my feet, feeling it throbbing within me. My smile was my wolf's smile when it came. "Who said you'll get a chance? Maybe it'll be me on your heels."

"She's not resting until she's expended some of that energy. If you think you're gonna cage her up in her room and feed her dick, you've got another thing coming, Mase," Zack said.

"Because you trained her."

"Damn fucking straight I did. That was the problem with Mum that you could never see. She never learned how to accept and control her power. She tried to fit herself into the mould everyone else wanted her to be in and then hated herself when she failed." Zack got to his feet, every inch of him bristling. "I never wanted another woman to be stuck in that kind of bullshit shame spiral. I wanted her to walk through this world an unapologetic queen who would take down anyone who tried to make her feel small."

It was then that I knew I loved Zack. I'd known all along, my wolf sniffing in frustration that my monkey brain had taken so long to clue in, but now that we were both on the same page, my fangs ached for his flesh. I stood as well, something that got everyone's attention, but I paid it little mind.

"You got your car keys?" I asked him.

"Of course."

"Then let's go. I know where we can go to let off some steam."

"Paige, you can't," Mason said, moving to get in my way but I froze him with a steely stare.

He cared, way too much probably. Always had, always would, but part of him was stuck back when I was just a dopey teen and he was a young man in his twenties, coming up the pack hierarchy. Nothing would work between us until he let that go. *If* he let that go. I shoved my hands into his jeans pocket, freaking him out initially before I fished out the ring of keys, walked over to the room where the guns were kept, and unlocked it.

"What the hell are you doing?"

"Dad taught me how to shoot. You remember that. I'm taking Zack out to the promontory. It will give me space to stretch my legs, and it's far enough out of town that we're highly unlikely to run across any of the contenders. And if I do?" I unlocked the safe and pulled out a pistol, making sure it was unloaded and grabbing ammunition too. "You'll remember I'm a damn fine shot."

I locked everything up again and then handed back the keys. "You're a good man. You know what you're doing and will work with the guys to keep me safe. Given the circumstances, I'm particularly grateful for that. But Zack's right—I'm not sitting in this house, riding Zack's dick twenty-four-seven to keep your paranoia and childhood issues in check. That's for you to deal with. When I get back, when I'm in the right mental frame, we'll talk about how you want to tackle security."

I probably seemed like some kind of ice princess right now, but despite the subordinate role I'd been raised to take, I was still born to rule. Back then, I'd thought it'd be at the side of the next alpha. Now? I fell back on my training, packing up the seething mass of emotion inside me and shoving them down deep. Being rejected by Mason nearly killed me the first time, but this time, I was using it as fuel to keep on moving forward. Whether he was coming with me depended on how effective the surgery was when they removed his head from his arse.

Zack seemed to read my thoughts, smirking as I strode out the door, the house, and into the carpark. As if to give credence to Mason's concerns, some of the contenders were perched on the footpath outside the house or sitting in their cars, waiting.

"Don't follow me," I said, in a normal conversational tone, one most couldn't hope to hear, but somehow, I knew they would. "If you want to do anything other than jerk off repeatedly to dreams of me, you'll stay the fuck away until I say so."

"C'mon, babe," Zack said, slinging an arm around my shoulder, just like he always did. "Show me this beach head of yours."

Chapter 22

I was always told the moment a girl takes her mate is one that transforms her life.

I gave Zack directions out to the prom, several hours drive from Lupindorf, and didn't say too much. He shot me sidelong looks. What else was he going to do? The coastal lands out here were resolutely flat and scrubby, not exactly picturesque. But I found that relentless monotony soothing somewhat, taking the manic energy in my body and coiling it tight, to be unleashed later.

Later came when we reached the sea, the sands blinding white, the water turquoise blue, and winds that had originated around the Antarctic circle buffeting us when we stepped out of the car. Despite being very pretty, the place freaking stank of rotting seaweed, which inhibited property development. When we got out of the car, walking up the tussock covered dunes and past the brightly coloured patches of succulent pigface plants, we were the only two out here.

"So what do you want to do? Some sprints to bleed off some ad…"

His words trailed away when I pulled my jumper off over my head, then my shirt. It took a lot to pull Zack's beast up to the surface, but his eyes flashed silver when he saw my sports bra appear, then get tossed onto the sand.

"You want me to chase you down." This was a statement, growled out not by him but his wolf. His eyes didn't shift from my nipples, like he could already taste them in his mouth.

"No, I'm going to hunt you." I pried off my shoes, socks, unzipped my jeans, and then pulled them and my underwear off. "If you don't give me a challenge, something to strive for, I won't give you what you want."

"And what do I want?"

"You know. You've been preparing me all this time for it, haven't you? Honing me into the perfect mate?"

"That's not what I was doing. Who knew the challenges you were going to face better than me? I wanted you to be strong enough to meet them, to go beyond all this bullshit, to be who you really are. Did I want it to be me you chose? Did I want you to look into your heart and see me? Fuck yeah, I did. I fucking love you, Paige. I always will."

"And I fucking love you, Zack."

My head tilted to one side, a strange power thrumming through me, letting me say what I'd known for some time but couldn't. He actually staggered slightly at my declaration, but I didn't need that right now. He'd told me what I was, so I had a name for it now, but I felt it more. Rising to the top, this godawful power that declared to any and all that he was mine, mine, mine.

"Strip down and then run, my love," I said. "I wish I could give you time to stretch first, but I can't. It's riding me hard, what's in me. I need you to run, Zack."

Some of the dominance he'd worked so hard to build in me trickled into my words, forcing his hands to his shirt, then his sweats as I watched him reveal that big, beautiful body of his. I hissed at the sight of him, hard for me, his knot swollen and painful looking, a trickle of slick sliding between my thighs as my body readied itself to take him. *Would it hurt?* I thought idly. No possible answer seemed to deter me. I would take him inside me, stretch my cunt around him, and milk him dry as I bit into his flesh.

"Now, Zack."

My voice was sharper, hoarser, harder.

He dropped his clothes in the sand and turned on his heel, running from a dead start off towards the rising promontory at the end of the beach. I counted my heartbeats, feeling the air caress my skin as he went. He got smaller and smaller, those powerful legs digging into the sand to push him farther. I grinned, dropped down into a semi crouch, and then I was off.

I usually fucking hated running and did it just for the endorphins and cardio, but right now, every muscle in my body had decided to cooperate to meet this goal. We cut through the air, my wolf and I, feet landing lightly on the sand, much lighter than Zack's bulk allowed. He was all intense stamina, but right now, I was speed. A manic thrill coursed through my veins, pumping, pumping all that fucking glorious adrenalin through me, making me feel more alive than any other moment in the world. I ran and I ran and I ran, the landscape feeling like it whipped past, the breeze tearing at my eyes, the gap closing, increment by increment until...

This was what I was born to do, I realised, right as I launched myself at him, grabbing him around the ribs mid-flight and swinging him around so he landed flat on his back in the soft sand. His eyes were wide, his chest heaving as I clambered up and over him—my love, my prey. He reached for me with shaking fingers, that need still pulsing inside, but I batted them away, linking mine with his, then pushing them above his head. *Stay there* was the unspoken command, and he did as I looked over the spoils of my hunt.

He was going to hurt going in. He did the first time I had sex a few years ago, one night after training. People had invested so much into my virginity and choice of sexual partners that I'd just thought *fuck it* and shoved my hand down his pants. I could see he was hard for me again, and right then, I wanted to see what that was like. His hand had gone to my wrist to stop me at first, then when he looked into my eyes, he held me in place, his hard cock thrusting up into my palm, like it did now.

"Jesus fucking Christ!" he snarled, the wind tearing at his words. "I've needed you so much since we got here. Paige, I—"

I put a finger to his lips as I moved astride him, not slotting him against me yet, just parting my thighs, working his cock in my palm and looking down at him—my mate.

My wolf was entirely on board, ready to wrest control and chomp him if I didn't. We weren't walking off this beach without joining, and I didn't want to. I rubbed the slippery pre-cum around the head of his cock as I leaned over and kissed him, just once.

"Come here, ride my face. I'll get you plenty slick enough to—Oh!"

He watched the sky and I watched him when he felt my cunt slide down his thick cock.

Then it all got kinda blurry, the harsh stretch of taking him with so little prep, the slick pouring from me, trying to ease this. My fingers, claws, digging into his chest, the thrust of his hips up as he fought my directive to stay still. The feel of his lips sobbing against mine as I worked him as far as I could get him before bumping against his knot.

My eyes closed when I felt it grind against my clit as I thrust down, something that happened over and over as I began to move in earnest. He disobeyed me, his hands going to my hips, fingers digging in, guiding me, dragging me back down upon him, not letting me dictate the pace.

"Yes, love…" he hissed. "Fucking need you so much. You're so tight and wet, but you're gonna take me." He wanted it to be a statement, but there was a lilt at the end that made it a question. One hand detached, sliding between us, the thumb massaging my clit, making me clamp down, drawing a strangled groan from him. I knew how he felt, as every fucking cell in my body sang at this, at this connection, at the feel of him inside me.

But not far enough.

I hadn't felt it before. We'd both seen his knot, sometimes I gave it a squeeze, which seemed to especially please him, but otherwise, we just ignored it. But not now. Something ached inside me, needing something else, something more. That didn't seem possible. Zack was both thick and long, high fiving my cervix on the regular, but not now, not this time. I moaned, the wind snatching my response away, my thighs spreading wider, my spine thrashing as I slammed down hard.

The first time we'd had sex, there was a lot of foreplay, lube, and patience, but despite panting like a woman giving birth, I'd been able to take him. Now I stared into the bright blue sky, feeling my body…shift. It wanted, needed Zack, all of him, as far as he could go and then maybe a little more. My eyes snapped down to him, going wide as I felt it. My heart smashed around in my rib cage, but his face just went soft, sweet.

"That's it, baby. This is it."

He rolled us over, so I lay on my back now, helpless beneath him as he nudged farther in, wriggling his hips slightly, which did insane things to my clit, until finally I felt it, a tangible pop.

"Fuck…fuck…fuck…" we both panted, pausing as if to mark what had just happened. Then I squeezed tight around him.

"Babe, no, too good…" he groaned, moving now, harder, faster, all the hard-won control immediately lost. His fingers were claws that stabbed into the sand, raking it as he drove himself deep into me. I was lost, buffeted around by great waves of pleasure, my screams like the seagulls wheeling above. I wasn't moving towards orgasm, I was just that endless crystal clear feeling of pure, bright pleasure that comes right before your body goes into riot, but mine didn't stop. It just crested higher and higher as my hips met his with every stroke, keeping him tight against me, not willing to relinquish an inch. And he couldn't, since the knot kept his strokes short, precise little stabs that cut me free.

He bared his teeth, trying to hold back, to wait for me, but I was already there. And besides, it was my fangs that mattered. I rose up, sweat matting my brow, my face a mask, a terrible creature that he caught sight of and then did what I never realised was possible. He bared his neck to me, the ultimate sign of wolfish surrender, only ever done under extreme duress, but he did it for me, to show that he would whenever I asked.

That was what I needed more than anything, which Mason

patently hadn't understood but my Zack always would. No matter his size, his strength, I ruled him, his heart, just as he ruled mine.

I sank my teeth into the thick muscle of his neck, clamping down, feeling his cum jet into me as I did so, and felt my own release slam into me at the same time. I held on, my screams muffled by him, our bodies jerking like fish on a line, until finally, we were mated.

"DON'T PULL AWAY," Zack said, holding me close. "Not yet. Still really fucking sensitive."

His knot had us locked tight. I was on birth control, but my body didn't know that as it held on for dear life while his cum flooded my cervix. I wasn't going anywhere. Little aftershocks racked my body, making him smile wickedly as his hand slid down between us.

"No, no, Zack… Oh!"

Just a featherlight brush, and another orgasm washed through me, shorter, sweeter, making my eyes fill with tears, so he did it again and again until finally, he was able to pull free.

"Why did we do this on the beach?" he mumbled, pulling me into his arms and down onto the warm sand. As always, he sheltered me with his body from the nipping winds. "I just want to snuggle down in a warm bed with you and do that at least five more times before Mother Moon rises."

"Only five?" I was joking, but my cunt twitched at that idea. I'd been kinda scared about the knot, but it was fucking fabulous. I felt the same way—loose, lazy, and so ready for more of that particular pleasure.

"That's why nix's have multiple partners, baby. When you go into heat, you'll be fucking voracious."

"You sound…turned on by that."

I looked up at him, searching his face.

"My brother's got it all twisted. I don't exactly want to think about my mum like this, but fuck, a queen of a woman with the kind of sexual power to bring a harem of wolves low? That's fucking hot. I love you, I'm not some toy to play with, but how can I not want to see me and the brothers you choose destroy you with pleasure? Plus, y'know, it takes some of the pressure off."

He shot me a cheeky grin, but I just stared, my mind already working.

"So you're just cool with me trying things on with all these different guys? What if I want to go through half the town?"

"Then you do. I've never stopped you from doing what you want, ever. Would I prefer to be part of the process, to meet whom you want to bring into our life, to make sure we all work as a team? Well, yeah. But if you're drawn to someone, if you feel like we felt just now, then they're there, part of us. I'll work out how to make it work. I always do."

"Mum used to always say Mother Moon puts people in our way for a reason and I thought it was always religious bullshit, but Zack…"

He wrapped an arm around my neck and pulled me close. "I know, love. Trust me, I know."

IT TOOK a while to retrieve our clothes, then we had to try and flick them free of sand before putting them back on. Maybe that was how they approached without us realising. Their scent must have been dragged away by the breeze, something I had to be more careful about going forward.

"So you've found your mate."

Both our heads jerked up to see Aidan and a few of the other contenders walking over the dunes towards us.

"By rights, that should nullify any pull you have over us. You belong to him now."

I took Zack's hand. "I do. I didn't plan it this way, it just happened, but I guess that finalises the contest for my hand. Neither of us wants to stick around in Lupindorf, so we'll still need to sort out who becomes alpha and if the contenders get community support—"

"So why do I still knot for you, Paige? Nothing's changed. As far as I'm concerned, you're still my fated mate, and I'm prepared to jump through whatever hoops you put out there to have my own pretty little interlude on the beach."

Chapter 23

I should've taken my gun with me. I should've gone to Nan's and Stevie's after the beach, then pumped them for information on whatever the fuck a nix was. I should've told Mason about the threat Aidan might pose, and whoever his dick posse was. I should've...

Instead, we drove home in silence, kinda shell-shocked. Not in a bad 'what have we done' way, more 'we just made the earth and the sun collide, wheee...' way. But we touched, his hand sliding from the gear stick to my thigh, mine stroking his, reaching over to the back of his neck and tangling my fingers in his hair. Then I was taking my seat belt off, ignoring the alarm dinging, and just breathing in his scent for a moment.

Fuck, I was in love. It sang within me, an endless perfect note, and nothing, not reality, not Aidan, no one right now could've taken that away. Zack pulled the car over, dragged me onto his lap, and then stroked my face like I was precious.

"You love me."

"So much. It feels like it just keeps growing and growing inside my chest until it almost hurts, but I don't want to stop it from hurting. I'm so full of you, Zack."

He smiled his crooked smile at my hurried words and then

pressed a kiss to my forehead before forcing me back into my seat, my belt clipped back on, until we got home.

He made me stay in my seat, walking around to open the door, sweeping me into his arms, then walking past the creepers lurking on the streets and inside the house. I was carried all the way into my bedroom, some of the enforcers turning to look as they paced downstairs, gun holsters now strapped to their chests. I thought we'd go to bed, that he'd strip me down and fuck me hard with that gorgeous knot of his, but he had other ideas.

"Sand is the antithesis of hot sex," he said with a firm shake of his head. "Sandblasting one's genitals is not sexy."

So instead, I was cleaned off rather meticulously, while I did the same to him, feeling the need to really make sure no sand got stuck to his knot.

"You're gonna make me cum," he growled out. "I feel like there's nerve endings there I never knew existed."

But I liked the look of the loss of control on his face. His hand slammed down on the tiles, his breath becoming ragged, his hand pressing down on mine, making my fingers grip him so damn tight, I was sure I was going to hurt him, until a few quick gasps alerted me to the streams of cum that came jetting out.

"On the bed, now," he growled out. "If I don't have your pussy on my face in five minutes—"

"You'll what?"

"We've never really explored sadomasochism, have we? How do you think you'll like getting your arse smacked raw?"

I got on the bed.

THE WORLD WANTED to press in on me, but I was lost in the feel of Zack's hair between my fingers, the drag of his lips against the soft skin of my inner thigh, the seep of my slick, readying me for him. He moved in, licking it away, getting a taste for it before burying his face in me.

"Fuck…your slick."

I was bloody glad he liked it because there was so much of it. It just leaked out of me when his fingers slid inside, when his nose brushed my clit, when he grasped it firmly between his lips, when he suckled lightly on it, occasionally brushing the hood with his teeth.

"Zack…" I moaned, clawing at him, trying to drag him up. "I need you. I need you now."

"Come on my tongue first, then I'll come up, slam myself deep in you, and fuck you through one orgasm and into the next. It'll be good, I promise."

I nodded reluctantly, but then it was no chore to surrender to that talented tongue, flick, flick, flicking until I screamed, eyes wide as he scrambled to do just that. As he rammed himself inside me, as my claws raked his back, it was hard to believe anything he'd said about other guys. There was only Zack.

I TOLD HIM THAT LATER.

The light was dying away outside, casting everything in the room a heavy gold. He just chuckled at my declaration, holding me against his chest, stroking my hair.

"No one's saying you have to take other mates, it's just for you, you'll be open to that. I'm done, locked down, yours forever now. You're my mate and that's all there is, but you, you can go through all of this again and again with other guys, if that's what you want."

"And you're OK with that?"

"I love you, which means loving what you are. There's a selfish kind of pleasure gained from thinking it could just be the two of us, and I don't mind saying I'll be enjoying that for as long as it lasts. Just talk to me. If you feel drawn to someone, let me know. Let me get to know them. I don't want to hang out on dates or watch you fuck or whatever, but just clue me in."

"It's that simple, is it?" I asked, looking up at him.

"It is for me. Now, did you have anything to tell me?"

I sat up, then flopped backward, resting my foot up against the wall, near his head. He kissed my ankle, then let his fingers trail up my leg.

"You know about Mason?"

"Not really. Tell me like he isn't my brother. We weren't close, and he left before I was even in my teens."

"Right." I looked up at the ceiling and then told him the story of Mason and me.

"THAT WAS the pain I felt when we met," he said. "You were aching."

"Part of me always will, I think. First love and all that, though maybe that was Declan."

"The enforcer with the freckles? What's the deal there?"

"Teenage sweethearts," I replied. "I loved him, maybe too much. We were stampeding towards my eighteenth, and I knew I was going to have to choose. What had been this special privilege all my life became this…life sentence. We started fighting, squabbling."

"That was probably part of your nix nature raising its head. Monogamy between two people is a happy choice for many, but not all."

"Maybe. He told me he wasn't ready to lock himself down, commit to becoming the alpha…to me." I inspected my fingers way too closely, picking at a hangnail. "We decided to end it. It was the right decision. We were miserable by this point, and we were only kids."

"And now?"

I snorted, letting my arms flop back over my head. Zack followed the movement of my breasts with lazy interest.

"And now he's the same old Declan—flirty and funny and attentive. But without all the teen angst. At the same time, he's also not. I don't know what Dad did with his enforcers, but Dec seems…more. More settled, more growly, more…"

"Was he good to you?"

"Of course. Dad wouldn't have let things get that far if he wasn't."

"Then he sounds like a possibility. If you want to pursue things with him, I'd like to meet him properly. Sit down and have a beer, find out what teenage Paige was like."

I shook my head and laughed nervously. "I am never going to get used to that."

"So who else?"

"I don't know. Mason's off the list obviously. I danced with Micah, and he held my hand a few times. Lorcan kissed the inside of my wrist."

"He did what?"

I went still, for a moment feeling that hereditary fear of pissing off a possessive wolf shifter.

"Um…we were testing a theory about this whole nix thing, before I knew what it was." His hand slid up my thigh, sliding way too fast, my skin damp from our previous lovemaking. "He said he saw himself kissing the inside of my wrist in his dreams, so we tried it out to see what it would… Mmm."

My story faded away as a finger very carefully swiped through the copious wetness that had collected in my folds.

"Keep telling the story, Paige."

"I…unh…"

"Yes?"

"He kissed my wrist, and it felt like a bomb went off inside me. I could see a girl running, wolves chasing…"

His finger slid down the hood of my clit, pulling it back slightly, then letting it fall back. The sensations were delicate, exquisite.

"He… We…"

"How did he make you feel, this Lorcan?"

It pressed down more firmly, making the fragile pleasure of before bloom more rigorously, my thighs falling open, my back beginning to arch.

"Paige?"

It slid down to trace a line around the place where I ached, where I needed his knot. I whined at the feeling of uncomfortable emptiness.

"Zack, I need—"

"I know what you need, that's why we're talking. Tell me about Lorcan."

"He was fucking quivering with need for me, and my slick was gushing. He offered to stay, crawl under the desk, and get me off with his tongue, and I nearly agreed to piss Mason off, force him to watch, to just be a selfish bitch and use him for my pleasure."

"That's it," Zack crooned, moving forward, pushing two fingers into the ache.

They curled up expertly, pressing hard on something that just made my clit throb. "Be honest with me. That's all I want. There's all sorts of games we can play if you're honest, and then we work to make sure no one gets hurt."

His words may have been all very wise, but they weren't my focus right now. I clawed at his arm, trying to drag him forward, bring him and his cock closer, but he just slid another finger in. The stretch, the rub of his knuckles went some way towards approximating the feel of his knot, which drove me wild. Short, stabbing movements pushed me higher and higher, his smile widening when my hands went to my breasts, tugging my nipples.

"Come apart for me, love, and then we'll snooze for a good long time. You've had a massive day."

So I did, wide eyed and screaming, before he bundled me up against him and drew me down into sleep.

Chapter 24

"Hello darling," Nan said when she opened the door, but she paused when she saw Zack and the prominent bite on his neck, proclaiming him as mine. "It's started then." She nodded, then ushered us inside. "I thought we had a little more time, thought it might've been that Klein boy who'd be first, but I guess when your love follows you from the big smoke, that's difficult to resist. I was fond of grand gestures too. Did I tell you about the time your pa picked every wildflower he could find in the fields outside of town and filled my room with them?"

She had, but I was always willing to listen to her stories, especially now.

"Of course, I developed allergies to the goldenrod, didn't I? My face swelled up and he thought I hated what he'd done, but we made up, which is always the best part. Sit down, sit down."

"Zack, this is my grandmother, April."

"A pleasure it is to meet you, young Zack. Now, coffee or tea?"

I'd warned health-conscious Zack that he'd be expected to have a hot beverage and there would not be a kale smoothie in sight. Which then started a conversation about the health benefits of green coffee and tea, and as a result, I punched him. He'd just grinned then and drove over to Nan's.

"Whichever suits you, April," he replied.

"Coffee then, at this hour of the morning. For energy, though I daresay you two don't need any more of that." She puttered around in the kitchen, boiling the kettle, setting out biscuits, another health sin he needed to commit to make Nan happy. But when she sat down, he wrapped his hands around the mug he was given and took two of Nan's Anzac biscuits, so he was sweet, literally.

"So congratulations are in order." Nan looked at the two of us with a soft smile. "Is he a good man, Paige?"

"The best, Nan. He looked after me when I took off for the city and helped me stand on my own two feet, then trained me to stay on them."

"So it's your fault she's too skinny. You need to feed her more if you want to keep her. In my day, men liked a girl with a fat arse."

"They still do to be honest," he muttered. "But I focussed on developing Paige's strength, her speed. I wanted her to have the ability to fight anyone who wouldn't respect her boundaries."

"You knew then."

"My mother was a nix—"

Nan wrinkled her face up at that. "Nasty word. Like calling a girl a slut in my day. So you grew up with a woman with the touch then. Was it a happy life?"

There was an edge to Nan's voice, something that both of us picked up. He shifted in his seat, consulting his undrunk coffee.

"It was a house full of love…but I wouldn't say happy. Mum didn't realise what she was until it was too late, was driven out of her town for stepping out on her first mate, my brother's father, with mine. She took Mason—"

"Mason Klein? I thought you had the look of him!" Nan said.

"And brought him to my dad's place. That's where we grew up until…" Zack shook his head. "My mother wasn't the most stable woman. She was always torn in two by who she was and how she was raised. I don't know if she ever worked out where she fitted in that."

"She hadn't found her pack," Nan said decisively.

"What?"

"We were always told, don't go making eyes at anyone until the Spehr girls were done. If they set a cap for the boy you liked, you would never keep them. That's what your family has done, Paige, schooled you girls into thinking one and done. He's the alpha, he's the power in the town." Nan's eyes twinkled. "The power is you, girl, but like your mate says, you can't let it twist you. It did that to your mother, poor thing that she was, and Zack's mother too from what he says."

She looked me clear in the eyes, her gaze steady, even with the faint circles of cataracts beginning to form. "Torn between two lovers…" Nan sang, her voice only wavering a little. "Used to love that song I did, before I saw what happened to your parents." She went still for a moment, just staring at the table, tracing the grain with her fingers, as the moment stretched on and on.

"You got yourself a good one, darling. A boy that understands what it is to have a girl with the touch." My grandmother's eyes slid sideways. "You know you'll never have her entirely to yourself. Adam wanted that for her, wanted her to have time to find herself, find them…"

"Of course." Zack reached over the table and held my hand, something that warmed me way more thoroughly than coffee did. "She's my girl. I love her, April, I don't mind saying. That means making sure she gets what she needs. Whatever she needs."

I took Nan's hands when I saw the suspicious shine form, her jaw tightening, but she just nodded quickly.

"He was right then. I wish he'd lived long enough to see it, but perhaps he does, from the pack lands beyond." She visibly calmed herself, then got up, picking up her mug. "I need to tell you the story of your family, Paige, the one those hoity toity idiots on the Spehr side will never tell you. We'll talk in the front room. Don't want talk like this upsetting the energy in my kitchen. The yeast won't rise and the milk'll sour."

I shot Zack a look at that, but we followed her through to a stuffy, airless lounge room, where the floral couches had neatly trimmed strips of plastic to protect the furniture. Nan sat and looked out the picture windows to her garden beyond, settling when she saw the willy wagtails playing.

"Your father was one of six men fighting for the hand of your mother," she said, not looking away. "She loved or could have loved five of them. She loved Adam the best, or that's what she told herself. Perhaps she thought he was the best candidate for father or for alpha. She wasn't wrong, of course. My boy, he was a good man. He did his best by her, tried his damnedest to make her happy, but that's the curse of the touched."

Her fingers tightened around the mug she held.

"Our hearts, they're split in two, one half with us, the other with our mate. Well the touched? They never know until they've found all the parts, and then they're done. They form their pack, then their hearts are whole and so are their mates. I know they told you your mother died of heart problems, love, and I guess it was partly true. She died of a broken heart, did Lucy."

She shook her head slowly.

"My Adam had to watch it happen, had to raise a little girl by himself. I think that's when he decided enough was enough."

"He knew…" I whispered. The rejection. Walking out the door. Dad's claws on the newel post to keep himself from running after me. Zack pulled me in close, but still, I shivered. His body laid out so neatly on the dais.

Daddy…

"You can't live your life full of regrets, darling. If he saw how you'd turned out, out from under those bloody Spehrs and their bullshit!" My eyes jerked up. Nan did not swear often. "I'm sorry, but they built a nice little power base on girls just like you, on their misery and pain. You strengthen their position, never forget that. With every single man in town sniffing after you, imagine the deals and negotiations that family has carried out to strengthen things. A bad business, Adam helped me see that. The women hate the Spehr girls for taking all that male attention, but the Spehrs raise their girls to be at odds with their own nature. Then you have those with no touch but they have the blood. Perfect little creatures they are, what they thought they had in you."

She jerked herself to her feet, but I saw the tremble in her hands as she disappeared deeper into the house. I set down the coffee cup and followed her down to her sewing room.

This was where the magic happened, the old-fashioned wireless on the sewing table, patterns and fabric hanging from pegs in cupboards, scissors and needles put neatly away. But in a cupboard tucked right up in the back, she retrieved a familiar looking leather satchel.

"Dad's bag…"

"Keep it here, love. It can't get in the wrong hands, not after he did everything he could to gather it all. You can sit in the front room for as long as you like, any day that you like, but please." She pressed the bag into my hands. "Read it. Read everything he collected."

ZACK LOOKED me over with concern when I returned, clutching it to my chest.

"I must put the meat on. We're having roast lamb for lunch, and that nice boy from up the street said he'd come by. You'll stay, won't you, love?"

"Yeah, of course," I said on automatic. It took Zack grabbing my hand and pulling me down beside him to reveal my burden. He took the bag from me and opened it to find it was bulging with papers. We started to pull them out, laying them across the coffee table.

They said we needed to look at history to predict the future, and if the papers were anything to go by, mine wasn't bright. Hangings and burnings, Whore of Babylon and witches, nixes and sirens and succubi were all fanned out before us.

"Fuck," Zack said.

"Fuck indeed."

Chapter 25

"So I'm gonna die screaming."

I flopped back against Nan's couch, the plastic coverings now sticking to my sweaty skin. The room that had been stuffy before, but now it felt volcanic.

"Paige…"

I got to my feet, started to pace back and forth. I needed to move, do something about what we'd just looked at.

"It's not that bad. Most of this stuff is from like, the Dark Ages or something."

"This is from 2019. 'The dark side of polyamory no one talks about,'" I said, swooping down to pick up an article Dad had printed from the internet. "Blah blah blah, workplace discrimination. Blah blah, have your kids taken away from you. Like fuck, this is now, with relationships between consenting adults. In America, which has a much bigger population than—"

"Paige…"

"What? What am I supposed to take from this, Zack? What Zen koan have you got to get me through this? You're telling me this is who I am. As a wolf shifter, I always risk fear and persecution if anyone ever found out what I was, but now this as well? I can see why Nance and the Spehrs try to keep a lid on this, because this," I gestured to the table and piles of paperwork, "is a life of ostracism and hatred and pain." I jerked my hand down when I saw the shake there. "I can't have kids. I cannot do this to another daughter. It's irresponsible and cruel."

"You're jumping to some pretty big conclusions here."

"No, I'm not. I'm really not. Female sexuality is demonic." I lifted the printout of a woodcut carved in the 1500s showing a hideous woman with a long flickering tongue and what looked like a small cave between her legs, complete with stalactites and stalagmites. "Women with power should be burned." I waved an etching of a witch burning. "Women as evil seductresses that damage the minds and bodies of innocent men." A colour printout of a beautiful oil painting with a thick gilt frame, showing an ethereal girl coming out from the lake's edge, to pull her prey under the water. "Show me one positive image of a…whatever you think I am. Just one. Just one role model."

"Here," he said, pushing a screenshot from the shifter social media site, Jungle, to me.

"Jungle, really? That's just full of menopausal shifter women swapping recipes."

"It's a little more than that. And when did you become such a social media snob? If you start posting photos with #blessed on Instagram, we're breaking up. Take a look."

I plucked the printout from his fingers, frowning the moment I read the group name. "'Nix and the Sacred Feminine'? Ugh, this is just more moony, girl power shit." He didn't reply, just waiting for me to keep reading. "Hang on, this post was written by Dad, about…"

I kept reading, seeing my dad's faltering attempt to introduce himself and then talk about me.

I'm Adam Meyer Spehr, Alpha of the Lupindorf Pack in Australia, and I think my daughter might be a nix. We have some weird traditions that were brought out from Germany. I was raised to expect that the eldest Spehr girl would take a mate and that man would become the next alpha of our pack. It's what happened to me, obviously. But there's something weird about our process, and it took me talking to shifters outside of town to realise.

Spehr girls don't have fated mates like most other shifters. They pretend they do, the young men who want her and want to become alpha step up and compete for her affections, but it wasn't until I had a daughter of my own that I realised how weird it is. I knew my Dianne was my mate the moment I locked eyes on her, so why the need for competition? If we were fated to be together, shouldn't that be it?

I asked my wife about it some time later, and I'll never forget what she said. It took a long time, and I'm ashamed to say, a lot of shouting, but while my baby slept in her cot, my wife let me know that while she'd felt our bond instantly as well, she'd felt the same with several of the men who'd fought for her hand. She cried and cried, not wanting to say the words, not wanting to hurt me, but I made her.

I'd heard about nixes, of course, though mostly when blokes were at the pub talking about girls who were loose with their favours before they found their true mate. That was always the big fear, that you'd be bound forever to some girl who everyone had been through. A shitty attitude, I've come to realise, but being an older bloke, that was a very different time. But I'd never heard anyone use the word you ladies do.

My wife passed on, but nothing was the same after that confession. I'd watch her all the time, see where her eyes, where her attention was, always wondering if it was on me or those other men. It created a rift between us, one that I think ultimately ended her life.

But I have a daughter. She's beautiful, smart, talented, like every man's daughter is, I guess. But if she's one of these nix things, what does that mean for her? Will she never find the satisfaction of a true mate? Never stop searching for the one, because there isn't one? I came here wanting to find some kind of reassurance that she's got a happy future ahead of her.

I had to force myself to read the last of it. It was hard, and my eyes had filled with tears, blinding me until I angrily dashed them away, only for more to come. This was so…Dad. Awkward, clunky, loving… My jaw locked down tight, feeling sobs form in my chest, but I didn't want to let them out. I hadn't earned that right, I felt. I'd been blithely doing my thing in the city, and he'd… My fingers went to crumple the paper between them, but Zack stood up and took it from me.

"Let me see what this group is. I'll see if I can join it."

"You have a Jungle account?" I croaked out.

"Don't get snotty. I run a lot of ads for the gym from it." He pulled out his phone, opening the webpage from the link only shared with other verified shifters, then searched for the groups. His thumbs danced over the buttons as he answered the questions to apply to join the group, and then closed out of the site.

"Just remember, you don't have to do anything. It can just be you and me if that's what you want. It's what your mum did, what most of your female forebears have done for some time. Your dad was concerned, felt like you might be happier being true to your nature, but he wasn't you. It's your choice, Paige. It always has been. I'll never pressure you to take other mates. I just don't want you feeling like you can't pursue things if that's what you want."

"Well, you've been working hard in here for hours!" Nan said, appearing in the doorway. "Come and have some lunch while it's nice and fresh. An old friend will be joining us."

"YOU."

The word slipped from my mouth when I saw Lorcan sitting at Nan's kitchen table, that black hair neatly combed back, a white button-up on over his jeans rather than the black T-shirt of yesterday.

"You remember Lorcan, do you? You two were inseparable when you were little, always up to mischief. You cried so hard when his family moved away, but I thought you would have been too young to remember him now."

"Zack Gillespie," Zack said, moving forward and holding out his hand to the other man, but Lorcan's eyes went from me, to my mate's neck, his face even paler than normal.

Finally, ingrained social customs had him standing and shaking it. "Lorcan Roth."

"Paige told me a little about you," Zack said as he sat down, his arm going across the back of my chair, Lorcan following his every move.

"She told me nothing about you, though I guess we weren't talking a whole lot last time I saw her. So, I can see congratulations are in order. Does this mean you're the new alpha?"

His tone was polite, but Lorcan's movements as he took his serviette and spread it across his lap were sharp, abrupt.

"Nah, mate, you know that better than anyone. The process isn't done until the lady says it is."

Green eyes jerked up, flicked from mine to Zack's and back.

"This smells lovely, April," he said, turning to Nan. "You didn't have to invite me around."

"Nonsense. Too much meat for just one woman, and boys are always the most appreciative of my cooking." A dark look was shot my way. "Girls are always too preoccupied with being skinny."

I snorted as everyone started helping themselves to meat and vegetables, taking an extra portion myself, then another when Nan continued to stare. It was only when she nodded that I started to cover everything in gravy.

"You drown out the taste!" Nan fussed. "You always did."

"A girl wants what a girl wants, I guess," Lorcan said, cutting into the butter soft lamb. "Don't they, April?"

I FELT like somehow I'd been transported into some kind of period drama or something. Everyone was being so polite, but no one actually said what they meant. My head ached from trying to decode all the double-talk, especially the light fencing of words between Zack and Lorcan. Zack ended the contest though, moving in close and brushing his nose against my neck. Nothing too handsy and likely to upset Nan, but it stopped the other man cold. He just stared, watching the two of us without blinking, and it took Nan glancing up to break the spell. But I saw the stark look in his eyes, flicking sideways at me until the end of the meal.

"So do you two remember running around all nicky noodle when you were little?" Nan asked with a chuckle. 'Nicky noodle' was naked apparently. "I'd turn the sprinkler on to water the grass, and you two would be naked as the day you were born, out there playing with it before I could take my next breath."

"Um…no," I said, focussing on my plate.

"I always thought that was some kind of repressed trauma or something," Lorcan said.

"Silly boy. You used to squeal just as loud as Paige here. You liked to pick up the blasted thing and run at her with it, splashing her with the sprinkler just to hear her scream, I think. Then not to be outdone, Madam here would snatch it off you and do the same until I'd have to come running out to see what all the fuss was."

Something rose at her words, just little fragments. Bleached out sunny days. Grass that crunched underfoot, gone dry under the merciless Aussie sun. The smell of water hitting sun-baked earth and him. My head jerked up and I frowned, for a second seeing a blurry image of a little boy where the man currently sat, but when it faded, Lorcan was still there.

"Well, that was an amazing lunch," Zack said, patting his stomach. "Why do I feel like falling asleep on the couch in front of the footy now?"

Nan flushed at that. He was golden now. New grandson-in-law, and he complimented her cooking? No quicker way to get to her heart.

"Why don't you boys go in the lounge room and turn the telly on while Paige and I do the cleaning up."

"We can help," Lorcan replied, getting to his feet and collecting his plate.

"No, no, I know it's all modern now, with men doing the cooking and cleaning, but you'll just make me cranky, putting things in the wrong drawers. Shoo! You two can have a little chat, talk about whatever nonsense men go on about, and I'll be back soon with some apple pie afterwards."

"Well c'mon then, mate," Zack said, standing up. "You can tell me more about what a rascal Paige was when she was little."

. . .

"SO," Nan said, always an ominous start to a conversation. "What do you think of Lorcan? You liked him very much when you were a little girl, and I heard you asked him back to the alpha residence yesterday."

"Are you…? Nan, are you trying to set me up with a family friend?"

I thrust my hands into the soapy water, scrubbing the plates like they'd personally offended me, then dumping them into the sink.

"Careful now. Those are your great grandmother's plates. Might be yours or one of Rose or Lynn's girls one day. Well, I just remembered how well you two got on together."

"I don't."

"For a while there, we thought… Well, your mother wasn't happy. Lorcan's a good boy, but that family of his. Not his fault he was born into a pack of villains, and everyone assuming the worst of him. He came back home, once his dad died, hoping to make a fresh start."

"Nan, I have no idea what you're talking about."

"Lorcan is a Roth on his father's side, but an Engel on his mother's."

My sponge came to a halt. Everyone knew the Engels. Hard to run an organised crime family in a small town without people knowing, so it was a disorganised one instead. Right or wrong, if something went missing, a car stolen, a cow poached, everyone looked to the Engels. The Engel girls were vicious at school, taking down anyone they thought 'messed with them.'

"Shit, so how did I end up hanging out with the kid of the local crime lord?"

"Paige, language!" Nan dried off the plate she was holding with a practised motion, then picked up another. "Delia Roth, Lorcan's paternal grandmother, was a dear friend of mine. One of life's little injustices that her boy found his true mate in an Engel, but the Mother wills what she wills. She asked me to keep an eye on him, their house being only a few doors down. Was such a pretty place when they first bought it." She shook her head. "I offered to help young Lorcan with it, try to put it to rights after his bloody cousins went through it." I cocked an eyebrow at that. "But too proud by half that boy." Her eyes slid to me. "He needs a mate is what he needs, and a good one."

"And so because I'm 'touched,' I can just take him on board? Nan, it doesn't work like that."

"No, it doesn't. From my readings, it's much the same as any other mate bond. You feel that inexorable pull that just starts out small. A look, a touch" —for a moment, I was thrust back into Dad's office, Lorcan's lips on my skin— "but suddenly, so suddenly and yet it feels like a lifetime, you know." For a moment, Nan wasn't an old woman whose mate was long in the grave. Age, experience, it all wafted away, leaving a young woman with radiant eyes. "Just as you knew with your Zack. They're a part of you, the other half of your heart. Or in your case, one bit of it."

"Maybe he's the only bit. Maybe I only need one partner. It's what all the other women in my family have done."

"Then you best look to the Spehr history then, to find out how well that went." She patted me on the arm. "Don't fret, love. Lorcan's a good boy and probably just as mortified as you are by all of this. If you don't feel the pull, then there's nothing to worry about, is there? We'll have some pie and ice cream, and I'll send him on his way."

THE PROBLEM WAS he'd rolled up his sleeves while we were in the kitchen.

The thing I liked most about the internet was it normalised some pretty crazy shit. There were posts and forums and Tumblr accounts all dedicated to the beauty of the male forearm. I'd tried to explain to the girls at the gym how hot Eliott Stabler's forearms were in *Law and Order: SVU* when he rolled up his sleeves, but the girls just cited that as further evidence of my daddy issues. Right now, I wasn't thinking about Daddy.

My eyes followed those long muscles all the way up to long, artistic fingers that held the spoon Nan gave him with a very masculine nonchalance I'd never be able to mimic. He twitched it as he talked about some shit. I couldn't focus, could I? He had that really lean look that some guys seem to manage and gym junkies always want to emulate, like the skin was wrapped tight around the muscles, showing every line, every vein, and my eyes could only watch them move as his hands twitched.

"Not hungry?"

I was jerked out of my daze by an amused aside from Zack. Nan's apple pie was to freaking die for, but I had a bowl full of it, the ice cream slowly melting into the soft, sweet mess, untouched. Zack's eyes were slightly silvered when he leant over, as if to brush his lips against my ear.

"You're needing," he whispered, little more than a breath out. "I can smell it. So can he."

I glared at my mate, knowing what this was, where he was going with it, and he just smirked and turned back to his bowl. Me? I went to pick up the spoon, shovel the food in my mouth, but it was bone-dry, would turn to glue if I did. Instead, I watched that twitch, twitch, twitch until finally my hand shot out and I closed my grip around Lorcan's wrist. The man looked stung in response. I couldn't have shocked him more if I'd gotten naked and danced on the table.

"Paige?" Nan asked quietly.

"Sorry, the twitching, it was bugging me." I pulled my hand back as I felt my cheeks flush hot. "I'm just a bit…"

Everyone turned back to their food and ate the glorious bounty Nan had prepared, but those green eyes flicked to me over and over, managing to catch me staring every time.

"I SHOULD GO. I've got a ton of stuff to get done around the house. Thanks again, April," Lorcan said, getting to his feet, and I felt actual relief. I was being weird, in my Nan's kitchen, and I couldn't seem to stop.

"We should too," Zack prompted, tapping me on the shoulder.

"We've got to pack away Dad's papers first."

"Oh, don't worry about that. I haven't got much on today," Nan said. "Just a little puttering around in the garden. I'll look after them. But you can always come by and take a look at them, love, you know that."

So we ended up saying our goodbyes together, awkwardly crammed in Nan's hall, and when we emerged out onto the street, I felt like I could take my first few breaths.

"Where's your place?" Zack asked, causing Lorcan to spin around, an eyebrow cocked.

"Look, mate, I dunno what you've heard, but my cousins were kicked out and aren't in the 'roid game anyway."

"'Roids?" Zack snorted. "You think I take them? Nah, mate, they make your dick shrink. So where do you live? I'm assuming it's either left or right."

"What the fuck do you want with me when you've got her? She smells…"

Lorcan's head moved restively, as if questing for my scent and pulling away from it at the same time.

"I know how she smells. She smells like that for you. Something you did back then tripped her trigger, and I want to know why."

"Zack, we don't need to do this," I hissed. "We can't just bring Lorcan into this."

"We can't just bring Lorcan into what?" Lorcan scanned the two of us, taking in the scar, Zack's arm around me, where I rested against his chest. "Are you…? Is it true?" He moved closer, then stopped himself, just holding himself very still before breathing me in. "Fuck…"

"Where is your place? I don't want to do this out on the street."

"Worried about her reputation? If she's seen walking into number thirteen, that's gone anyway."

"Thirteen, huh? So this way."

Zack's hand closed over mine and dragged me up the road, Lorcan keeping pace with us.

"Sorry about the…well, fucking everything," he said when we walked into the front garden. Someone was obviously fixing the place up, the foot-high grass slashed roughly down to the ground, piles of cuttings from overgrown shrubs in a neat pile. "If you're gonna do this, you may as well come in then."

Lorcan unlocked the door and then led us in.

I SAW why he wasn't keen on having us over. Someone had trashed this place. You could see the remnants of graffiti under the undercoated walls, the couch looked like it'd gone ten rounds in a prize fight, and the windows were smashed into spiderwebs of fragments.

"I'd offer you a drink, but I don't think that's what you're here for. What are you here for again?"

Lorcan's jaw worked, and his hair was no longer so neat, his hand raking through it. He shifted on the heel of his feet, back and forth, but that's not what caught my eyes. It was those fucking hands, complete with knuckle tattoos, a large silver skull ring on one. They were blunt tipped, long and pale, and they scrubbed so furiously at his scalp. His bicep bulged under his shirt as he moved too damn much.

I wanted to still him, knew that if I stepped forward and put my hand on that beautifully wrought forearm, he'd go still, so very still. And then I could trace every inch of those very pretty arms as he stood there, looking down at me, quivering.

"Hungry now, princess?" Zack's voice was a low buzz that jerked us out of this trance.

"Is that what this is?" Lorcan snapped. "You gotta hard-on for whoring out your mate?"

"Don't use that fucking word around her."

The growl, the clear and obvious menace there stopped both of us still.

"So what is this, then?" he shot back. "You got the girl. She marked you. Lemme say something true, mate. If it was her fangs on my throat, I sure as shit wouldn't be sharing her with you."

"Wouldn't you?"

This wasn't my Zack, my sweet, caring, growly mate. This was a devil at the crossroads, offering you riches and gold if you just signed over your pesky soul.

Lorcan shifted where he stood, his eyes going greener, brighter.

"I wouldn't be giving her to some bloke I met off the street, and

I sure as shit wouldn't be bringing her to a shithole like this. She deserves a lot more."

"What are you doing, Zack? You're just rubbing shit in Lorcan's face, stirring up trouble," I growled out.

"I want to know."

"Want to know what? Where he lives? How we used to play together as kids? Both of us can barely remember that."

"Well you mightn't, but I do." I felt bad. Lorcan looked stung, like I'd slapped his face or something. "It took me a bit for me to connect the dots. April coming by, talking about her granddaughter and how she used to look after us helped me realise who you were. Those days were one of the few pleasures of my childhood. I carried them around in my heart and pulled them out when shit was going down like other people would family snaps. And then there was the fucking dreams."

He swallowed hard, shaking his head.

"Came on with adolescence, just these intense fragments. The smell of her hair, the feel of her fingers in mine, her breath on my skin. Spent my time at high school fucking a whole lotta girls to try and find her." His eyes narrowed down. "It's you. I shoulda fucking known when you came to town. That feeling that woke me up was so bloody familiar, wasn't it?"

"She's it for you," Zack said in a low rumble.

"Of course she fucking is. Why would Mother Moon grant me a true mate I could actually have? How would this be any different to the endless skull fuck of my existence?" He strode forward, stopping just short of me, but his focus was all on Zack. "How can you fucking do this? How can you hold yourself back from her? Act like you're oh so cool?"

"How can you?" Zack asked.

Lorcan's eyes snapped to mine, his breath coming in hard, too hard for an argument. His fangs dropped down, his lips parting to give them room, and suddenly, I couldn't think of anything else other than sliding my tongue into that gap.

"We need to know," Zack said. "I'll do what you want, it'll just be you and me, babe. I'll throw you in the car, buy you all new shit, move you into my place, and keep you tied to the bed, pleasuring you over and over until neither of us can move. You'll be mine, all mine, and I will fucking glory in that. But I need to know that I'm not just another man stifling your nature, locking you down, putting you in a box that you've got no right being in. He's drawn to you."

Lorcan spluttered at that, shooting him a filthy look.

"Is that what you think it is? I want her more than my next fucking breath."

"And what do you want, Paige?"

This will change things, I thought as both of them turned to me. I couldn't come back from this, put this genie back in the bottle. I'd be taking a step towards…becoming something I had no preparation, no guide for. I should've waited, got on the Jungle group, talked to other people about whatever the hell they thought this nix thing was, and then discussed with Zack in a civil way about how to deal with the situation.

Instead, I went forward without any of that.

I felt like a tightrope walker without a safety net, making careful steps closer, sure at any point, I'd go plunging to my death. But I walked into the harbour created by their bodies, letting mine brush against Zack's as I reached out for Lorcan's.

He flinched when my fingers landed on the brachioradialis, the muscle that sits on the top of the forearm, but he didn't pull away. He just watched me stroke my hand along the surface, and it felt as smooth and firm as I thought it would.

"You rolled your sleeve up," I said by way of explanation, but it didn't work well. He looked at me in confusion. "I saw your arms, the muscles, the veins…" I turned his arm and stroked down the sensitive skin on the inside. "And suddenly, that's all I could think about. You were tapping your spoon, making the muscles jump, and I…"

"And you what?" His eyes were silvering, his beast coming out in his hoarse voice.

"And I needed you to be still." I shifted away from Zack, which hurt a little, but that was OK, Lorcan would kiss it all better, wouldn't he? I stepped into his space, letting my fingers trail down to circle his wrist. "I needed you to stop so I could look at you."

"You're not looking right now, princess."

"No, I'm not, am I?"

I tipped my head up, and he tracked my movement, his tongue flicking out to run along his bottom lip, and I wondered if he felt the small gap between his and mine. I jumped when his hands went to his shirt, unbuttoning it with a flattering swiftness and then wrenching it off like it offended him personally, and then there it was.

His body was very different to Zack's but no less beautiful. It wasn't the super heavy muscle developed through years of weight lifting. This was the hard body of one built through work or activity. I reached out, unable to stop from touching that pale skin, moving to the other arm with the sleeve tattoo, tracing the arabesques and curlicues, finding the savage wolves hiding in all that beauty

"Why weren't you like this yesterday?" I asked.

"Because yesterday I hated the whole hoopla, hated this town, hated myself."

"And today?"

"Still all of those things, but I want you more." His hand went to my hair, his fingers digging in hard as he loomed above me. "Tell me you want me back. Tell me you want this, or you need to take you and your kinky arse boyfriend outta my house."

"I…"

He smiled slightly, a look of sheer fucking mischief, and I thought he should've led with this yesterday. He was as magnetic as the sun, and I couldn't look away, even though it hurt my eyes. I tried to lean up, to press my lips to his, but he held me where I was, though I could see he was pleased by it. He lowered his mouth closer, closer, and then said, "If this is when your boyfriend asks to ride my arse while I fuck you, I'm gonna be pissed."

"What? No," Zack said. "Though a conversation needs to be had. What do you want me to do, babe? I'll leave you with the keys, walk back to the house. You can come back to me when you're ready."

Lorcan growled at that, spinning me around, arms like steel bands across my chest, but that made me painfully aware of how my hard nipples were.

"You want your mate to watch me with you?" Lorcan suggested, his voice like slow-moving poison now. He nipped my ear when I didn't reply. "I wouldn't mind leaving someone else to do the aching for a fucking change."

"This doesn't change anything," I said to him and to me.

"Fairly sure I'll disagree if I get my hands on that pretty little cunt."

"You touch her with her permission. You only go as far as she says," Zack warned.

"I still knot for her. I can feel it throbbing right now." A gentle hand stroked down the side of my face. "She's still my mate until this goes away. You have to know what that means."

Just as when he kissed the inside of my wrist, the first press of his lips to my neck set off explosions within me, only his arms stopping me from arching upwards.

"Sssh…" he said, placing another and another until my head swam. "I'm going to take you into my room, and you're going to try very hard not to judge how shitty it looks. Then I'm going to strip you bare, because I need to kiss every inch of you. Tell me you want that."

My eyes flicked open, and I saw Zack standing there with eyes that burned fiercely with a weird mix of passion, fear, and pain.

"Zack comes with us. That's my condition. He's my mate. He doesn't get left out. He leaves of his own volition."

"Sure thing, princess."

And with that, he spun me around, taking my hand in his, and dragged me down the hall.

Chapter 26

He wasn't kidding. Old sheets had been tacked over more smashed windows, the carpet worn to the backing in places, covered in stains I dared not guess the origin of in others.

"C'mere," he said, tipping up my chin, dropping his mouth down to mine. "I've been dreaming of tasting those lips for days. You bit them yesterday when I kissed your wrist, and I've never been as hard. Tell me you want this."

"You're going to ask permission for every step of this?" I asked, unable to stop my hands from running over those cobblestone abs. "Could make things kinda prolonged."

He grinned, a not entirely nice thing, but he was moving in close, drowning me in a crisp, masculine scent as he trailed his hands up my arms.

"Tell me I don't need to. You give me a free rein, I guarantee you'll go back to your mate a happy girl."

"Paige…" Zack said.

"Oh, now you've got qualms?" I said, shooting him a harried look.

"Just be clear where your boundaries are."

"Right, boundaries." I turned back to Lorcan. "No pain. I don't get off on it at all, which fucking rules out surprise anal. Actually, to both of you, surprise anal is always off the table. Just leave my butt alone until I can trust you to know what you're doing."

Oddly, that got me a chuckle from both of them.

"I don't know what all of…this indicates to you, but I'm pretty vanilla. If you try and choke me or face fuck me, I will pin you to the ground, find the nearest thing that'll work as an impromptu dildo, and ride your arse like a pony with it. If women are into it, I'm cool. I'm just not."

"Fuck, that put some vivid mental images into my head. OK, I can work with that. Mostly I just wanted to kiss you." His lips brushed mine, finally, briefly, my head whipping up to close the gap, but he held off. "A lot. Like way more than you can possibly want."

"That definitely works," I panted before he claimed my mouth with his.

I DIDN'T KNOW what I was expecting from Lorcan. Who he was and his behaviour seemed to bounce around from smart arse shit yesterday to dutiful young man at Nan's to this… What was this? If I had to choose a word, it was reverent. He stroked my hair, my face, seeming to need something for his hands to do as his mouth conquered mine.

First with teasing little glancing kisses, pulling away before they could deepen, then darting back for more. His tongue grazed mine but retreated until I dug my hands in his hair and pulled him closer. He groaned into the tight grip, so like my OTT display yesterday, but I didn't care. He said he needed a taste, well I did too, of mint and our meal and coffee and him. My teeth sunk into that too full bottom lip, marvelling at its plush depths before my tongue surged forward. We were eating at each other as his hands went to my waistband and mine to his, my fingers nimble, flicking open the button, sliding down the zipper and pushing my hand in.

"Fuck!"

He tried to claw my hand away when they closed around his rigid length, but I just purred. I hadn't seen a whole lot of shifter dick, but compared to humans, they were always so damn thick and long. I rubbed a thumb over his slick head, making it glossy with his seeping pre-cum.

"You keep doing that, and I'm going to embarrass myself," he rasped, trying to pull my hand back, but I slid it lower, lower until he let out a noise from the depths of his soul. I spanned my fingers across the tightly stretched skin of his knot, giving it an impulsive squeeze, fascinated to see more clear fluid gush from his cock.

"You said you kept getting hard over and over."

"Wanted that to be in you," he ground out, but I dropped down, sitting on the edge of the bed and pulling him closer as I saw Zack shift into view.

Hot brown eyes watched me trace the central vein of Lorcan's cock with my tongue, the way I flattened it just under the head where it was the most sensitive. Zack's hand went to his sweats, rubbing the big lump there as I traced the rigid head, licking away the other man's pre-cum like you would an ice cream.

"Well, if you're sure about this," Lorcan ground out, gently putting his hand on my head to coax me to swallow him down, and I did.

Not far. Zack always reassured me the most sensitive part was the head anyway, and I could never get past the feeling of choking. Lorcan certainly didn't seem to care, babbling a stream of sweet nothings as I started to move.

"So good, so good…" He stroked my hair, my jaw, tipping it slightly so he could go a little deeper. "Oh fuck, Paige. Tell me where you want this, because I'm gonna come. I've been fucking rigid all through your nan's dinner, imagining all the—Fuck!"

I looked up into his eyes, saw the tension and the awe get washed away by a great wave of pleasure. My hand wrapped around his knot and squeezed hard, then his growl filled the room, long and strangled as his body went stock still.

Cum jetted into my mouth, over and over, while I was frantically trying to swallow, but some still dripped free. He tried to pull away, but I still suckled on him, more gently now, moving my lips in little bumps, and he didn't soften an inch, just as he said. Only the sensitivity seemed to fade, as his little almost pained gasps gave way to long, full throated groans.

"How the fuck do you do that?" he hissed, yanking me free and throwing me on the bed, then pulling my jeans off in one sweep. "Why do I come so hard? Why won't my dick quit?"

He said the wrong thing in the right way when he followed me down, shoving my shirt and my bra up around my neck.

"Are you some kind of witch or something?"

That should've conjured images like I saw in Dad's papers, of screaming women standing on piles of kindling, burning alive, but as his lips went to my collarbone, my breasts, I just smiled.

Maybe they had the right of it, those medieval men, because there was a power here. My fingers tangled within Lorcan's hair, those black strands so stark against my skin, and gripped them as his eyes rolled up to meet mine. He watched me unblinking as he circled my nipple with the tip of his tongue, too soft, too imprecise for what I wanted, but it was coming, I knew. I smiled at him, and his eyes shone silver as he closed his lips around it and then sucked.

Jesus. My head was thrown back, unable to deal with the incredible intensity as I felt twin tugs on my nipple and my clit. His teeth scored my tender tip, pulling harder and harder until I began to squirm. I felt the bed dip, a heavy weight displacing it, and opened my eyes to see a naked Zack had crawled on, his hand stroking his cock.

"I told myself I'd watch and wait, let you do this on your own, but…I need my girl."

I nodded, watching him move closer.

"Our girl," Lorcan growled.

He was bent over my body, protecting it like a dog with a bone, which I guessed he was.

"If you're good to her. If you're worthy. I'll share with anyone she chooses, as long as they prove they're good enough for her."

Lorcan trailed his kisses down my stomach, moving to my inner thigh to the sound of my pleased moans.

"Beyond this, you might not get another chance at touching her for a while. If she wants her hand held or long romantic walks or just to get to know you, then that's what you do," Zack insisted.

When Lorcan pulled back, the diffused sunlight hit his face, revealing the complete destruction of his expression.

"When you first met her, would you have done absolutely fucking anything for her to touch you? Even just a graze of her finger, her breath on your skin?" he asked.

"Yes."

"Would you fight every single one of those fucks who think they're owed a piece of her because the base of their dicks swelled?"

"Fucking promise I would."

"I don't know you or Paige." Lorcan looked down at me, that expression softening. "But everything inside me tells me to burn the whole fucking world down if she asks. Do you want me to stop? We can do things right. I'll come to your door, court you better than your granddad did your nan. Tell me you want this. Tell me you want me."

This was sheer fucking insanity. Wolves are ruled by their instincts, while shifters try to be anything but, too many cautionary tales of jumping in when things 'feel' right, only to repent like hell at leisure. Being mated to someone lasted a lifetime, so you wanted to do things properly.

But I couldn't remember any of the advice I'd been given. I just knew I wanted them, that when Zack moved closer, sliding a hand on my shoulder, when Lorcan stared at me and ran his hand down my thigh, I couldn't say no. I wanted to say yes, yes, yes to fucking everything. So I did.

Lorcan slid to the edge of the bed, dragging me over with him, slinging my legs over his shoulders before regarding what was before him. He stroked one solitary finger through my folds before looking back at me.

"I want you to burst, drown me in your slick. I want to be covered in you, dripping, so that when you turn around and scurry away from this shithole with that mate of yours, I'll have something of you still with me."

He didn't wait for me to reply, since I'd given my permission. Instead, he bent his head down and kissed me.

It was all so delicate at first, like he wanted to take tiny sips of me, little kitten licks to make me aware of everywhere I ached. But I was more than conscious of it.

"Lorcan…" I begged.

"You fucking destroy me when you say my name like that," he growled out.

"I need…"

"I know, I know, I just wanted…"

Me, he wanted me. I felt that as his mouth plundered me, thrusting his tongue inside to lick my slick from the source, his fingers pinching at my clit, making the ache sharpen so swiftly, a little scream escaped me.

"Babe?"

Zack was all concern, leaning over me, watching what Lorcan did, but when I reached out with a shaking hand and wrapped it around the base of his cock, all was forgotten. I parted my lips and licked up his length as I squirmed.

"You're fucking brave," Lorcan said, pulling away for a second, only to shove those beautiful long fingers inside me. "She's close. She might chomp you in two."

"Could you resist if she offered to suck you off again?"

He snarled at that, watching me squeeze Zack's knot, then lick the pre-cum that trickled out of the head.

"Never. Her mouth was like hot fucking velvet." His eyes dropped down to me. "You ready to come, love? Come hard for me."

He pushed my knees up to my chest, splaying myself completely open, and then his tongue slid up as I took Zack's cock into my mouth.

I was caught on the spike of each of them, one pushing in while the other backed off, the rhythmic tides swelling in me. Lorcan had cunning fingers that found my G-spot automatically, while he licked my clit and my cunt frantically to capture all the slick seeping out.

"Fuck!" Zack yelped as my groan travelled through my chest, up my throat, and into him, my lips working up and down his cock. "Babe…so good…" he panted.

"You're going to come now," Lorcan said, dominance vibrating in his voice as he pulled his hand back and then shoved another finger in, the stretch making me writhe. Because I needed it in ways I'd never known before. My body was hot, throbbing, aroused, and that was its natural conclusion. To stretch around their knots, take them deep, let them lock right up inside me, and then fill me with their cum.

But Lorcan made good on his order, his lips fastening around my clit, and then he sucked hard. It was a marble in oil, rolled over and over and over, a vicious pleasure swelling inside me, filling me up until I did just as Lorcan asked.

I burst.

My spare hand clawed at the bedding, my back arching up off the bed, letting Zack push a little deeper.

"Jesus, babe, I'm coming!" was all the warning I got before he exploded too.

I swallowed and twitched and jerked and licked as Lorcan rode my spasms, forcing me on and on, every muscle in my body straining to process the feeling.

"You fucking near drowned me."

Zack pulled away, collapsing down onto the bed, his fingers tangling with mine as the other man rose. Lorcan's face glistened, looking entirely like the cat that got the cream, and he made no move to wipe it off, not even when he threw his body down next to me.

"You're feeling all soft and swollen now?"

I nodded.

"I can stop now. I already got way more than I ever thought I would. If you're done, I'm done."

But he wasn't, his dick rigid between us.

"But, baby, if you let me wedge my cock into you, I swear it'll feel so good. You're already so sensitive. It won't take much to set you off again. You'll want it, need it."

"No knotting," Zack rasped between pants. "Not yet. Not so soon."

Something unfriendly flashed in Lorcan's eyes, but he nodded as it faded, seeing the wisdom.

"Just lift your leg and put it around my waist. That's it, sweetheart. You can feel it, can't you? All that deliciously sensitised flesh just rubbing against each other. It'll get better, I promise. Other leg now. That's it, baby. I'll do all the work now. You just feel."

"And my hands?" My voice sounded rusty and disused. I reached up with them as well, tangling them in his hair, then tightening my grip to the sound of his groan.

"I do like that," he hissed. "Makes me feel for just a minute that I'm yours. That you own me. Just a little harder. Ah…yes, just like that. Now I'm gonna rub my cock on your dripping wet cunt. Your slick makes the nerve endings come alive."

"The Mother's little joke," Zack sighed. "The thing that makes her able to take us is the thing that destroys our control."

"The Mother's Tears." Lorcan's eyes falling closed as he did just that.

I jumped at the feel of him, big, broad, and blunt, slicing through all my softness like it was nothing, slipping in my slick, dragging intense sensation in its wake. He was gentle at first, as if just waking up my flesh again, helping it to remember the ecstasy it'd just experienced before creating more.

He nudged my clit, making me twitch, but again, gently and persistently, he teased it from oversensitive to just glorious. His eyes slid open when he heard my first gasp, then he smiled when he caught the second, shifting to draw a circle around the mouth of my cunt, just teasing me with the tip until I growled my readiness.

"Mmm…you feel like silk, satin, everything that's good in the world." He paused and then stabbed inside me, filling me up, forcing a stretch, making my nails dig into his skin as I let out a long moan. "And now you're mine."

For some reason, I thought this was going to be all gentle and sweet, but on the first stroke, I knew this was what I needed. My fingers left his hair, slapped on his hips, and my nails dug in.

"That's it," he ground out with a smile and a frown. "You feel it."

And I did. There was something wild and untamed about Lorcan that he'd been holding back all this time, and now it was off the chain. *Slam, slam, slam,* his body buffeted mine, but I levered myself up by my thighs wrapped around his waist, meeting him stroke for stroke. He was hammering me hard, frantic trills of pleasure flaring brightly in response, but it wasn't enough.

What we were trying to do, it wasn't right, not by our bodies' dictates. This was the warm up, the sweet coming together, but it was always only foreplay. Those silver eyes opened, stared down at me, and I knew. My body was shifting. It knew what it wanted, what it needed from him.

"You're…"

"Paige!"

With every downstroke he was pushing deeper, impossibly deeper, until all artifice and skill was lost and there was just need. Lorcan's eyes shone like the moon as we ran together in the forest in my mind. Was I the wolf? Was I the girl? It didn't seem to matter, because soon, we would be one. My lover let out a long, tortured groan, the clasp of me around him, drawing him deeper, more than he could take.

"Yes… Yes…"

Right when the perfect moment should have come, right when all the boundaries and bullshit should have been thrown aside and what was true should have come forward, Lorcan yanked away. I came, achingly empty as he slapped his cock down on my clit, pushing it to keep on twitching but not around what it should. He sobbed when his cum jetted out, his tears hitting my skin at the same time as his seed did. And what a sour harvest that was.

I pulled him down on top of me, cradled him in my arms, and fought the urge to growl when Zack came closer.

"You've only just met. I rushed things. I'm sorry."

His excuses would make sense later, I knew that, but all my wolf knew right now was betrayal. This was part of my heart. I'd found him and been denied, and he wept from the pain of it.

I did too. That hurt at first, fighting to get free, my body warring with itself until it won. I stroked Lorcan's hair and cried for him. I cried for all the women and their well-documented torture and murder in my Dad's papers. I cried for Mum, being forced to endure this same pain by her own family. Worse because she didn't even get this. And I cried for my dad, reaching out to strangers on the internet, trying to find a way to help me, right when I refused any help at all.

When we came back to ourselves, Zack was cradling me against his chest and Lorcan was wrapped around mine.

"It was the right thing to do," Lorcan said finally. "I didn't want it to be. Mother, how I didn't want it to be. People make bonds hastily and then spend their life regretting it. I guess we've gotta see if there's anything beyond this little experiment."

When I reached up to touch his face, he rubbed his stubble against my palm, closing his eyes for a minute.

But of course, moments like this were always going to be short ones.

A loud crash alerted us to the intruders, then a shouted, "Lor! You in here?" confirming that. Both men were up off the bed, yanking on clothes to meet the threat head-on.

I was much slower. Imminent doom might've been, well…imminent, but I was drained, hollowed out, and just a husk remaining. My clothes felt weird and wrong against my skin, but I pulled them on anyway, especially as the noise got louder.

"Taking it up the arse, Lor?" one of several thuggish looking guys sneered, the three of them clustered together. Fuck, it was Jim, Marty, and Baz Engel.

"How the fuck did you get in here? I changed the locks."

"Like that'd keep us out. Worried we're gonna try and poach your boyfriend here?"

No one answered. No one said a thing as I walked into the room. The Engel boys, their eyes flashed silver as they watched me approach.

"You've got the heir here?" Eyes slid to Lorcan. "Why didn't you ring us? Half the fucking town's panting after her."

"And you fucked her." Marty was the smaller, weaselly looking one, his face screwing into a weird combination of anger and envy.

I walked up, slid between my two men, putting my hands on either of their waists, only then feeling the steady thrum of tension.

"Get out," I said, shoving dominance into my words. Marty stumbled back and the others flinched, but they tried to stay where they were, growling in response. I stepped free of the men, Lorcan trying to stop me, but Zack shook his head. This was what he'd always trained me to be. "Pick your flea ridden corpses up and get the fuck out of this house and never come back unless invited."

It took a lot, exerting this much will, shoving it into not one but three big men, but I saw their feet slid backwards, taking one step, then another, my determination beating down on them, breaking down their objections with each begrudging step, one after the other.

"You'll regret this, bitch," Baz, the oldest Engel said. "Lot of riled up, frustrated men in this town. Only so long before they start pushing back."

"Don't care about them. I care about you lot fucking off. So go!"

They stumbled out the front door, snarling as they went, but run they did.

"Pack a bag," I said to Lorcan when he came to stand beside me. "I dunno how committed you are to this place, but we've got plenty of spare rooms at the alpha estate. If we go in the direction I think we will, we'll be leaving Lupindorf, go to the city. You could come with us."

His breath on my neck was my only warning, then a kiss, soft and sweet on the base.

"Being a kept man. Not exactly what I had on the agenda right now. But yeah, the only thing that stops me from lighting this place on fire is the arson charge. Gimme five."

Cool air let me know he'd gone, but that was quickly replaced by another warm presence.

"You need to be careful with that meddling, Zack."

"I know. That didn't go to plan."

I looked over my shoulder. "There is no plan now, only unchartered territory. You better be as foolhardy as I think you are, because this is gonna get messy." I turned, softening towards him. "I love you with everything I have, but you are a micro-managing, manipulative fuck sometimes."

"I know." A long sigh and a soft hand against my face. "I'm sorry. I'll tell Lorcan the same when he comes back."

"Tell me what?"

He carried a bag stuffed full over one shoulder, and something told me he hadn't really unpacked what was in it since he got home.

"I'm sorry, mate," Zack said, holding out a hand. "I thought it was for the best. For both of you."

Lorcan looked at it, then shook it with the hand covered in tattoos.

"Got it. Don't do that fucking again though. You're her mate, I respect that, but you don't get between me and her. Whatever poly fucked-up thing we're rocking here, that's my bottom line."

"Done."

"Then let's go home," I said, looking out onto the suburban street. The banal arrangement of neat lawns and parked cars seemed ill-fitting with what had just happened between us. "All I've gotten today was more questions, and I need some answers."

Chapter 27

Zack had told me to get in the back seat with Lorcan. He couldn't stop meddling, I knew that, but I saw the wisdom in his words when I settled against the seat, the warmth of Lorcan's body against mine.

I'd known him a few hours, but damn did I feel that pull. I took his hand because not touching him physically hurt. I thought he felt it too because he stared into my eyes as his thumb rubbed across my knuckles. No, there seemed to be no postcoital regret there. He leaned forward, kissing me slowly, thoroughly, as Zack turned the ignition. We only pulled back when we were gasping for breath, and even then, we both went back for more.

He grinned at that, his face becoming radiant. So much so, I wondered what the hell had happened to him to make something as small as this change things for him. Initially, I felt ridiculous. We'd known each other for just a few hours, and a bunch of them were not especially conversational, so why did I notice these things? Why did I care?

Because I did. I turned as far as I could towards him within the seatbelt's constraints, put my hand on his waist, then plucked at the hem until I could slide in under his shirt and to him. He let out a little hiss in response, frowning for a second.

I was making something out of nothing. This was just heat, my call, skin hunger. I knew this guy's first and last name, the name of his grandmother, where he lived, and that was about it, and I was gonna get all moony eyed? All my conditioning rose up and shouldered forward, wanting me to pack what I was feeling up and away to protect myself from what was surely coming.

So why did my eyes drop down as I rubbed my hand across his taut abs, feeling the muscles quiver slightly at my touch? Why did my eyes meet Zack's in the rear vision mirror? We hadn't moved yet. He was waiting, but for what? Why was there pride shining in his eyes as he watched me, along with fear and jealousy, but mostly pride? Why would I have been just as happy if the roles were reversed and it was Lorcan driving?

For some reason, as I stroked Lorcan's satiny skin, hearing his breath pick up with every stroke until finally he gripped my wrist tight, the contents of Dad's papers came back. For all their historical record of the ways women had been hurt, judged, or even massacred for displaying any kind of power, right now, they coalesced in my mind as something else. Despite knowing what their future was, the consequences of pursuing their nix nature, they had anyway.

Because that was the thing. People tried to use social mores to condition people into certain forms of sexual and emotional relationships. Some things were normalised and some were taboo. And while that made sense in some instances, like taboos against sexual assault, animals, and grooming or abusing children, others tried to flatten the great myriad of sexual identities into neat little boxes, and woe to anyone who did not conform.

But under repressive dictatorships where same sex attraction equalled death, the human heart persisted and people reached out for those they loved, damn the consequences. When people were raised under strict religious rules that outlawed certain forms of consensual sexual activities, some were forced to step beyond them to be who they were. The human world was teeming with countless attempts to tame love and sex, make it neat and tidy, and support existing power structures.

Just like my family.

"It's either stop or I end up coming buckets all over your mate's back seat," Lorcan ground out. "Fuck, I've never felt anything like this. You hit me like a freight train."

We could do just that. We could turn the car off, go back to that sad little room, and strip off again, be exactly who we were meant to be on that bed, over and over until we collapsed, or I bit him, or any of the many possible endings.

Or we could move bravely into the future. That's what Dad had wanted, what he'd been trying to do for me all this time. I saw him lying on the dais, on the bed in the hospital, watching me leave on the night of my eighteenth. If I was going to honour his memory in any way, it was to find a way for me to be happy.

When I unclipped my belt, when I crawled onto Lorcan's lap, his arms went around me, his lips found mine, and I devoured it, the potential, the possibility, him. Right now, he was mine, I felt that intensely, and only time would tell us if that was a feeling that would stay, one he shared. Then I pulled away, even as his hands grabbed at me and his lips followed, while I turned around and put my hands on the centre console and kissed my mate, my Zack.

"Something's changed," my mate rasped when he pulled away. "Something's different."

"I'm me." He frowned a little. "I know what I am, what I will always be. This is a gift from the Mother, no matter what people think. I get to have you, have all of you in all the amazing, intense ways a shifter can have their mate…" Zack's eyes shone suspiciously at that, boring into mine. "And I get to do that with more than one person."

Our eyes slid over my shoulder towards the backseat before returning to each other.

"Then you know what to do, going forward?" he asked.

"I do. Let's go to the alpha residence, do what's needed."

Chapter 28

"Where the hell have you been?" Mason snapped out the words, taking in me, Zack, and Lorcan in quick succession, breathing deep and then frowning. "You fucking stink of sex."

"That's because we've been fucking, Mase," I replied.

Declan let out a snort of laughter, then tried to cover it with a cough, and I just winked at him.

When we'd arrived back at the alpha residence, the creepers who liked to lurk on my front doorstep had multiplied. There was a big cluster of guys there, all shouting something as we passed, so we'd gone around to the rear carpark, protected by the high back fence. Mason had come barrelling out, glaring at us when we got out of the car.

"Well, you need to stop doing that and start sorting out the bouts, because Aidan has the men riled up."

"Damn, there goes the afternoon DP I had planned," Lorcan drawled, sidling up to me and pressing a kiss to my forehead. I knew he was joking, but a little shiver went through my body at that idea. "Watching your arse stretch to take my knot would be one of life's considerable pleasures. If you take it anally, does that still count as claiming you as my mate?"

His tone was light, teasing, and I knew he was just saying shit to stir Mason, but why did I feel a gush of slick at that idea? Something Mason detected too, if the sudden clench of his jaw was anything to go by.

"Paige, you've kept these men placated by promising them a fight for dominance and the opportunity to ask you out. You need to honour that if we're to have any chance to keep them out of here."

"Fine. Anyone who's a contender can gather in the foyer of the house. If they want to take me out, they can put their offer on the table, and if I respond to any of them, I'll go out with them."

Zack nodded approvingly.

"Zack and Lorcan will attend." That had Mason spluttering. "In their present state, stinking of sex, as you say, because what else would give them hope? They're proof that I put out, and if that's not an incentive for those who want me, then I don't know what is."

It took Mason a while, but finally, he nodded.

"They're going to know what you are." His voice was much softer now. "You marked Zack, made him your mate, yet you've obviously slept with Lorcan. I…" His eyes dropped down. "I wanted to protect you from that."

I felt it, a quiver, a flutter of fear. Wolf shifters valued monogamy above all other things in a relationship. In my mind, I could see the men's faces, the sneers and the sly smiles when they worked it out, what I was. It meant the gloves were off, that I wasn't a 'good' girl, exclusively someone's mate or potential mate.

"I am what I am. I'm still trying to work out what that is, but I'll be damned if I let this town take that from me. It'll be a useful screening tool in my negotiations. If a guy isn't man enough to accept me the way I am, then he can fuck right off." Mason flinched at my words, and so he should. "Doesn't stop them from becoming alpha though. To me, that's a separate issue. I'm not staying after this is done."

I looked around me, at this castle of a house, and it hurt to think about leaving, but what else could I do? It was going to be hard to get acceptance for what I was in the city, let alone here.

"The men aren't gonna like it," Mason said.

He was right—they didn't.

ZACK AND LORCAN moved in closer to the big chair we'd dragged into the foyer. It was enough like the throne kept on the stage to convey the same impression, and I'd sat down upon it with each of my guys standing behind me, the enforcers fanning around the back. And then I told them what I told Mason.

"So, as I said," I continued, "for some of you, becoming alpha is the issue. You have a mate or you know who yours is, and it's not me. You can compete in the fights, show your dominance, come out on top, and me and mine will vacate this building and transfer ownership over to you."

I scanned the crowd, searching for the disgruntled faces.

"As for the rest of you, you know the drill. Deep down, you do. If I have to take this to the whole town… Fuck, if I have to take this to the human police, I will. I'm not yours to win like a meat tray in a pub raffle, no matter what you might think. From my research, my understanding from my father's papers, unlike most wolf shifters, I don't have one true mate, I have several." A rumble went through the crowd. "What you're feeling right now is my call. It's obscuring things, stopping you from being able to find your actual true mate in some cases. It makes you…responsive to me, up until the point I either leave town or I find my true mates."

The 's' in mates seemed to go on forever, a hiss taken up in the crowd until it coalesced in one word—nix.

"A nix, yeah."

The hiss became grumbles, a rising wave of comments, judgements, declarations, all threatening to drown me. I saw the looks, silver eyed and hungry. I saw the balled up fists, the drawn back lips, the flash of fangs, and the snarls, right up until Mason stepped forward.

"Enough!"

There was a reason he'd been Dad's beta. The way they measured dominance here, he was second only to Dad, and when he spoke, his will smashed down on everyone. You could've heard a pin drop.

Just not for long.

"So we should've fought things out that night," Aidan said with a sneer. "We could have settled things there and then. You would have been under the winner before the moon fell."

"And whoever did that would have been raping me."

The quiet was instantly restored. Sexual assault was way more taboo with wolf shifters than humans. I'd have loved to tell you it was due to our matriarchal religion and tradition, but it was more practical than that. Taking what a woman didn't want to give meant you were assaulting someone's future mate. The thought of someone attacking the one person who was your other half was enough to deter almost anyone.

Aidan's sneer faltered at that, the subtle shift in body language of his supporters telling. They moved farther away from him, as if not wanting to be tarred with that brush.

"Zack, Mason, and I will be visiting the local gym today to start the ball rolling on the fight for succession. We still have five days until the nominations close. I'd spend my time bolstering community support to make sure you get to compete. And for those feeling the pull of my call, wanting to see if you're one of my mates?"

I shifted on the chair, taking a deep breath to try and just get this out.

"You can step forward today, make your case. I'll consider the offers, and anyone I feel drawn to, I'll make time for. Just like any wolf shifter, I want to find my mates as quickly as possible. It'll alleviate the…pressure some of you are feeling and allow me to leave Lupindorf, get back to my life."

"No."

Interestingly, it wasn't my suitors who protested, it was my family. Nance strode into the room, my uncles and some of my cousins behind her.

"There's been no consultation, no approval process."

"I don't need it," I said, meeting her blazing eyes.

"You're just going to turn your back on what? Hundreds of years of tradition? Your own family? No, no, this is not—"

"And what's your alternative?" I arched an eyebrow, then scanned the crowd. "Am I not the heir?" There was nearly unanimous agreement. "We tried it your way, we tried to put Selma forward."

"She can step up once you've found your…harem and left."

"No," several men replied in response. Some were already mated and saw this as a great loophole, others wanted my favour. I'd been thinking hard before Mason let the men in, but this was going to work, I could feel it.

"It's done, Nance. I'm sorry for what it means to you all, but the Spehrs are finished in this role. They should've been some time ago. If there's good men who find their mate early in life," my eyes strayed sideways to where Callum stood quietly, "who'd be worthy leaders, why shouldn't they have a chance at alpha? There's a whole world out there where people get ahead based on merit. It's about time this town did the same."

I'd never seen my aunt so angry. Her face was bright red, her eyes blazing silver as she just stared at me. Alan, Bill, they came to stand beside her, some sort of moral support, but what would that do? Their power came from me, and I wasn't going to give it to them anymore. It'd mean a change. I'd need to look into ownership of the alpha estate. Was it in our name or the town's? Maybe a nominal fee or even rental situation could be worked out with the next alpha? I shook my head. We needed to get through the initial steps first.

"So if you are purely interested in the battle for succession, the roster will be drawn up once we know what the town wants. We'll be in touch with everyone who puts their name forward, but you don't need to stick around for this."

I was relieved to see a bunch of men turn and walk out the door, though I noted a few of my potential suitors didn't like the loss of some of their support base, particularly Aidan.

"You're really going to do this?" Nance asked. "Interview…men for you to collect, like you did Barbie dolls? This house—"

"I know the history of this house. I was raised in it like you were."

"Your father—"

"Knew all about what I am. He was trying to find a way for me to accept that and be happy. He stopped me from taking Mason as a mate, knew the expectation of having just one would kill me, just like it did Mum. That's why he thinks she died, Nance."

I watched my aunt flinch at that.

"Go about your lives. Do what makes you happy. Find your mates. Focus on you rather than maintaining a bloody stranglehold over this town. See my family out, Mason. If I'm going to get to the gym in time to start talking about the bouts, I don't have time for this."

That was high-handed and bitchy, but damn, these people knew what I was, could guess at the misery they'd put me through, and hadn't flinched for a minute at the prospect. I couldn't afford to either. Wolves responded to clear and definite displays of power, and I was demonstrating mine.

"Proud of you," Zack murmured, moving in closer and putting his hand on my shoulder.

"If these boys need a demonstration of what they're getting themselves in for, I, for one, am ready and waiting," Lorcan muttered.

My eyes jerked up, shocked, then I laughed. I settled back in the chair as the suitors lined up to make their case.

I was in for a long afternoon.

Chapter 29

I was starting to see a pattern.

We'd ended up moving things into Dad's office. The first few blokes had stumbled through their offers, eyes more on the other guys than me. I got it. Asking someone out was nerve-racking enough, doing it in front of an audience of your peers was crushing.

So everyone had lined up in an orderly fashion as I moved into the office, Zack and Lorcan by my side, and then Mason ushered them in, one by one.

"I... You're so beautiful," guy number twelve, I think, stammered out. He took a step closer, then another, drawing growls from the guys. "I just need to touch... It'll..."

There were those that came in like this—silver eyed, half feral, the bags under their eyes and personal grooming making it clear how they'd been coping since I got home. I felt sorry for them, what they were going through. It was as if I were a bomb that had gone off in this town, laying waste, no matter what I'd intended.

"I need..." The man's words came out a long, drawn-out growl now, his beast too close to the surface. The guys moved in, blocking all sight of me as I called out for Mason to remove him.

For these men, the call I was emitting made them savage, and not in a hot way. All they were aware of was their own artificially enhanced desire, their wants and needs. I was but a receptacle for them, willing or not.

"NO!" the man howled, his fingers going to claws, his face wildly distorted as he almost went to fur. The door slammed open, and Mason and several other enforcers barged in, grabbing the man in a headlock before dragging him away. Mase looked at the way the two guys were hunched over me, ready to attack, and he nodded.

"Who's next?" was all he said though, but he was surprised by the answer.

"I am," Declan said, walking over and taking a seat as the men slowly moved back, letting me see the pleasing way he filled the chair, all laid-back allure.

He was one of the other ones, the ones that had potential. When Declan looked at me, he saw a woman. A woman he liked, if that smile was anything to go by. One he liked the look of, as his eyes slid slowly over my body. So I did the same, cataloguing all the ways that teenage body I'd enjoyed so much back in school had changed.

Then he was all loose-limbed swagger, his body hard and lean, but his shoulders had broadened exponentially and being an enforcer had packed some serious muscle to his frame. He wore a blue button-down work shirt, unbuttoned at the neck, a sprinkling of reddish hair and freckles on the brown flesh revealed there. His jeans hugged a tight pair of hips, thickly muscled thighs, and clear evidence that everything had grown proportionally. He smiled when he caught me looking, pressing down on his obvious erection with the heel of his palm.

"Let me take you out."

"Where, when, why? Usually, there's some details to go with the offer, Dec."

"Where? I'd probably take you to the steak house you always liked. They still do a damn good T-bone, and no one can put a slab of meat away like you do, love. I still get a little hard when I see a girl with BBQ sauce on her chin. Then up to Lasseter's hill before the sun sets. The flowers are pretty this time of year, the place is quiet. We could be alone and…talk."

He waggled an eyebrow at me.

"Why? Because we were good together. You were my girl and my best friend rolled up into one, and I'd be an idiot to not see if that's still true. I didn't want us to break up. You know that."

I did. We'd cried hard about it, holding each other close as we realised what we needed to do. I'd been devastated mainly, not realising what a rock he was in my life until he was about to be taken away. But I'd also been scared of what that would mean and… I looked at the door, the wavy glass inset into the wood. And excited to see what would transpire between Mason and I when I turned eighteen. So there was a weird feeling of coming full circle, to see him sitting there, that cheeky smile on his face, but now with heavily lidded eyes that promised to show me allll the tricks he'd learned while we were apart.

So did I want to go back there? Was there anything other than nostalgia and the echo of teenage feelings?

"But mostly, I want you to go out with me because I want a chance to get to know this Paige and I want you to know this Declan. You were always my favourite people, but you left town, trained to become some kind of kick arse fighter, built a whole other life. You were my best friend and I lost you, and I don't want you slipping through my fingers again."

"PAIGE?" Zack prompted.

I came to with a jerk. A parade of memories of Declan and I together had been taking place, overruling what was right in front of me, but that's where I needed to focus.

"You know what I'm going to say."

"Let me hear the words from those pretty lips. You know I like hearing them. 'Yes, Declan! More, Declan! Give me all the steak, Declan!'"

The guys growled when he threw himself at my feet, landing on his knees, his hands held out in exaggerated prayer. His eyes shone, of course they did, with thinly concealed amusement, and I found myself doing something I hadn't realised I missed—smiling.

"When? You didn't say when."

"Right now, if I could swing it. Definitely tonight. Weather seems like it's gonna hold. We could… What?" My grin spread wider at his hurried discussion before he stopped himself. Still some of the old Declan then, throwing himself headfirst into things.

"Make a tentative booking. I've got some stuff to do first." I waved vaguely at the door. "But I'll make sure to let you know."

"You won't regret it." He moved to come closer, to put his arms around me and hug me like we used to, but he stopped short when he looked at the guys. "How do I…?"

I got to my feet and wrapped my arms around him, feeling and smelling Declan. There was an emotional punch I hadn't expected when I did, but it didn't stop me from burying my face in his chest. When you break up with someone, you try and turn off that tap, of desire, of need, of love and affection. It doesn't stop overnight, if ever, and sometimes the healing process was just learning to live with the fact it never does. I pressed my face to his chest and realised something.

I'd been damn lucky with the men I'd had in my life growing up. Probably a lot to do with the whole pack princess and that, but Dad had made sure I was surrounded by men who cared about me, who valued me. When I hugged Declan, I welcomed that back into my life. It didn't change anything, and yet it did.

"Damn, I don't want to let you go."

I felt the same but forced myself to do so. I may be a nix or whatever, but getting my emotions tugged hither and thither by these men was really intense. I smoothed my hair back from my face and took a step backwards, but he reached down and tipped my chin up.

"So I guess I better let those other losers in, huh?" I nodded. A thumb brushed over my lips. "Save some of those kisses for me."

And then he turned on his heel and walked out, whistling jauntily.

"You OK?" Lorcan asked, taking up the space Declan had vacated.

"It cuts both ways," I said in a low voice. "Being around me seems to hit you hard." He nodded in agreement. "But when there's someone I feel a connection to, it hits me too. I made Zack my mate yesterday. We did…whatever we did today. Why do I think that if I was just allowed to do this on my own, I could spend days, weeks, years finding my mates?"

"The call says otherwise," Zack said. He moved in closer, then stroked my back to soften the words. "The amount of energy you'd have to expend to keep it up, to prevent those you weren't compatible with from just taking what they wanted… I think rather, you'd have been taught to expect and embrace these connections like all shifters do when they find their mates." He lifted my plait and placed a kiss against my nape.

"Fuck 'em," Lorcan declared, brushing his hair out of his eyes. "They want you. Plenty girls make a guy work for it, so make them. You don't owe them shit. If being with us—" He stopped, then corrected himself. "If being with your mate is what you want, then why fucking shouldn't you?"

He looked harried and brittle and ready to slam open that door and kick everyone's arses, which for some reason, I needed to see, even if I was perfectly capable of fighting my own battles.

I nodded, pulling away from the two of them, the small distance between us feeling like way too much. But I went to the door and opened it and gestured for Mason to come in.

"You need to let the crowd know I'll only be able to see a few more."

"Well, they won't like that. We're keeping them controlled through a series of flimsy promises. That gets harder when they get broken."

"Not broken, delayed." I settled my butt against the desk. "It's hard, draining. Guys come in here spilling all their hopes and dreams and fantasies. Some are about me and they cut me to the core, others are totally alienating because they have absolutely nothing to do with me as a person. My father only just died, we only just buried him. I took Zack as my mate yesterday, and if I were any other wolf shifter, no one would expect to see hide nor hair of me for days, maybe weeks." I felt a flush as the memory of yesterday rose. How could it feel like so long ago? My eyes darted to Zack as I remembered sprawling out on the bed together. "But I don't get any of the same consideration?"

"You chose this," he said, his arms crossing his chest.

"God, were you always this much of a cold bastard?" I asked, shaking my head. "How can you act like this? Have you ever felt the pull like I feel? Like not having your hands on them is too much to bear for a second more? Your skin screams for them, to just—"

"Every day," he said flatly, staring into my eyes for a second too long, then shaking his head. "I'll tell them five more, make up some excuse, then go to the gym, Paige. This can't be delayed forever."

"You don't get to dictate to me, Mason Klein." I was using my best lady of the manor voice. "You get to manage security around my dictates. I'll let you know when I'm ready to leave. I stink of sex, and I need to get cleaned up before I go anywhere." I turned on my heel, marching back to the desk. "Send in five with the silver eyes. None of them seem to be viable. I'll listen to the fevered imaginings of their horny little brains, and then the boys and I are going upstairs until further notice."

I sat my arse down, legs crossed, back straight, like a queen, then gave the furious shifter a little hand wave to indicate he could go. He did as I asked without a word, but he slammed the door, hard, as a token act of rebellion.

THE HUNGER GREW as I walked up the stairs. Each step was like some kind of foreplay as the two men climbed ahead of me.

Mason had stayed true to his words, clearing the house of intruders after I saw the last five. They were as I expected, just vomiting freeform montages of their favourite PornHub clips at me and wondering why I didn't climb on and take them for a ride immediately. But I told them politely, firmly, that I wasn't going to accept their kind offers, and while some looked insultingly at Zack or Lorcan for confirmation that they were gonna back me, off they went. I felt tired, irritated, faintly dirty, and not a little soggy when we exited the office, but hitting the stairs was a whole other thing.

Wolf shifters experienced a heat—harder, more intense sexual energy, easier arousal, greater receptivity to their mates. While I was fairly sure mine hadn't hit yet, something was definitely in play. Jeans and sweats were like fucking catnip for me. The soft grey fleece moulding itself to Zack's arse when he moved and Lorcan's jeans quite blatantly hugging his had me stumbling over the top step. The two of them turned as one, then gave me that uniquely male look of satisfaction when they worked out what had happened.

Zack hauled me to my feet, shoving me up against the hall wall and slamming his lips down on mine, right as his hand collared the side of my throat. Yes, yes, this was what I needed. I clawed at his clothes and made little needy noises when they didn't instantly fade away. But he pulled back, pressing his forehead to mine before turning to Lorcan.

"Take her in her room and wash her very thoroughly."

"Yeah? How come you're tapping out?" Lorcan asked, eyes glittering.

"Because it's come to my attention that I'm a micro-managing, manipulative fuck sometimes. I'm not getting between the two of you again until I'm invited."

And with that, he pushed himself off the wall and disappeared into one of the spare rooms.

Things got a little awkward after that. Jumping into bed and making heartfelt declarations to almost strangers would probably do that to a person, but Lorcan just nodded to himself, then held out a hand. He wasn't sure if I'd take it, I realised, feeling the little jolt when our hands connected. But he took the opportunity and pulled me close, tucking my arm under his and then steering me into the room.

THE AWKWARD WAS STILL THERE when he started to strip off. He'd been naked before obviously, but I wasn't really focussed on it like I was now. He yanked off his T-shirt, tossing it on the bed, snapped off his watch, unbuckled his belt, and I watched it all like I could determine the world's secrets in those quick economical motions.

"Changed your mind?" he asked.

I realised he was staring at me, hands on his fly, not willing to take a stitch more off until I did. Actually make that ready to put more on. His hands dropped down, reaching—

"Don't."

He froze where he was, then straightened up, searching my face for answers. Of course he did. I was acting fucking weird.

"I haven't changed my mind about anything." And wasn't that terrifying? The life of a wolf shifter was always a weird place between thought and instinct, and it was the beast that ruled my mind now. "Especially about the surprise anal. If you're gonna stick around, you'll find I won't budge on that."

His grin was sudden and blinding, dazzling me in its light as he swaggered over, and I just followed every movement. I wanted to suck him up, every move, every muscle, file him away in my brain for retrieval later. But he came in close, close but not touching me, until I was pulled away from the wall and then turned around to face it. His breath was on my neck, his hands sliding down my hips to cup my arse to the sound of his low growl.

"Had some dickheads try shit you weren't ready for?" His thumbs pressed into my glutes, filling his hands with me. "Some trust, a whole lot of patience, weeks and weeks of teasing? I think I could broaden your horizons, love, in ways that'll fucking rock your world."

See, this was what I needed, what I wanted, not some burbled diatribe about how some rando wanted me. His lips barely brushed the skin peeking out the top of my shirt, but I felt every kiss.

He smiled when I turned to face him and trailed a hand down his chest, just feeling all the things we'd rushed through beforehand. He loosened my hair, working my plait free, pulled my shirt up over my head, and then undid my bra with a kind of practised finesse that had my eyebrow jumping upwards.

But he didn't notice. His hands went to my ribs, not daring to go any further.

"You're beautiful."

"So are you."

His smile grew broader as I traced his happy trail, his head tipping sideways as he gave me a nipping kiss.

"We don't have long if the pissed off dude with the massive hard-on for you downstairs has anything to say about it, and coitus interruptus is my least favourite form of sex. How about I wash you down, rub my rigid cock against that fucking fantastic arse, and get you all soapy before I start flicking your clit."

"And what about you?" I forced out, feeling every word he said throbbing between my legs.

"Oh, I'll come with embarrassing swiftness all over your arse. It's the first step, love, marking it as mine."

"We better hurry."

We didn't.

Chapter 30

"Zack Gillespie," the gym owner, Brock someone, said. I forgot his last name, being a little distracted. He was a big, blocky looking guy with reddish skin that had seen a lot of sun over the years, but it wasn't him I was focussed on. "Never thought I'd see a fighter of your calibre in my gym."

"How's it going, Brock? You might not be so happy once we put our proposal to you."

"You want to take over my gym and run the succession fights out of it? Mason's saying the town will foot the bill, so I'm not too fussed. It's well past the 'new year, new you' season, and I've got a few guys who are semi-serious and looking for an opportunity to test themselves. If people didn't know about Gruf's Gym before this, they sure as shit will afterwards. The fire department's already had a chat though. We aren't gonna be able to fit the whole town in here, which will create a fuss. I think we've gotta look at streaming it somehow."

Brock and Zack walked off as they discussed things further, their voices fading away. I soaked in the stinky sweat sock smell of the place, which Brock had tried and failed to mask with the chemical stink of wetsuit cleaner. Weird trick, but the stuff was the best thing for getting the stench of body odour out of synthetic fabric. But while the scents were familiar, comforting, it wasn't until I climbed into the empty ring that I felt it.

Everything seemed to settle. Mind and muscles became relaxed but alert, thoughts stopped, time stopped, my knees softened, leaving me poised, alert. When I heard someone climb into the ring, I turned to face them, pulling my fists up, ready to defend.

We were paranormal creatures, so he shouldn't have looked any odder than the rest of us, but there was something almost unearthly about Micah. He strode across the canvas, sweat glistening across his bare chest, just a pair of athletic shorts on, slung low on his hips, and some wraps around his knuckles. His hair had been pulled back into a short queue, but strands had come loose, falling around his face as he came closer. Those pale eyes bore into mine as he approached, then when he got close enough, he reached out and tapped his knuckles to mine.

That was apparently some kind of sign, and the two of us started to shuffle, dancing around each other, not brave enough to touch yet. Getting the blood up, our lungs pumping, our muscles flexing. This was it, this was being alive. For some reason, my run on the beach, hunting Zack down, came to mind. But this was different. We moved in almost lazy motions, bodies long and loose but ready to snap into action when the time came.

Which was now.

His hands dropped, his smile growing wider. His focus was on my body, not me, and he was just enjoying having me here with him. More fool him. I waited until his hands started to fall and feinted with one fist, while his came up too late to block, leaving his side exposed. I struck like a snake, not hard but enough to give him a jolt, right in his ribs, a cheer going up around the ring. I didn't pay attention to them, just him, which made me wonder if this was his plan all along.

Some of the contenders had tried to do the right thing, offering to take me out to nice restaurants, bring me flowers, shower me with gifts, and there was nothing wrong with that but it just didn't appeal to me. Flowers, however pretty, didn't get my heart pumping or make me feel fucking alive. Micah shot me a rueful smile, those grey eyes flashing fire, more than I'd ever seen in him, but I just got a nod, his fists lifting up. No more cheap shots for me. So on it went.

This was fucking foreplay. After my first hit, no serious strikes were laid. We weren't trying to hurt each other, just get under each other's guard. Get close enough to lay a tap or a toe on the other person, dancing away before they could retaliate, then hunting for the next opportunity while trying to stay clear of their jabs.

He got faster, tighter controlled, more precise in what he was doing, obviously confident I could take it, and I always loved those moments. It was like my opponent finally saw me—hello, daddy issues—and every hard won punch or breath they took to hold me off was some kind of validation.

My head was singing with this pure kind of energy, which was always a worry. Zack called it letting my bullshit get to my head, where the fucking joy of moving your body overrode everything else. I was skipping faster, not slower, and my muscles felt like they were only just starting to burn when he moved like bloody lightning. Ducking under my punch, wrapping his leg around mine, he used the most basic of throws to put me on my arse.

"Fuck!"

I looked up at the artificial lights, hearing how hard my breathing was coming now.

"You gave your excitement its head again, didn't you?" Zack said.

"You OK?" Micah asked, trying not to smirk as he walked over, feet on either side of my legs before putting a hand out to haul me up.

The tilt of my head was my only warning before my feet shot up, landing on his waist, and I used my body weight to shove him down onto the mat with an *oof*, then rolled up and on top him, straddling him and pinning him down.

"I won," the stupid man said.

"Like fuck, you did."

"Nah, I won all right." There were chuckles from around the ring when he bucked his hips up, making it clear what he meant.

Very clear from the sizeable lump there. I snorted at that and made to get up, but he pulled me back down. "Go out with me."

"Ooh…" came some responses from the peanut gallery.

"C'mon, dickheads," Brock said. "The boy's making his play, and he doesn't want you mob watching him when he crashes and burns so get to work."

"You're still looking, for mates, right?" The smile faded, but the intensity in his eyes didn't. "Mason said—"

"Yes."

"To what? Me taking you out or—"

"Just yes."

I got up now, unmolested, then held out a hand to haul him up. His hair tie had come loose in our playing, and something in me wanted to gather all that auburn hair and bind it back again.

This is it, I thought. When I wasn't thinking, wondering, scared about being who I was, I knew. Who I was drawn to, that's what I needed to follow.

"Give me some notice, let me organise things, as I think it's gonna get hectic, but yes, Micah."

"Well, all right."

He grinned and then jogged off, getting out of the ring to finish off his training.

"You're trusting your instincts," Zack said when I walked over, handing me a clean towel. I wiped the thin layer of sweat off, then looked past him to where Lorcan was working a speedball quickly and methodically.

I nodded, then looked back at him. "Seems like the only way. A lot will settle down when I find all my mates, but, Zack, that means a lot less time for you. We only just settled the bond yesterday. You must be needing me."

"I've always needed you, babe, from the minute you walked into my gym. But a wolf on the hunt, he's a slow methodical beast right up until he needs to run." He wrapped an arm around my waist and hauled me up and over the ropes. "A relationship is never easy." He cupped my jaw, kissed my lips to soften his words. "But it's worth it, so fucking worth it. Now c'mon, lemme show you how this is gonna go down."

We sat down with Brock and some of his team, and they spelled out what they thought would work. None of my guys could be involved in the running of the thing, for fear of appearing biased, so a group of older, mated fighters would come in and do compere and referee duties, as well as judge each bout. They were well respected in the community, one was the dad of a school friend, I thought, so that should build confidence in the process.

"Let's do it," I said, and when I pushed myself away from the table, I felt lighter somehow.

"You look like it's chicken and licking day," Lorcan said when we got out to the car.

"What the hell is that?"

"The female equivalent of steak and blowjobs day," Zack replied.

"So I get chicken and you…" I grinned, suddenly able to imagine them doing just that, perched on a chair with a box full of KFC as both of them parted my legs.

Well, that did sound like a great way to spend the day.

"So?" Lorcan asked, leaning against the car, slowly looking me over. "Whaddya wanna do next?"

I looked up at the sky, saw it was starting to go dark, and remembered I'd said I'd get back to Declan about that date.

"Let's head to the pub for a celebratory drink, and I'll contact Dec, see if he still wants to go out."

"Not the fighter?" Zack asked.

"He didn't specify now, and Dec did."

"Well, all right then."

STEVIE'S PLACE was well and truly full, but while the music was still pumping, the chatter died away when we walked in. The guys scoped the place but I went straight up to an empty spot at the bar, and the woman herself met me there with shot glasses and tequila.

"So the fights are set up?"

"How the hell did you hear about that so fast?"

"A few of your referees drink here," she said, nodding to a group over in the corner who were casting a curious eye over us. "So a new alpha will be decided within a week. How do you feel about that?"

"One of them for me?" Lorcan asked, throwing himself down on a stool, but Stevie just looked at me. I let out a long breath and then pushed a shot towards him. He grinned impishly and then downed it. "Your boy wants to play some pool while you're out, do some male bonding or some shit. Make sure I'm OK to keep around or something. He can't like, kick me out, can he?"

He was being a dick, as per usual, but there was a flash of vulnerability there, so I moved in and kissed the tequila off those lips until it was gone again.

"I'm the one you've gotta worry about." For some reason, that put a smile back on his face. "Though I never put much thought into what happens if you guys don't like the other men. You're my fated mates, not each other's."

"Don't much like people scoping me out. Doesn't tend to end well." He shook his head. "But I'm willing to give it a shot."

In response, he snuck another one of my shots, to my spluttering disgust, then ducked out of reach before I could belt him. Zack had the balls set up and a cue in his hand by the time Lorcan ambled over.

"So the harem idea was just a joke. I never thought you'd take me up on it," Stevie said, her eyebrows shooting upwards.

"Me either." I looked at the bar, at the scratches on the polished wood. "I worked it out, what I am, why Dad wanted me to leave." I met her eyes, not wanting to shy away from her reaction. "I'm a nix, Stevie."

She was slow with it, just a nod at first, her eyes not leaving mine, but there was no rush of disgust or disbelief there.

"Thought you might be. The way the guys are acting… Y'know, in other places, it's not that big a deal. You have more than one mate. So what?"

A long shuddering breath I hadn't realised I was holding came rushing out at that. We weren't super close, but for some reason, her even tone and her words made me feel better. We could do this. Get the fights sorted, pack up Dad's stuff, finish off things with the suitors, and then get the hell out of this town. In the city we'd just be a face among many, with people too busy with their own love lives to care about mine.

"So Lorcan and Zack?" she prompted.

"Zack I made my mate the other day." I took a breath, then another, feeling it, that day rise up inside me again. My eyes slid sideways, across the pub to where he leaned over the pool table, taking his shot. How the hell had I found someone like him? Someone who seemed to know what I needed before I knew I did. "Lorcan…that's still new. And I have to text Declan about a date."

"Damn…" Stevie said, and when I looked back, she lifted her drink in salute. "Well, I'm glad you're embracing what you are. There's no changing it. You can only be true to yourself."

When she downed her glass, I did too, the burn down my throat making me feel like there was something more to this, but I didn't know what.

"Have a few drinks on me." She pushed the bottle my way as more drinkers clustered at the bar. She had other bartenders, but the press was growing. "And ring that other boy of yours." She winked before moving back to deal with her customers, my phone feeling suddenly heavy in my hands. Mason had given me his number before we left, all the enforcers' numbers, but as I scrolled, I felt something I hadn't for some time.

Dad had always ragged on me for being ready and waiting when Dec came to pick me up. *Treat 'em mean and keep 'em keen*, he'd said. But I was keen. Keen to see his smile when he walked in the back door, keen to wrap my arms around his neck, to feel his lips on mine. Keen to be swept out of the house and into a swirl of fun and romance. From watching a movie together, to hanging out at his house playing computer games, to going to parties with our friends, I wanted that and couldn't see why I was supposed to pretend that I didn't. I pressed my thumb down on his contact and initiated a call.

"Paige?"

He picked up on the second ring, sounding slightly breathless when he said my name.

"Yeah, it's me. We finished up at the gym. It's all looking like it's gonna go ahead smoothly. The fights will begin in less than a week."

"That's good, love. You must be feeling like a weight has lifted."

He was walking somewhere, I could hear the crunch of his boots on gravel.

"Yeah, in a way." I sank back against the bar. "I don't know if I'd had time to think about it, but choosing the next alpha was this knife over my head the whole time. Like, what would have happened to us if the alpha thing was off the table?"

I heard his little snort down the line. "I gotta admit, I thought a lot about that over the years. Pretty sure I took a position as an enforcer to be in the running, just in case you came back. But, love…Mason."

His name was a slap, sending a rush of complex feelings through me. Too many to parse.

"This…being a nix thing. It was a shock, but the more I think about it, the more it makes sense. You were always it for me. I've never found another woman I was drawn to like you, but you were always pulled towards more than one bloke. He told me one day when he knotted for you, so I put it from my mind. That meant you were his, that he was your true mate and I had to get my head out of my arse and stop thinking about you."

Something clawed inside me at that, a tightness forming as I saw him doing exactly that, all the girls in town seeing that big frame, those pale brown eyes. My hand formed a fist without even thinking.

"So you never knotted for me?"

I just heard one breath, then another, deeper, harsher.

"Let me come and get you if we're gonna talk about my dick. I wanna see your face and have your scent in my nose if we do. Let me drown in it."

"I'm at Stevie's bar, but I'm just in gym gear. I'm sweaty and too casually dressed for a restaurant. I could go home and—"

"I don't want a date, not really. I just want you, Paige."

"Come and get me. I'll be waiting outside. I just need to tell Zack and Lorcan where I'm going."

"Already in the car, I'll be there in five."

And that was why I could never understand my dad's advice. Dec didn't play games, didn't hide his interest. If he liked you or didn't, you knew. I put my phone back in my pocket and walked over to the pool table.

"Got a hot date?" Zack asked, and when I looked at the two men standing there, I wondered how I could say yes. I still felt the ache of them inside me from what we'd gotten up to together, but I was about to walk away from that and go off with someone else.

But I'd come back, I knew that as much as breathing.

"Yeah, Declan's picking me up. You guys'll go back to the estate after here?"

Lorcan seemed to need to hear that, when we'd connect again, something softening in his stance.

"Figure we'd have a pub meal here." he said. "Play a few rounds of pool, and hopefully, I won't piss your mate off enough to tell you to kick me to the curb."

"Not how it works," Zack said. "Just keep her happy. Piss me off all you like, but keep her sweet."

Both their eyes came to rest back on me, full of a hot sweetness that was almost too much to witness. Why me? Why did I win the wolf lottery? But pondering the origins of good luck was a waste of time. I had it, I just needed to appreciate it.

"See if we have any popcorn," I said. "We can sit down, watch a movie, and make out like teenagers. Salty, fatty carbs for the win."

Zack gave me a censorious look that promised six am morning runs in my near future, but Lorcan looked so pleased by that idea, I couldn't regret it.

"Done. Now, should we wait outside with you for lover boy to arrive?"

"He said he'd only be five minutes, so he's probably already there."

I walked around the table, reaching up to kiss Zack, hearing the chatter in the pub die down slightly when I did so, but that was nothing compared to when I kissed Lorcan. I didn't care. It meant I could hear the whistle of his breath, the small groan in his chest all the more easily, but when I pulled away, I just walked out, not bothering to look at how people reacted.

MAYBE IT WAS that obliviousness that got me in trouble next.

Declan hadn't arrived yet, but night had. The air was cooler, the breeze tangling in my hair as I stepped out, while people were walking up the street towards the pub, one pulling away from the pack.

"Paige?"

I looked up at the sound of my name, thinking it was Declan with all the need injected into my name, but it wasn't. Aidan's mates hung back, watching the two of us as the big man came and loomed over me.

"Didn't recognise you, out from under all those enforcers. You coming for a drink?"

I needed to get onto that Jungle group, talk to some other nixes, and find out how the hell this worked, because that same light, bright feeling I felt around Declan or Zack or Lorcan rose when he moved in closer. He was a really solid bloke, the muscular breadth of his chest apparent in that tight T-shirt, and his dark blond hair looked so soft, my fingers itched to stroke it, while his face was all open, sweet, invitation.

So why did I take a step backwards?

His expression darkened slightly, but he smoothed that away quickly. But not quickly enough.

"Everything OK, Paige?"

I looked across the footpath where Dec was hanging out the driver's side window, looking across the roof of his car at me.

"Yeah, I'm good." I turned back to the other man. "Look, Declan asked to take me out in that session today, so I need to honour that."

"Fair enough." His grin was quick, allaying fears he was going to create a scene. "Maybe I'll get my chance tomorrow. You're hearing contender's propositions?"

Well, I was now.

"Yeah, I'll get Mason to send word around. Though being a weekday, I guess it'll have to be after work."

"Oh, I don't think anyone's boss would deter them from fronting up whenever and wherever you wanted them." Those almost amber eyes held mine, heat flaring deep inside them. "I look forward to talking to you more later."

I almost shook myself, feeling really weird when that intense gaze was redirected back to his friends. They walked inside the pub, leaving just me and Declan on the street.

"Hey, you look all shaken up."

A warm hand went to my shoulder, and I found even warmer eyes when I looked up.

"Let's get out of here, Dec."

"I thought you'd never ask."

Chapter 31

They said that smell was powerful when bringing back old memories, and I saw the truth in that when I got in Declan's car. It wasn't the same car, since back then, he'd had a beat-up old station wagon filled with school books and fast-food wrappers. Now he had a big ute, and it was in a considerably neater state, but it still smelled of him. He shot me a shy look when I got in the passenger seat, watching me all too closely as I put on my seat belt. This was just a car, we were just two people going for a drive, something we'd done so many times before. But when his hand went to the ignition, his other to the steering wheel, of course, memories of just what we used to get up to in the old car surfaced.

The motor was humming, the car ready to take us out on the road, but we just stared at each other. Did he feel his hand sliding up my thigh as we devoured the other person's mouth in the messy, undisciplined ways only horny teenagers could manage? Did he feel that thrill of excitement as he traced the elastic of my underwear, asking for unspoken permission, which I moaned into his mouth? That prickle as his hand slid underneath, just letting me get used to the feel of a foreign finger where no one else's had been as my core clenched in anticipation of what was going to come next. The parting of my thighs, that sharp intake of breath from both of us when his finger swiped through my sodden folds.

"*You're wet...*" *he hissed, like I'd just given him the greatest gift.*

Of course I was. For all his complaints about giving him boners in class, he had me dripping on a regular basis. I'd been horrified when my slick first came in, then even more traumatised when Dad tried to explain why I suddenly was sporting wet knickers. Nance had stepped in to give me a brisk but damning over-view of shifter biology and the expectations on me as heir.

"*Your slick is the Mother's gift to your true mate. You should keep it for him only,*" *she'd said between tightly pressed lips.*

Maybe that was why teenage Declan had looked stunned to find me sopping wet for him, his fingers growing bolder, his eyes widening as I became even wetter.

"*Fuck, Paige...*" *he'd groaned, brushing my clit, then sliding a finger inside me, and my eyes had rolled back as he did so. I'd made myself come before, the internet being way more useful about that than my family, but this had felt so different. That unfamiliar touch stirred something deep in me that—*

"OK, what the hell are you thinking about? Because my dick feels like it could smash diamonds. Your scent just went into fucking overdrive."

I looked up at the here and now, Declan, and saw the man not the boy after a few blinks.

"Sorry, just getting in your car reminded me of what we used to get up to."

"Fuuuck... I was trying real hard not to think about that. I figured we could grab some takeaway and go up to the lookout and talk."

"You mean Makeout Point?"

"Shit, maybe we need to..." His voice trailed away, his eyes dropping down to my mouth and staying there. "Tell me what you want to eat, because if I don't start driving soon, we're gonna give the patrons of Stevie's bar a damn good show."

"Chicken," I blurted out, then smiled when I remembered Lorcan's words. "I feel like chicken."

. . .

ONE OF THE things about being a passenger is you're free to look around while driving. My eyes catalogued the way Dec's big hands spanned the steering wheel, and I assumed my forearm fetish had somehow been circulated amongst the guys, because he wore an old soft flannel shirt with the sleeves rolled up. I watched the way the muscles flexed as he turned the wheel.

"How fucking hungry are you?" he asked.

"Um…hungry. Why?"

"Because if you keep looking at me like that, I'm gonna assume you want me to feed you my dick, not KFC." His eyes were darker when they looked at me. "This is a date. I'm not supposed to get my cock out on a first date."

I thought about what had happened earlier today, then snorted before schooling my face into hopefully a more neutral expression.

"Eyes on the road, got it."

"And here was I hoping you'd misbehave so I could spank that arse," he muttered to himself as we pulled into the drive-through.

"What is with everyone focusing on my arse?"

"So it's not just me. Good to know," he shot back, then wound down the window and ordered us some food.

"C'MON, let's get out of the car and go sit on one of the picnic tables," Declan said when we got to the lookout that showed you a panoramic view of town. "Otherwise, there's gonna be a whole different kind of finger licking going on."

His voice was dark and assertive, which deviated enough from the old fun-loving Dec that I stared up at him when he took my hand and led me to the picnic area.

"You sit there, I'll sit here," he ordered, pointing to either side of the table.

"What are you worried about? That I'll jump you?" I laughed as I looked through the bags of food, pulling out items I'd have to run my arse off for later.

"I never forgot about you, not ever, but when you were away, I missed your laugh and the look on your face when we were being dickheads together. I used to ask your dad how you were doing and snoop the gym Jungle page to see pictures of you looking like a fucking bad ass. But since you got back..." He shook his head, a limp chip dangling from his fingers. "You asked if I knotted for you?" I looked across the table at him and found it hard to hold his gaze, all that lazy good humour scrubbed from his face. "It came in when I saw you that first time, at the house. I saw you, Paige, all grown up and looking like you could kick everyone's arse, and damn, did my dick swell. I thought it was just memories, connection, but when I took a piss, I knew."

He shook his head, as if that would be enough to throw off this mood, grabbing a chicken burger and taking a bite, but I just waited, watched, knowing there was more to come.

"That story I told at the wake, of you and me? It was a regular feature in my spank bank, I don't mind saying, but fuck, I've never said a word about that to anyone. It was so hot and desperate, the way it is when you're a kid, but suddenly, I was feeling the same damn way—painfully aware of where you were, how close, and breathing in your scent. I know why Mason's such a hard-arse, even if I don't agree with his methods. This doesn't change what you're doing, how you're dealing with us, but Paige..." He looked up at me, his eyes fading silver. "We burn for you."

"You're hard all the time?" I asked, feeling twin thrills of fear and arousal. He nodded. "You come hard, but you're ready to go again minutes later?" Another nod. "And it just doesn't stop, does it?"

"If you knew what it took to prevent myself from throwing you in the backseat of my car, you wouldn't have looked at me like that. It isn't your problem, love. Just wanna be clear on that. I dunno if the other guys have it as bad, because my mind's flat out digging every scrap of memory of your body touching mine, pulling them up, and presenting them like nuggets of gold at the worst possible time. Memories of you."

I sighed, feeling my muscles tense, ready to fight an enemy I couldn't see. I hated this, my call or whatever. It was messing with people's heads, people's lives. Surely there was a better way than driving half the blokes in town mad.

"It's this nix thing. It'll go away once I work out who my mates are. Then everyone can get back to their lives."

I heard the burger plop down on the paper, the hiss of his breath.

"You know what? When I heard about it, being a nix, you know what I felt?"

"What?" I asked, a glutton for punishment, my appetite dead as I stared down at the greasy food.

"Relief. There's something I'd carried with me, known, since we broke up. Do you know what that was?" I shook my head. "You loved me." It was a declaration and a question all at the same time, and when I looked up, his eyes speared into me. "You loved Mason. For ages, I couldn't work out how the Mother got it so wrong. Usually, if you got that deep with someone, you knew they were your mate. If you didn't, if things didn't progress, then you pulled back and knew it wasn't right. You didn't pull away from me because you didn't love me."

I stared into his eyes, all those painful ghosts of feelings I'd felt when he'd finally broken up with me rising.

"You pulled away because you loved him too and he was ready to be alpha."

The ambient sounds of the bush setting slowly seeped in. The creak of cicadas, the hush of wind in the leaves, the late chirp of bird calls. They dragged me back, out of high school, out of heartbreak, back to here.

"I'm sorry. I'm the fun guy, and here am I, vomiting my feelings up everywhere. Eat your food and I'll take you back. We can try this again another time if you like."

I reached across the table, taking one of his hands in mine, staring down at the freckles across the back, the slight smattering of ginger hair, and just held on. Did that small feeling of connection make him settle the way it did me? I hoped so. But when he turned his hand over to thread my fingers through with his, it wasn't enough.

We'd held each other through so much of the travails of being teens, that was what had been hard about us breaking up. It meant I couldn't reach for the person I'd been reaching for all this time, that I was in this on my own. Mum had died when I was so young and Dad and my family had clustered so tightly around me, I hadn't felt her loss that much, so losing Declan was the first one I really remembered. It was so bloody confusing, walking away from one part of myself to go towards the other.

"I think you're what clued Dad in that I was a nix," I said finally. "He saw how devastated I was, yet emotionally, I had already been reaching out to Mason. That shouldn't happen. I saw it as one thing or another, because that's how I was raised, but what if it'd been different? What if you were my boyfriend all through school and you hadn't been feeling the pressure to become alpha? What if you could've just been the warm, funny, sexy guy who was helping me find my feet as a woman and Mason was the hands off, solid rock he always was? Then when I was ready..."

He wouldn't have seen it the way I did—Lorcan and Zack's bodies replaced by his and Mason's, coming together in my bedroom at home once I was eighteen, nineteen, whenever I felt it was time. What would it have been like, shared between two men that loved me, stroked and teased until I opened, ready for them, taking one swollen knot and riding it to completion, then another? But when I looked up, I saw the aftermath of something similar.

"That kinda hurts, that that choice was taken from me."

He moved now, coming over to my side, then collected me up and pulled me into his lap. It was funny. I'd been trained to be self-sufficient and confident in my ability to look after my own problems, but there was something in me that loved this—feeling so small and vulnerable when they held me. I wanted to be able to kick arse, and I also wanted big strong hands that stroked my hair and my skin, settling me against them. I wanted us to be strong together.

"I'd have done anything to have what you described, you know that, right? I let you go because I thought——" I shifted in his arms, silencing him with a kiss. We couldn't do this, get lost in the past, in memories, because while teenage Paige and Declan were gone, we were still here.

It was gentle at first. We were grieving, again, and our mouths told that story. First, there was that rush of Declan, of that tap I'd so firmly turned off rushing back in again. He tasted the same yet different, and I needed to know exactly how. Then we pulled back, our foreheads pressed together, just breathing for a moment.

"Fuck, I never thought I'd get to do that again. Never. I locked it all down tight, thinking there's no way you'd go out with me again."

"Dec…"

"This doesn't have to go anywhere. I might not be your mate, but having this, just this…"

I ran my fingers through his hair, then down to that thick beard.

"We're gonna see where this goes," I said. "You might have to come back to the city with us."

"I'm there, love. One hundred percent. Already talked to a cousin of mine about some possible work at a workshop he owns."

"You thought about this?" I asked with a smile.

"You know me. I don't hold back shit. I wanna know." His grin faded. "I have to know. Am I just buzzing around, bugging you, or is there…?"

He didn't want to say the words, and neither did I. It was too soon to know, with him, with Lorcan, with whoever I might take as a mate, but considering the possibility he wasn't? I didn't want to think about that. Seemingly of the same mind, he swept me onto my feet and dragged me back to the carpark.

"We can't just leave that mess there."

"We'll come back for it. We're not done yet, not for a while."

He got inside the car, turning it on and leaving me blasted by the headlights, and a familiar tune came from the stereo.

"No," I said, shaking my head and backing away, but he just grinned as he swept me into his arms, proceeding to move my body into the form Mrs Pfister insisted we practice before the school formal. "No, I suck at this. You know it, I know it."

"You just never loosened up enough to let someone lead." He pulled his body against mine. "You can stand on my toes if it helps."

"You better have work boots on."

"Steel caps," he said with a grin. "I'll be fine. Just let yourself go loose and feel the music."

That was what Pfister had always said, and maybe if she'd done so with a low-down growl, I'd have listened. Right now, I looked up into those eyes, saw that slow smile, and then we moved.

Zack thought it hysterical that I could master fighting steps way more easily than dance ones.

"We need you doing capoeira, babe."

I'd just flipped him off and then focussed on taking him down. But I came back to the here and now, feeling the rhythm in our movements like I did an opponent's strikes, trying to do as Declan said and let go and follow him.

"That's it." He nodded encouragingly, placing my arms up around his neck so our bodies were pressed even closer, his hands sliding down to my hips. "You're dancing."

"I'm swaying with you while you dance."

I yelped when he dipped me down, his smile growing wider as I wriggled, then he yanked me back before swirling me around. I remembered this part, that wild swing round and around, until finally, the song ended and we were left panting. He picked me up and put me on his bullbar, stepping between my legs in the next moment.

"Feels so good to have you back in my arms, love." He moved in closer, slowly, surely, waiting for my hand to snake out and grab him around the neck before he closed the gap. I frowned for a second, just stroking the slope of those broad shoulders, the thick bush of his beard.

"Those arms have changed a lot since we were in high school."

"Yeah?" He whipped his shirt off. Damn shifters, always ready to get naked at a moment's notice. "Better?"

"You're fishing for compliments." My voice was a growl, but my hands? They were curious, stroking over the muscles, the scatters of freckles, sliding down his sternum, the other hand reaching out and tracing the hard bead of his nipple.

That was the thing, wasn't it? I'd never have completely new sex with Declan. I knew his lips would fall open when I pinched it. He'd told me he felt it in his cock when I did that during a make-out session. But there was enough different, fresh, freeing about this that my gasp matched his. I stared into his eyes as I gave it a solid tug, seeing his hips thrust forward, his hand reaching out to bring my lips down for—

The ring of my phone cut through the night air, the music, the hum of the car engine. I shot him an apologetic look as I pulled it out and saw an unknown number.

"Paige Spehr speaking," I said when I answered the call.

"Ms Spehr, sorry for calling you at this hour, but I thought you needed to be the first to know. This is the coroner's office. We examined your father's body before it was interred as a precaution, human rules and all that, as well as taking the usual battery of blood tests required. We didn't expect to find anything, so we didn't bother to mention it, but…"

Everything fell away as I waited for him to finish the sentence.

"We've reason to believe your father died as a result of foul play. I understand the prohibitions against exhuming bodies, but I really feel…"

The phone dropped to the ground, my fingers hanging limply by my side, while Declan said something, did something, but all I could hear was the erratic beat of my heartbeat thudding in my ears.

"Paige? Paige?"

Declan's face swum up into my field of vision, but I just shook my head. *No, no, no,* that was what beat in my blood.

"Mase, I need you up here, now. Yeah, I'm with Paige at the lookout. Right, well, hurry."

Chapter 32

One of the mindfulness meditations Zack had taught me to do was imagining your thoughts as dead leaves falling on a flowing river. The thoughts passed by without comment, without response, while realising they always will, but you kept bringing your brain back to the exercise as a way to try and train it to be less caught up in the 'reality' of your thoughts. Well, it appeared I'd been too successful. When a large hand steered me into the local hospital, I was the leaf, thoughtless, empty, dead, and I was pushed along by the current that was them.

"It's come as quite a shock."

I blinked, saw that Mason, Declan, and some guy sitting behind a desk were all staring at me, prompting something inside me to focus.

"The alpha was a picture of health when Paige left town five years ago. She had no reason to expect him to die so suddenly, so she's taking it very hard," Mason explained.

"Of course, and her assumption was actually a good one," the man said. *Coroner*, my brain supplied belatedly. *Brian...someone*. "I suspect the alpha had been administered a drug called coumadin. The tests they did when he was admitted showed abnormal clotting rates consistent with being prescribed this drug. It's used for preventing blood clots in those with atrial fibrillation and other conditions that would cause your blood to abnormally clot, and while it can be dangerous if not used correctly, it's very effective. The problem is there's no record of Alpha Spehr having been prescribed the drug. With shifter health and healing powers being what they are, there's little use for them locally until our elders get to a very advanced age. The alpha was still in the prime of his life." The man's hands formed a steeple. "This puts me in a difficult position. Our samples are all tested in human labs, and the findings are sent as an alert to me and human authorities. We're going to need to bring the local police in on this, if only to keep the human ones from intervening."

"I'll contact the senior sergeant in the morning, if that's all right," Mason said. "I need to get her home, get her safe. The police and the coroner's office will have our full cooperation, but…"

"I understand. I admit, I was a little concerned, dropping this sort of information on the heir."

The implication being I might wolf out and rip his head off. He couldn't have been more wrong. My beast felt completely divorced from me right now, because my thoughts and my feelings were as well. I got to my feet, going for the door, and the guys scrambled to say their goodbyes and follow after me. I couldn't take a full breath until I was outside, looking up at the night sky, seeing the slice of Mother Moon left to us.

She was in her slow process of turning her face away from us, and that made perfect sense, so I just stared and stared until someone put their hand on my shoulder and ushered me over to the car.

LEAVING town had been a little like a butterfly shedding its cocoon. If you'd ever looked into it, seen the process on YouTube or whatever, you knew it got quite brutal. Well, mine had been a step worse. I'd had a reliable car, a bag full of junk, and a bank account with some cash, and not much else. I hadn't emerged from my cocoon, beautiful wings unfurling, I'd been ripped from it, forced to get those premature wings flapping, because it was fly or die.

So being taken out of the car, walked back into the enforcers' quarters past the curious eyes of the other men, down the hall to an all too familiar room, it felt like I was taking several steps back. Like I'd returned to the cocoon, pulling it tight around me. Mason laid down on the queen-sized bed that smelled of him and then pulled me after him. I obeyed, because that was what I did. When my world fell apart, this was where I went.

"You can leave me with her, call her mates, let them know what's happened."

"No, I can't, and deep down, you know that."

"What? You want to make this about you right now?"

"No, I want to make it about her. She needs us, Mason. I used to think it was just you and was prepared to step back, get out of her way. I only ever wanted her to be happy, and you know that. Deep down, you do."

My eyes closed when I felt Declan's hand on my skin as I snuggled down against Mason's chest, sucking great lungfuls of him in, one after the other of that deep, spicy male scent. The smell of safety, the smell of comfort, the smell of home.

But Declan was right. When he settled down on the bed, cradling his body against mine, fingers pushing back my hair, his scent mixed with Mason's and they became something more than the sum of their parts.

Something that gave me permission to let go.

The next breath was a long shuddering one. I'd thought I'd been doing so well, just taking one step after another, focussing on settling the succession and coming to grips with what I was. It was all about just keeping on moving forward, I'd thought.

Well, I was about to go screaming back.

The tears felt like acid as they fought their way free, my ribs shaking, my whole body tensing against them. But they leaked out anyway in poisonous trails that scoured my skin, and letting one out meant letting them all out.

"It's OK, Paige," someone insisted, but they fucking lied. It wasn't, he wasn't. He was dead, not due to some physical malfunction of his brain or body but because someone decided to take him from me. My fangs snapped down, and my fingers went to claws, fabric shredding underneath them.

"Paige…Paige!"

One set of arms went around me like bands of iron and held me still, stopping me from striking out at the shadowy form. He smelled like home, but it was a lie, all of it. This wasn't home, it was some kind of fucking trap for wolves like me, caging me in. My first instinct when I saw Dad die was to run and keep on running until I couldn't anymore, and I should've honoured that. She knew, deep down inside, my wolf, she knew this wasn't right. But I'd let myself be lured back and sucked in by them. I thrashed against my bonds, despite the desperate sound of my name repeated over and over. I wasn't going to do this, lie down, cuddle between them, and cry piteously for my murdered father. I wasn't.

Because that'd make it all real. Instead, I did the only thing I knew how to do—come out swinging.

"Let her go," came the steely order from the darker one. *Mason*, my beast said with a sneer that matched the one on my face, but he just stared me down, eyes shining like the fucking moon.

"Yeah, let me go," I snarled, my wolf in my voice. "Open the door, Mase."

I spat the last word, but he just shook his head, dodging when a clawed hand went smashing into the wood where he'd just been.

"He was murdered. You were his beta. Your whole fucking purpose was to protect him and keep him alive."

Mason's head jerked like my fist had actually connected, but I was a fighter, so I knew how to go for the low blows.

"I know."

"Someone came into this house and gave him…whatever that was."

"I know."

"They took him. They took Dad. They looked at him, at all he did and said to try and help people in this motherfucking shithole of a town, and they said no, no more of that. You had to have known. You had to have your suspicions."

But those lips remained resolutely closed.

"Let me out of here. I'm not staying in the place with the very people who failed to help him when he needed it."

"No."

"Mase…"

"Shut up, Declan."

"I'm not asking, I'm telling you," I said, ignoring the little aside between the two men. "Let me out so I can do what you failed to do, or I will fucking hurt you. I'll find them."

"Find who, Paige?" Declan snapped, my eyes jerking sideways. "You're hurting and you don't want to be. You think we don't feel what you feel? That we don't want the person who did this to die screaming? You need time to process, to let the pain inside you out. Give it some time, and then when heads are clear, we hunt them, together."

"Not together," Mason insisted.

"No," I nodded to Mason, "you're fucking right there, just not in the way you think."

My attention was wrenched back when I heard someone at the door, Mason moving to block me, but he was too slow. I struck him hard with an elbow to his ribs, taking advantage of his faltering stance to push past him and the concerned enforcers clustered around the door. I strode out of the room and down the hall to the sound of Mason shouting, "Don't let her leave!"

They hunted me, making my wolf fight to come to the surface, and I snarled my scorn when they fanned out, surrounding me.

I knew I was just acting out. Like an overtired kid, I was lashing out at those closest, rather than the real villains, but I had a child's control right now. I hadn't fought my beast this hard since going through puberty. Because in her mind, this was all too simple—hunt those who dared harm the pack and take out anyone who got in the way.

I threw back my head, let out the mangled gargle of a howl an in between form allowed, letting everyone, every fucking citizen of this town, hear my challenge. I would find who did this, and they'd better be quivering in their little hole right now, because when I got my claws on them...

"Fuck, we're gonna have wolves pouring in here at that," one of the men said.

"Forget that, focus on her," Mason ordered.

"You need to let me out," I said between pants. "I need to get out."

"Not like this, not yet. You'll hurt someone and hate yourself for it, or worse, you'll hurt yourself," Mason said, positioning himself between me and the door out.

"You can't protect me. You can't protect anyone."

"Maybe," he tilted his head in my direction, "but I'll never stop trying, and you know that. You have to go through me to get out of here."

"Fucking gladly." I fell into a loose stance, despite my muscles locked tight.

"Whaddya wanna fight him for?" someone drawled. When I turned around, the one who'd taken me down in the ring stood there. *Micah.* He smirked, all insolence, drawing a long snarl from me, but those grey eyes just flared brighter. "You already put him on his arse. Just like I did you." I growled, my teeth baring. "You reckon you're all that, city girl who learned to fight?"

"Jesus, Micah, shut the fuck up," Declan hissed.

"You gonna be all pack princess? Have the fellas let you beat them up for thrills because they're dying for just one little touch from you? Let you keep that illusion that you're hot shit alive?" He tilted his head, that shit-eating smile spreading across his face. "Fight me, and if you can put me down, you can walk out of here."

Anger was a fire that burned up everything indiscriminately, and I was a raging bushfire out of control, but right then, it all narrowed down, focusing on Micah. That arrogant smirk, those big fists smacking into each other. If he thought he was going to take me out, he had another thing coming. That grin only widened when I took a step towards him, his hands going up, gesturing for me to come closer like a dog. I came all right, running from a standing start, my wolf stretching within me as I made my way. She shifted when I did, when I threw my body into a flying kick, arrowing in for that smirking face.

Trouble was, he was smirking for a reason.

At the last possible moment, his foot snapped up, smashing into my guts, aborting my strike and leaving me to fall heavily onto the ground. Every scrap of oxygen had been forced out of my body.

"Paige!" Declan came stampeding over, but the others held him back.

If I'd thought I was in pain beforehand, I knew how wrong I was. My body was in riot, desperately working to suck more air in, but it felt like I'd forgotten how. My diaphragm ached, and my throat constricted because I was trying to draw it in too fast, forcing me to purse my lips. It was counterintuitive, but it always worked.

"Flashy, princess," Micah said with a broad grin. "Leaves you fucking open though, doesn't it? So you giving up? I fucking stink and wouldn't mind rubbing one out in the shower before bedtime."

"Fuck you…" I rasped, getting to my feet.

"Well now, that'd be even better." He looked me over with insulting slowness, as if imagining how that'd go as I raised my fists. Over my dead body would be how it went.

He bounced on the balls of his feet, hands up, looking like he wanted me to hit him rather than caress him, and I was all too happy to oblige. I struck out, and he countered, blocking my blow with the flat of his arm, so I was moving on, striking again and again from different angles, with different fists, and he intercepted every single one of them. My muscles bunched, trying to get faster, meaner, harder, and he did the same with a grin. I watched the sweat trickle down his face, saw the shake in his arms, but he never let a hit land. His grin just got nastier, his wolf's fangs in his mouth now when I backed off. I was just wasting energy. He wanted to follow, I could see it in the flash of those silver eyes, which gave me an idea.

I turned on my heel and walked to the door.

It was the ultimate insult to another wolf. They weren't threat enough for you to consider guarding your back against, and anyway, I wanted out the door, not him.

But I got him nevertheless.

I grinned as I heard the feet, the shout of my name to watch out from my loyal mate.

Mate?

That almost derailed me, but the moment his hand hit my shoulder, mine locked around his wrist, pivoting under him, pulling him off balance and tossing him over my hip.

I could see now why he'd grinned. I liked the look of him sprawled out on the ground too, that smirk wiped clean. He was much prettier without it. I walked over, smiled his smile, and then moved past him.

Except his hand whipped out and grabbed my ankle, yanking it out from under me and sending me smacking down across him, which was where it all got ugly.

I'd been trained and trained well, and so had Micah. We had skills, but they weren't being used right now. Our beasts were too close to the surface to use mere monkey fighting tricks. His fangs were bared to me and mine to him as we got in each other's faces, claws raking at the other's flesh. The scent of his blood stung my nose, and it made my eyes go red.

"They're gonna fucking kill each other! Get the stun guns!"

But they weren't worth paying attention to. I was in another cocoon now, a brutal, snarling, slashing one where all my rage was safe to let out. We rolled, end over end, kneeing, scratching, biting, tearing, yanking hair, until finally, it all stopped.

I was over him, crouched like an animal, my fangs at his throat, listening to the rapid tattoo of his heart, right before I was about to stop it.

"Fucking hell! We—"

"Back off," Micah croaked, flapping a hand, but that was all he moved. My fangs tightened a tiny amount, but he just reached up, slowly, so slowly, and then lightly brushed through the brambles of my hair.

It wasn't just that which brought me back, my human side

fucking aghast at what I'd done. As it came online, it rapidly catalogued all of the ways I was hurt and had been hurt. Including the much heavier, much denser one inside my chest.

Daddy…

I yanked myself back, still straddling Micah's hips, and saw the mess I'd made. Tears formed as I saw the bloody carnage I'd made of his chest, his arms. They were healing rapidly, the cuts and the bites, but some of them would scar.

"Jesus…"

I went to scramble back, away from this, this aberration, but he gripped what was left of my shirt and held me there.

"Don't." He shook his head, sharp and decisive. "You need to feel strong. You're afraid when you don't. What you heard, you can't fight or fuck. You can't do anything about it, not yet, and what you'll have to do will be painfully slow and meticulous, searching for clues. Fuck, you might never find out who did it."

My fangs had receded, but they came back at his words. He saw my snarl and nodded.

"Where does that leave you? If the fuck who murdered our alpha continues to walk the earth, walk through this town?"

"Fuck, you punch hard," I said, my hand going to my jaw, feeling a click there, but he just smiled, knowing that I wasn't talking about his hits.

"So do you. Whatever your mate taught you, you're a goddam powerhouse."

He let go of my shirt, and for some reason, I felt a sense of loss at that. It was minor compared to the whirling cyclone inside me, but still. I got to my feet, then bent down, helping Micah to his. Deliberate or not, he ended up standing a few finger's breadth from me.

"I'm sorry." Fuck, that was a lame response to what I'd done, my hand going out and touching one of the bites I'd left on him.

"Don't be." He shook his head, smiling just as bright as he did before, then leaned in to speak directly into my ear. "Next time your fangs are in me, I want my knot buried so deep in your cunt, you'll never get free of me."

At the sound of a growl, mine, Declan's or Mason's, it didn't seem to matter, he pulled away, walking over to the kitchen where I heard the unmistakable crack of a beer can being opened. I didn't have one, didn't have it in me to have one, so I drifted instead to the now unprotected door. I opened it out onto the night sky and looked up at the moon as my feet crunched on the gravel, thinking I was finally free, even if every scrap of emotion was burned out of me. But that's when Mason emerged out of the shadows.

I shook my head, feeling the ache at the back of my skull that told me I had to shift. I'd let my wolf come too close to the surface, let her savagery out, and she wasn't going back in the box just because I said so.

"I'm not a little girl anymore, Mason. You can't keep me caged up for my safety."

"Were you ever?" The hard tone, the sadness there had my eyes swivelling around to meet his, as bright silver as mine were, I was sure. He snorted, then smiled, his fangs on display. "This wild girl, she had to be lurking under all those labels—heir, alpha's daughter, nix. A little savage in a party dress."

"That makes you happy?" I frowned, unable to reconcile that with my father's beta, but maybe that was a label too. Which made me wonder what the hell we all were once we tossed them aside.

I was about to find out.

Zack's car roared into the carpark, and Lorcan was out before the car rolled to a stop, yanking his shirt off, kicking his shoes off.

"What the hell happened?" Zack shouted, people spilling out of the enforcers' quarters now, but I didn't bother to answer.

"You need to run," Lorcan said, looking me over with eyes that were almost black in a way that somehow perfectly contained all the desperation and need in me. Because there was an answering one in him. "We go to fur, go to the forests. Let's go."

His hands were on me, shoving my shirt off over my head as I tried to yank off my sweatpants.

"Paige?"

But no one was answering. Zack hadn't felt it yet, but the others did, my mates, my pack. A howl built in my chest, but I swallowed it down. We would use it to power our paws over the asphalt, over the dirt. Silent as ghosts.

Lorcan pulled me to him and slammed his mouth down on me, forcing still swollen lips apart to admit his tongue, sucking on my bleeding flesh before he stood back and shifted into a huge black wolf. Other wolves milled around the carpark when I turned and stared back at Mason, blood trickling down my chin. He just nodded, something dark and satisfied in that, before he strode over to the gate and slammed his hand down on the button to open it. He was in fur moments later, the biggest black wolf of all, giving us only one look over his shoulder before taking off out the gap.

Fucker.

Instincts yanked me off my feet and after him, taking fur, a black wolf at my shoulder keeping pace, others, some grey, some pale, some reddish. We ran and ran, Mason's wolf's tail a red rag waved in the faces of bulls, our paws eating up the ground beneath us but not fast enough.

Cars beeped and veered as we moved through town, but on we ran until all the man stuff fell away and there was just this—grass, dew, bugs flying up in our wake, their chirrup marking our passing, and the moon.

It made sense that we'd return to that clearing, the one where I'd howled my pain at my father's passing. The need to do so again, a cry of a different kind, was harsh inside me, but I'd come back here and tell the moon of my father's betrayal when I had his killer's blood in my mouth. Instead, I went back to skin as they did, my mates. I knew them now, fur's much clearer, cleaner instincts riding me. The five of them stepped forward, while the other enforcers stayed in fur, forming a ring around us as I moved closer. Lorcan stepped up first, but Micah was only seconds later. Declan's eyes darted around the circle, but he took his step in confidently enough. Zack just nodded. He was already there, inside me, thrumming like a struck string. And then there was Mason.

Did anyone else see the fight in him, with all those tiny little micro expressions? Did they see under that mask of dutiful beta, of good man, of brother? I did, lifting my chin and staring up at him, proud as a queen, because I was his and he was starting to realise it. It felt like the earth shook when he stepped in, joining his brothers in more ways than one. And now it was my turn.

I walked into them, into their bodies, felt their fingers on my skin. I leaned up, moving close enough to kiss but didn't, and just breathed them in until I came to a stop. They wanted it, felt the ache for it, my bite, but there was only one who would get it tonight. A dark star in a night sky, Lorcan hung back slightly as if not entirely sure about putting himself forward, which was maybe what drew me to him.

My hand snaked up and around his neck, his head coming down easily enough. His fingers were still clawed when he grabbed my arse, those sharp points dimpling the flesh there. But he was gentle, too gentle when I kissed him, and soft enough to fall head over heels into and drown me with all that swelled inside him, my teeth aching with need for him.

"Mine," I said, stroking his jaw.

"Yes, fuck yes, Paige."

"On your knees then."

He dropped down with gratifying swiftness, staring up at me, the moon. Right now, I was his Moon Maiden and he shuffled forward to worship her.

His cunning tongue, his hungry mouth, I didn't really need them. I was ready with every fibre of my being, but I tousled his hair as he lapped at my cunt, slurping lewdly on my slick. Then I pushed him down onto the pine needles while the others paid witness, covering his body with mine, and Lorcan's eyes went wide.

"You OK?" I asked, my last vestiges of humanity there. He nodded furiously. "Then tell me you want this."

He grinned, quick and spontaneous, his brows creasing.

"Fuck, I've been waiting my whole life for this."

So I grabbed that thick, hard cock that had served me so well and made him mine in a series of rocking movements, the two of us gasping with each inch that sank in.

"Jesus…" His back arched as my body shifted, readying to take his knot. He kept babbling that as it eased in, stretching me to my limits, to the point where I began to doubt I could take him, and then it was done. I panted, feeling him locked down hard, his eyes wide and glowing like the moon, so bright, I finally had to shut mine and just feel.

They invaded my body like they did my heart. I took them into me, locking them inside me, as they did me. Lorcan… Lorcan came rushing in as the mate bond snapped around us, as I drowned in him, a flood of pain and shit, of teeth clenching tenacity, and finally, of love.

When I opened my eyes, he'd rolled up into a seated position, arms wrapped around me as we rocked together. Just tiny little movements, but it felt like the world moved with them. A tear fell free as we did, his finger reaching up to trace its path, and then he thrust up.

I don't know how to tell you what happened, it was all such a rush. He was a complete stranger and my mate, and he was buried inside me, my cunt clutching at him, like I needed to grip him harder, hold him closer, but he just shook his head. His smile, infrequent and all the more beautiful for it, came as he stared at me.

I heard a wolf howl far away, the sound growing louder, higher as I curled my body around his, pushing his head to one side. I felt my fangs snap down, the saliva fill my mouth as he filled me, driving up harder and harder, his strokes growing ragged and spasmodic.

"You're gonna come for me now, beautiful girl, and then you're gonna mark me hard, mark me deep, make my body ache for you like my fucking heart does."

So I did and he did, our bodies exploding the moment my fangs sank into him, pulsing and pulsing, one orgasm triggering the next and the next, until finally, when the moon was lower in the sky, we had no more to give.

A black wolf with eyes like the moon sat at the edge of our clearing, but when I noticed it, it turned and ran away.

I was lightheaded, loose kneed, and stumbling when I got to my feet, but hands shot out to hold me up.

"Fuck," someone said. "Anyone think of bringing a car out with us? Because it's a long way to walk back to town."

Chapter 33

When we finally got back to the house, I said a few words to the enforcers, thanking them for their forbearance.

"You've found them," Will said, "your pack. The hot and cold running Viagra feeling seems to be settling down. You're a mad woman, being prepared to take some of those fuckers on, but…" He nodded, and some of the others did too. "It's good. Look at you. You're all glowing. Micah looks like a fucking streetlight."

"Get fucked, Will," the man in question snapped back.

"We'll be able to strap him to a bullbar and use him for a spotlight when we go rabbiting," someone else said.

"As I said previously, get fucked."

And with that, they all filed inside to celebrate with the time-honoured Australian tradition of getting pissed. Especially when I said they could ring Stevie and order some more piss on my tab.

"Did you guys want…"

I was gonna ask them if they wanted a beer or something, anything to process what had just happened, but with that dense, implacable gaze they all had, focussed entirely on me, I could see that wasn't needed.

"Just you," Lorcan breathed into my hair, rubbing his chin

against it, like a cat marking its territory. "Just you. God, how the fuck do you keep your hands off her and get anything done?" he asked Zack. "I can't get her close enough or touch her enough."

"You just do, because she needs you to. You'll find that more and more, that you'll find depths inside you that you didn't know you had, because she needs them to come to the fore. Everything becomes about her." Zack looked around at the rest of my men. "If you come upstairs with us, you'll sleep curled around her body, will be ready to answer what's in you. You need to be prepared for that."

"I'm in. Have always been in," Declan said. "I'm just wishing I hadn't lost all that time, that we'd known this before."

"One hundred percent." Micah shifted on his feet, those eyes glowing in the darkness again. "I know I've got a way to go, that I don't know her like you mob do, but I want to. There's a hunger in me, in my blood. It can't stay away until I know there's one in her too."

Mason looked slightly uncomfortable when everyone's eyes turned to him, his eyes dropping, his head shaking. My breath stopped, trapped in my chest, waiting for his response.

"The most important thing your dad taught me was hope. I came here a fucked-up, angry kid, and he turned me into a man. He said that wasn't possible without some kind of hope. Hope for the future, hope of finding a mate, hope of moving past the chaos I grew up with and finding something healthy. I took what he meant too literally, thinking I had to have something that was as far away from my parents' relationship as I could to be happy."

When his eyes met mine, it was like looking into a whole other man's gaze. We'd shared caring looks and hot ones, desperate ones and sweet ones, but none of them were like this. It was like finally, finally, he stopped seeing what he thought I was and saw me.

"You know I've always loved you."

No, no I did not know that, and I needed to hear it a lot more to really take it on board.

"I loved you as a little sister first, I guess. Then I loved this woman-slash-child who was taking her first steps towards adulthood, and then you were an adult and I wanted to hold you to me, protect you from all the shit in the world, and lock you away in my heart, where I hurt most for you. But I look at you now and know that you don't need that from me. You're a fighter. That's what I love about you now."

He shook his head.

"I knew that really deep down. Zack didn't make you into something you weren't before, he just taught you how to direct that instinct." A strange smile spread across his face. "I was worried that would terminate things between us. What the hell did I have to offer you but protection? I still don't know, Paige, but all I can offer you is me. That's it, that's all I have."

I felt that night on my skin as I walked towards Mason. I was just a girl, standing in front of a wolf, asking him to love her. And when he reached out and pulled me into his arms this time, dropping his mouth to mine, everything I'd ever wanted that night came rushing in. He cradled my cheek with his hand, trying to pause and just look at me, but we couldn't.

I'd needed to kiss Mason Klein every day since that night five years ago, and I hadn't been able to. A wave of resentment threatened to swell, but it couldn't get traction, not when he was here, now, in my arms, touching and kissing me.

I'd need to deal with it, the pain, specifically the pain caused by his goddamned stubbornness. I needed assurances and apologies and, to be honest, proof that he wasn't going to pull that pigheaded bullshit again. But not now, not tonight, not yet.

"We need to set up a bigger bed," Zack said when we finally drew apart. Always the practical one. "Packs stay together, sleep together, bond."

"I'd be clawing at your door in fur if you sent me back to the enforcers' quarters," Declan said. "I need…well, a lot of things really, but skin contact." He drew me out of Mason's arms and then tucked me under his chin, arms wrapping around me. "I'm done sleeping without that."

"We need to take your father's bed, then add one of the spare ones next to it," Mason said, eyeing me to see if that would be OK.

I remembered crawling into that same bed and crying my eyes

out when I'd just gotten back, but nodded anyway. It was just furniture, not him.

"And then there's…"

Dad's murderer. I couldn't say the words, my fangs already returning at the thought of them, but every man grew solemn, nodding, showing they knew exactly what that meant.

"Every man here will make it their full-time job to investigate what happened to the alpha," Mason said. "We'll tear the place apart if that's what it takes."

"We can get a PI in from the city," Zack said. "I know some guys in the business who are good and reliable."

"No one will rest until the alpha's killer is brought to justice," Declan said, surprising me the most, his usually light-hearted demeanour thoroughly thrown aside as something much darker and more intent bled through.

"But not tonight." Lorcan pulled me close with fingers a little tight with need. He thrust his nose in my hair, breathing me in. "Just tonight, can we have this, us?"

I wasn't sure if he meant me and him or all of us, but I was going with the latter. I kissed him, just a long slow steady press of the lips until the tension leached out of him, and then we walked inside, up the stairs to my father's door. They waited for me to open it, and then we all moved in, working as a team to strip the bedclothes off and replace them with new ones, remove the bedside tables, and shift the massive bed frame to allow another to be put alongside of it. And then, when everything was fresh, new, and remade, I looked around and saw all of them, waiting.

They watched me with hungry eyes when my first knee was put on the mattress, then each movement until I was lying on my back, staring at Dad's ceiling. Lorcan moved first, sliding down beside me, pulling me to face him before tucking me against him. Then the rest came, each dip in the mattress a weight on my heart that steadied, stilled me.

Did they feel it click into place? Something small, temporary, an acknowledgement of the step we'd just taken, but also a promise for the future. I'd claim them all, take all of their knots deep inside me, dig my fangs into their necks, formalise what I already knew, that they were mine, mine, mine. But right now, I was content, with this, with what I was and what we were.

We were pack.

We were strong, we were united, and when we found whoever did this to my father, we would be bloody of tooth and claw, and then we would be triumphant.

Strange things to fall asleep to, I guessed, but we were not human. We dreamed the dreams of wolves, of running together free, of blood, of Mother Moon.

Chapter 34

In the end, it was the lack of hydration that got me.

At some point in the night, I woke up and saw the moon starting to fade, her last rays of light coming in through the gauzy windows in front of the bed. It formed a circle across the bed, and that made sense. I smiled to myself, then felt what had woken me. My throat was bone-dry from all the screaming, fighting, fucking, and mating, but not enough H_2O. I was seriously going to need to start carrying a water bottle around again with these boys. It took some work, but I eased out from under the bodies that had pinned me to the bed. Jesus, Zack had always smothered me, but now I had five willing to take up that duty.

I stood at the end of the bed once I got free, just letting the moonlight caress my skin, and sent up a silent prayer of thanks to Mother Moon. Like any parent, her decisions hadn't always made sense to me at the time, but now that I saw the bigger picture, I could see it. I'd thought I knew what I wanted and had felt like I was going to die when that was taken off the table. I looked back at those beautiful forms, completely at peace right now. This was what I needed.

My last prayer went to my father. I liked to imagine that in the mottled shapes of the moon, I could see him in the pack lands beyond, looking down upon me. He'd be proud, I realised, of the men I'd found, the ones I'd taken as mates. Lorcan might've pressed the boundaries a little, but… Tears formed as I saw in my mind's eye all of us sitting down to eat at the table, talking shit over one of Nan's roast dinners, together, a family.

"I'll find them, Dad, I promise," I whispered. "They tried to take that from me, from you, but you'll see. We'll have that dinner, that family, and when we do, we'll raise a toast for you."

MY MISTAKE CAME from my wolf's nature. My instincts should have told me there was someone in the house, but they were dulled, soothed by the sense of my pack I felt throbbing inside me, calling me back to the room as I went downstairs to get a drink. I should've heeded it.

Because I thought I had all the time in the world. That I could walk into the darkened kitchen and open the fridge door and grab a bottle of water, drink it down, then go back upstairs and crawl into bed, teasing my loves with my mouth and hands until they woke up hard and hungry, wanting to slake that appetite on my skin.

It was a rustle that alerted me. An innocuous enough sound in the city, but my head jerked sideways, my eyes searching the dark for its source. They were dulled by the artificial glow of the fridge, so I shut it, leaving the bottle inside it and padding out into the dark.

Later, I thought about all of the shoulds. I should've shouted out for the guys, for the enforcers. I should've gone to fur, my nose more sensitive, my fangs more deadly. I should've turned the light on, to unmask what I thought was a mouse scurrying around in the dark.

But instead, it was a rat.

The rush of air on my face was the only warning I got, then the rapid skitter of human, not rodent, footsteps. My fangs snapped down, my hands went to claws, but that wasn't going to do much against a baseball bat to the head. At least I thought that was what it was. All I knew was a brief, explosive moment of pain when I felt the impact of the bat like an IED to my brain. It was so sharp, so intense, I couldn't even force out a scream.

And then there was nothing, just me, lying on the floor in a slowly spreading pool of blood.

Chapter 35

Mason woke way too early from habit, but he knew this day would be different the moment it all came back. The forest, his girl… His thoughts didn't get past that bit. They couldn't. He'd prised them away from thinking about Paige that way, over and over, but now… When he took a deep breath in, his chest seemed to expand further, his lungs filling more completely. That was fitting. She was as necessary to him as oxygen, and now he had more of all of it. He rolled over, looking over Zack's shoulders, expecting to see her buried beneath the pile of bodies as she had been last night. It'd made him smile, that deep need for her being expressed even in sleep, but this didn't.

Her spot was empty, Lorcan's hand reaching out into the space she'd left. Mason frowned, looked around the bed, hoping that she'd just wriggled free to go and snuggle into Micah or Declan. He was up and off the bed, wriggling back into his jeans, then grabbing the gun he'd stashed in the chest of drawers, making sure it was loaded and the safety was still on.

"Micah, Declan," he said, a short sharp order with enough dominance to jerk them out of sleep. They just stared at him bleary-eyed for a moment, and he didn't wait for them to focus. He was out the door and down the stairs in seconds.

She's gone for a run. She's making breakfast. She's having a shower. She's talking to the other enforcers. She's searching her father's office. His brain frantically threw logical reasons why he hadn't woken up next to the woman he loved, but none of them stuck. She didn't know, he'd never told her of the rush of pure unadulterated fear he felt when he didn't know where she was. As a teen, that had been brotherly, protective, but as an adult, that just increased. Now? His hand clawed at his sternum, the customary ache turning into an outright stabbing pain.

Because he smelt it first, the blood, and then he saw her.

"No…" he whispered, because it couldn't be true. Now when… Not after… He took a faltering step forward, something he reamed himself out about afterwards. He kept saying that stupid word over and over as he forced himself onwards, his feet almost silent on the wood floor. He didn't pull his gun, scan for whoever did this to her, because he couldn't look away. She was sprawled out on the floor like a dropped doll, her closed eyes making her look like she was just sleeping there on the polished floorboards, the blood matting her beautiful chestnut hair making a lie of that.

His brain raced, trying to insist that he initiate lockdown, go through all of the fail safes Alpha Spehr had put in place if Paige got attacked.

"She'll need protection from everyone, if what I think is going to happen eventuates. She'll need you to stand firm against the lot of them for her, even from her own family."

But instead, he fell to his knees beside her, and he begged. For her to wake up, to open her eyes, for her to be OK. To forgive him, then, now, for all the ways he'd failed her, as he should've the moment she came home.

"No, no, no, no, NO!" His voice rang out throughout the living area, but it made no difference. She didn't move, she didn't waken. Instead, she lay there, a bloody naked facsimile of her father when he'd found him.

His tears touched her skin before he could bring himself to. His fingers shook, his whole body quaking in an attempt to process this. Finally, he forced them down, wrapping around her wrist. *Warm, alive!* his brain shouted at him. He made his fingers press down on the veins there, the time between his search and the feel of her pulse feeling like an age. It was strong, slow but strong.

"What the fuck?!" Declan shouted.

"Call an ambulance now, Dec!" Micah said, dropping down beside her. "Tell those fucks they better be here in twenty seconds or I'm coming for them myself. Mase…"

He couldn't respond. He had no words. Everything inside him was just smashing at his lips, caught all snarled up together in a log jam that stopped everything getting out but this.

"My girl…"

She was, he'd always known it. She beat inside his heart, came in and out of him with every breath, saturated him so deeply, no one else could get in. She was his motherfucking world, and he'd held out on her, let her walk out and away from him. His hubris, his arrogance shocked him almost as much as her current state, as Micah bent over her, listening to her heart beat, the one that beat in him, as Declan shouted at emergency services. Some instinct had him shuffling forward, smoothing her hair back on the uninjured side, not wanting anything to obscure her face.

"Jesus," Micah said with a start when her eyelids fluttered. "No," he snapped, his hand shooting out to hold Mason's still when he went to pull away. "Hold on to her, Mase."

"ETA two minutes. I'm getting the boys in. We go into lockdown. Codes changed. No one in or out but enforcers and her."

"What the fuck happened?!"

Feet came thundering down the steps, but he couldn't focus on them, on the shouts. It all faded away, the sharp scream of the approaching siren unlocking an answering one inside him.

"Sweetheart…" His voice couldn't convey all the pain inside him. "Hold on, my love. You're such a ballsy little fighter. You never back down, never give an inch. You've gotta hold on. Fight this, fight them, fight the fucking monstrous cunts who…" His hands started to ball up hard, needing to hit out, strike, but even as he felt his mouth fill with fangs, he continued.

"All that's good in the world is in you. You go, the light goes with you. The moon won't rise, it can't, not when her favourite daughter is laid low. There is no moon, no sun, no day or night, no rain, no life without you. I…"

He choked on it, his past cruel declarations stabbing into him like sharpened knives, making him bleed when his life blood was already leaching out with hers.

"Just wake up, sweetheart. Wake up, smack me in the face, kick me in the nuts, bring me down, baby, because I deserve it. I fucking deserve it for walking away from you." He shook his head over and over, hearing the shouts and stampeding feet, officious voices asking him to step back.

"He can't," Micah said. "I think…I think he's holding her here."

He grabbed that flimsy idea, ridiculous and not standing up to close inspection, but he didn't care. There was no life but for hope, and right now, all of his was tied up in her.

It always was.

"I'll do anything, Paige. Absolutely fucking anything if you wake up. You're not my girl, you're my whole fucking heart."

"Well, if you let us get through, we can make sure hers keeps beating. She needs to go to hospital."

The voice cut through the haze, then the men, his pack, her mates, all came into sharp focus. Micah looked desperate, Declan horrified, Zack pacing back and forth, but it was in Lorcan he found what he was looking for. Did his own face look the same? That devastation so complete and utter as to be seamless?

Lorcan knew.

He knew what it would be like, if they didn't get her to the hospital, if they didn't help her body's natural healing abilities bring her back. To them.

Mason shook his head, scrambled to his feet, moving to allow the paramedics closer but still holding on to her.

"All right, we're going to stabilise her neck and then get her onto a stretcher. Staff at the hospital are on standby."

And so they did, while Lorcan took her other hand, the two of them walking out with her when they moved her stretcher, and the heavy steps felt way too close to the way they'd carried her father to his final resting place.

Come back to me… That beat inside him now, over and over, a call to arms, an imperative, a destiny. He'd give anything he had for that to happen, anything, including this fucking town if that was what it took. He looked the alpha estate over with a dark eye as they slid her into the back of the ambulance, him taking up one side, Lorcan the other, and despite everything that had happened or hadn't, he knew the other man would join him in tearing it apart to find those that dared hurt his mate.

Mate…

One last knife to the chest, he let it twist, breathing little sharp pants as he considered what he'd turned his back on, but he'd have plenty of time to kick himself in the arse when she was safe, stable, healing.

The doors slammed shut, a thud on the back letting the driver know he was good to go, the sirens, as far as he was concerned, announcing their intent to the town. They might've thought to bring their best and brightest down for reasons Mason would never understand, but that would not stand.

If they wanted a war, he was more than happy to bring it.

What next?

THIS BOOK WILL BE OUT MUCH EARLIER THAN THE DATE ON AMAZON.

Coming soon!

COME OUT SWINGING

What next?

Get it here!

So, who the hell killed Paige's dad? And will Mason pull his head out of his arse? Will whoever is pulling this shit finally take out the Scooby gang? Find out more in what I think is the final book in Paige's story!

Want another shifter tale set in the same world?

Get it here!

Never tell them what we are, Shannon's grandmother had always said.

Working as a faux-Reiki healer in her local veterinary clinic, Shannon uses her psychic abilities to help sick or anxious animals, worried that one day people were going to see past the New Age façade she'd constructed.

With good cause.

What next?

Men from the newly created Capricorn Institute bring her to the newly renovated prison on the hill to work her wiles on their beasts, creatures she'd thought she'd only ever seen in a zoo, but they don't respond to her psychic overtures like a normal animal would.

Because they aren't.

Beautiful, wild, Shannon's about to find out the truth about the Big Bad Wolf and all of his apex predator friends. These sexy shifters track her every movement, memorise her scent, because even from behind bars, they're hunting her. Physically, psychically, these men will use whatever tactics they can to get what they want: her.

THERE IS AN EXTENSIVE TRIGGER WARNING INSIDE THE START OF THE BOOK. PLEASE MAKE SURE TO READ IT.

This is book one in a brand new super steamy series from the author of the Pack Heat series. If you love hot shifter romance, you'll love Tail 'Em. Some MM

Acknowledgments

To my author group: a better group of ladies can't be found. You gave me permission to step out on my seriously crowded dance card and spit this baby out. The support, as always, is amazing.

Super editor Meghan Leigh Daigle cast her eagle eye over this one. She's an outstanding editor, if ever you're looking for one!
   https://www.facebook.com/Bookish-Dreams-Editing-105567517555119/

Cover was created by the team at CJ Romano
   https://www.facebook.com/groups/coversbycjromano

Special thanks to Mollie, Teresa, Richelle, Jami, Amanda, Steph, Lizzy, Rebekah and Jennifer. This was a labour of love and you helped support me all the way through it.

Super special thanks to the trope advisors, Kayla, Sarah, Amanda, Jessie, Terrin, Met and Clare.

Printed in Great Britain
by Amazon